LEAP OF
FAITH

Other Books by Sharon Zukowski:

The Hour of the Knife
Dancing in the Dark

LEAP OF FAITH

A Blaine Stewart Mystery

Sharon Zukowski

A DUTTON BOOK

DUTTON
Published by the Penguin Group
Penguin Books USA Inc., 375 Hudson Street,
New York, New York, 10014, U.S.A.
Penguin Books Ltd, 27 Wrights Lane,
London W8 5TZ, England
Penguin Books Australia Ltd, Ringwood,
Victoria, Australia
Penguin Books Canada Ltd, 10 Alcorn Avenue,
Toronto, Ontario, Canada M4V 3B2
Penguin Books (N.Z.) Ltd, 182–190 Wairau Road,
Auckland 10, New Zealand

Penguin Books Ltd, Registered Offices:
Harmondsworth, Middlesex, England

First published by Dutton, an imprint of Dutton Signet,
a division of Penguin Books USA Inc.
Distributed in Canada by McClelland & Stewart Inc.

First Printing, October, 1994
10 9 8 7 6 5 4 3 2 1

REGISTERED TRADEMARK—MARCA REGISTRADA

LIBRARY OF CONGRESS CATALOGING IN PUBLICATION DATA:
Zukowski, Sharon.
Leap of faith : a Blaine Stewart mystery / Sharon Zukowski.
    p. cm.
ISBN 0-525-93897-4
1. Private investigators—New York (N.Y.)—Fiction. 2.Women detectives—New York
(N.Y.)—Fiction. I. Title.
PS3576. U44L43 1994   94-14438
813'.54—dc20   CIP

Printed in the United States of America
Set in New Plantin Light
Designed by Leonard Telesca

LEAP OF
FAITH

To my nephew, David Zukowski,
and my godson, Drew Kelly.
The next generation.

. . . they risked more than death—they gambled
with new life.

Designs on Life,
Robert Lee Hotz

It takes a leap of faith to get things going
It takes a leap of faith you gotta show some guts
It takes a leap of faith to get things going
In your heart you must trust

"Leap of Faith,"
Bruce Springsteen

Chapter 1

• • • • • • • • • •

"I want to hire you."

My attention was wandering, as it usually does during early-morning meetings. I'm a night person. It was eight o'clock in the morning and I was in my office, not home drinking coffee and trying to wake up, because the message said the meeting was urgent. Holding back a yawn, I looked at the woman sitting in front of my desk and tried to guess her net worth. I'd heard so many different figures.

Twenty? Thirty? Forty million dollars? Take your pick. No matter which figure you settled on, it'd be more money than I'd ever see in my life—unless Ed McMahon makes good on the sweepstakes promises he's been sending me.

Judith Marsden was well into middle age and trying to hide it beneath heavy makeup and hair dye that left her looking like an aged castoff from *Seventeen* magazine. A lot of money was being spent on cosmetics, but the Marsden fortune wasn't being squandered on clothes. Judith was wearing a rumpled black corduroy skirt, black turtleneck, and pink cardigan; the entire outfit probably cost less than twenty-five dollars. Judith nervously twisted a button until it fell off. She dropped it in her pocket and looked at me. Judith was waiting for an answer.

Judith and I were what my grandmother would have called nodding friends. I'd known Judith for three years but never had more than a ten-minute conversation with her.

As board members for a summer camp for inner-city kids, we nodded hello over the conference table at meetings, made small talk around the coffeepot, and never saw each other for anything but camp business. Since I couldn't imagine why an upstanding citizen like Judith E. Marsden required the services of a private investigator, I asked.

Judith repeated, "I want to hire you. Blaine, I'm desperate. I don't know where to go for help."

"Most of the people who come to see me are desperate. Tell me about your problem."

"Do people ever hire you to find someone who's missing?"

I hate missing-persons cases and rarely take them. You have to be persistent, willing to waste a lot of time, and very lucky to find a person who's decided to get lost. I'd rather spend my time where the odds of being successful are better.

Judith was anxious; I hated to disappoint her. As gently as possible, I explained, "My company, Aldridge and Stewart, specializes in civil and criminal law. My partner, Eileen, is an attorney. She handles the courtroom work. My division does corporate investigations, background checks, white-collar crime, insurance fraud, and corporate security. We don't handle missing-persons cases unless there are exceptional circumstances surrounding the disappearance."

Judith didn't look satisfied. I reached for my card file to find a telephone number of an investigator who specializes in missing-persons cases; he'd appreciate the wealthy referral. "Let me refer you to someone who can help you. You'll get better results from an expert."

"I don't want a referral. I want you. Not a stranger. I know I can trust you. What circumstances do you consider exceptional? I think mine qualify."

I sat back and thought. Business was good, I didn't have to take every problem that walked through the door. Accepting or rejecting a case is always an instinctive decision. My instinct, which resides in my stomach, was twisting and turning, warning me to send Judith away.

Judith studied my face and decided she didn't want an answer. She quickly asked, "Are you married? Do you have children?"

I should have told Judith my personal life wasn't any of her business, but I didn't. Curious about her sudden change in tactics, I quickly said, "I was married. My husband was killed four years ago."

I stopped talking and thought about the things I'd never tell Judith. When Jeff died, I was three months pregnant. A few weeks after we buried Jeff, I lost the baby too. I doused my grief with alcohol and stayed drunk—until I realized the liquor did nothing but intensify my nightmares. The memories still torment me, especially during the night when ". . . I can't tell my courage from my desperation."

Realizing an awkward silence had taken over the room, I simply said, "We wanted to have children. We didn't."

"Then you'll understand."

"Understand what?"

Taking a deep breath, Judith blurted out why she was sitting in my office, trying to hire me.

"I want you to find my son."

Chapter 2

•••••••••

What son?

Rapidly scanning my memory, I searched for the remnants of a conversation where Judith had mentioned children. I couldn't recall any. I'd never seen any pictures. Never heard any funny stories, parental complaints, or boasts.

My overactive guilty conscience stirred; maybe there were extenuating circumstances. "Judith, I'm sorry. I didn't realize you have a son. How old is he? How long has he been missing?"

"Don't be sorry. Only a few people know about Jerry Junior." The heavy makeup around Judith's mouth cracked as she forced a smile to her face. "I don't like to talk about him. The doctors at the clinic tell me I'm silly and superstitious, but I'm afraid I'll jinx the pregnancy."

I'm convinced getting up early makes people crazy; Judith's statement was additional proof of my theory. I glared at her. "Your son hasn't been born yet, but he's missing and you want me to find him." Judith nodded. I snapped, "Is this some kind of stupid joke?"

The tears filling Judith's eyes weren't tears of laughter. She hadn't come to my office to play an early April Fool's joke. I apologized. "I'm sorry. My imagination isn't as good as it used to be. You'd better explain."

"It's a long story . . ." Judith's voice cracked and died, but her lips continued moving.

I turned to the coffeepot on the credenza behind me, filled two mugs, and swiveled back to Judith. After passing her a cup, I leaned back in the chair. "Take your time and tell me everything. Don't worry about how it sounds, or what order you get the events. We can sort the details out later."

Judith sipped the coffee and grimaced. I added Judith to the list of people who complain that my coffee is too strong. She carefully put the mug down and clenched her hands into fists; her knuckles turned white from the strain.

"I come from a small family. I have a brother and a sister, that's all. I couldn't wait to grow up and have my own children. My life plan was simple—get married and have babies. Lots of babies. Whenever I met a man, my first thought was always: Will he be a good father? When I met Jerry, I knew the answer was yes. We married a year after we met. Everything was wonderful. Except I couldn't get pregnant. We finally went to a doctor. That was the day my neat plan exploded."

Judith glanced at me, trying to judge my reaction. I drank my coffee and kept my face quiet. She pulled a tissue from her sweater pocket and clutched it in her hand. Ready for action.

"On my sixteenth birthday, I went out with a boy—Carl Lindsey. I'll never forget him. Carl was eighteen. He was the captain of the tennis team. My parents liked Carl. They thought he was a nice young man . . . It was our first date."

Sweat beaded on Judith's forehead. I held my breath, knowing how the story ended. I wanted to stop her. Judith's voice rose and picked up speed.

"The team was having a party to celebrate a winning season. Everyone was drinking. Rum and Coke. I didn't like the taste. The rum made me gag. It burned my stomach. But I didn't complain. I didn't refuse any of the drinks either. I wanted Carl to like me. You see, he was a senior, I was a sophomore. I was hoping he'd take me to the prom."

Judith paused. The silence lengthened until I thought she wouldn't continue. Another taste of coffee gave her strength to go on.

"I got drunk—I was sick. Throwing up. Carl decided to take me home before I ruined the party. I didn't want my parents to see me drunk so he drove around to give me time to recover. It started raining. We parked by the tennis courts. Carl kissed me. I tried to push him away. He wouldn't stop. He tore my blouse . . . grabbed my breasts. I slapped him."

Tears dribbled from her eyes. I cleared my throat and said, "Judith, stop. This isn't necessary."

Judith couldn't stop. The words were self-propelled, rolling out without restraint. I held my protests behind clenched teeth.

"He . . . he raped me. When I close my eyes, I feel his fingers closing around me. I smell his sweat. I hear the rain hitting the roof of the car. I hear myself screaming. I feel him pushing inside me. Hurting me. I never told anyone. Not until I started getting sick in the morning. I was pregnant."

Judith closed her eyes and bowed her head. "I was so scared. I thought my life was over. My parents . . . my parents made the arrangements. It was the worst day of my life."

"You had an abortion?"

Judith grimaced. "Abortions were illegal thirty years ago. It wasn't easy. I don't know how, but my parents found a nurse who moonlighted helping wanton girls like me. The nurse gave me a lecture about being promiscuous, an abortion, and a shredded uterus—I'll never get pregnant again. . . ."

Judith's mouth set in an angry red line as she relived the past that still twisted her life farther and farther away from its neat plan. It's been years since I tried to force my life into a tight box; I don't like the pain when the lid slams down on your fingers.

In an effort to drag Judith back to the present, I asked, "How does this tie into the missing child?"

"Jerry and I wanted to have children more than anything else in the world. After a year of trying to get pregnant, we started worrying. Our family and our friends said we were too anxious. They said to let nature take its course. Six months later, we went to the clinic."

"A fertility clinic?" Judith nodded. "Which one?"

"The Metropolitan Fertility Clinic." I scrawled the name across the top of my pad and motioned for Judith to continue.

"It didn't take the doctors long to discover I was infertile. The abortion—carrying a baby is something I'll never do. Jerry got sick about the same time. It was cancer. We knew he wouldn't live long."

"Did you ever consider adoption?"

Judith was adamant. "Never. Jerry was a proud man. He was also a very rich man. He didn't want his money to go to some other man's child."

The color drained from Judith's face. She backpedaled and tried to soften the harsh words rolling around my office. "That's not entirely true. We both wanted *our own child.* Our own flesh and blood, not a stranger's jetsam."

My stomach twisted again. Judith's cold words destroyed the sympathy she'd earned. I shook off my distaste and harshly said, "So you and Jerry decided to use his money to hire someone to carry your own flesh and blood."

"You make it sound like something dirty. What we did wasn't sordid. It's beautiful. The clinic found what they call a gestational surrogate. She's not the baby's real mother—I am. The sperm is Jerry's, the eggs are mine. She's only lending her uterus to carry the baby because I can't."

Lending her uterus? I was horrified. After nine months, Judith expected the rented uterus to disgorge its contents without a murmur of protest. A thousand negative remarks came to mind, but I kept quiet. Judith wasn't in my office for a discussion of the ethics of modern medicine.

"Now you're afraid she's run away with the baby?" A ragged sob was Judith's answer. I waited a second, then asked another question. "How far along is the pregnancy?"

"Seven and a half months. We have a C-section scheduled for April twentieth."

"What's the name of your surrogate? Where does she live?"

Judith hesitated long enough for me to wonder about the answer that was coming. People may be desperate when they come to see me, but desperation is never a guarantee they'll be truthful. Embarrassment, pride, and fear turn on an internal censor that rewrites the disagreeable parts of their story. Clients have many reasons for editing their stories, but they all make the same delicate hesitation before they tell their white-washed tales. Truth or lie? I can almost see the question being decided.

"Her name is Hannah. Hannah Wyrick. You know her sister Nikki. They live together."

The name was instantly familiar. Writing Nikki's name on a check and tossing it on the kitchen table was the last thing I'd done before rushing out of the house to make this meeting. I couldn't hide my surprise. "My cleaning lady and your surrogate mother are sisters?"

Several months earlier, Judith listened to my complaints about dustballs taking over my house. She smiled, wrote Nikki's name and phone number on a piece of paper, and gave it to me. Her recommendation was one of the best I've ever received. My house has been sparkling ever since.

Judith nodded. "They're twins. Almost, but not entirely, identical. Nikki's hair stayed blond. Hannah's turned dark brown."

At least I wouldn't need a description. I shook my head again and asked, "How long has Hannah been gone?"

"At least a day. The clinic called me late yesterday afternoon. Hannah missed her appointment, and the nurse wanted to know if I had seen her. I tried calling Hannah. When she didn't answer, I went to her apartment. No one was there. I didn't worry until I got back to my house and found a note. It was shoved under the front door."

Judith fumbled in her purse. With shaking hands, she pulled out an envelope and slid it across the desk to me. "After I read it, I called you."

The envelope was standard issue—white, business-sized. The type of envelope that's on sale in every stationery store in the city. No stamp, no postmark. Judith's name had been carefully typed on the front. I removed a thin sheet of paper from the envelope and unfolded it. Judith watched and struggled to keep the tears in her eyes. The typing filled the top quarter of the page.

"Dear Judith:

"I know this will cause you pain. I'm sorry, but I can't think of another way. I've been lying to you. I can't do it any longer. I've been awake every night since the doctors gave me the baby, thinking and crying.

"From the minute they put that tiny baby inside me, I knew giving him away would be wrong. I'm the baby's mother. I can't give him up. It would be wrong. I hope you'll understand and forgive me. He belongs to me—no one else. Some day, when the boy is old enough to understand, we'll come back. He'll need to know about his father.

"I am sorry. —Hannah."

A postscript ran across the bottom of the paper: "P.S. If you go to the police, we'll disappear forever."

I examined the letter again. The words didn't change. I was stalling, looking for something that would convince me to take the case. I sighed and looked at Judith. Tears ran from her eyes, eroding furrows in the makeup on her cheeks.

People tell me I've become jaded and cynical from my years as a private investigator. They're wrong. I keep my emotions hidden. I let them out late at night when I'm alone and can examine them in private. Judith's streaked face and bloodshot eyes overrode my misgivings. I folded the note and dropped it on my desk.

"I'll help you find your son."

Chapter 3

New York City was in the middle of a harsh winter, reminiscent of the one that delivered the great blizzard of 1888. Back-to-back storms buried the city under eighteen inches of snow in less than forty-eight hours. Before the snow had a chance to melt, an arctic wind blew out of Canada and left frozen mounds of snow on the streets and sidewalks.

For ten long days the temperature never moved above twenty

degrees. On this, the eleventh day, a thaw arrived. By noon, it was almost freezing—a welcome change from the frigid air. I walked up Fifth Avenue to the clinic, enjoying the warmth and worrying about Judith. More accurately, I was worrying about the effect Judith's case would have on me. Like many alcoholics, I have a very fragile grip on sobriety. Accepting this assignment without thinking about its impact on my brittle nondrinking status could have been a mistake.

After four years, the pain of losing my baby had lessened. Not disappeared, as my well-meaning friends promised it would. The grief strikes at the oddest moments, always when I'm unprepared and most vulnerable. The sight of a mother pushing an infant in a stroller, a woman in maternity clothes, even a silly commercial with cute kids sends a thunderbolt through me. My eyes water. I blink the tears away, hope no one's noticed, and wonder about what might have been if a traitor's betrayal hadn't destroyed my life.

When I drank, wiping the sadness away was easy. I'd get drunk and stay drunk until I couldn't feel anything. Sober now, it's more difficult to recover. I stumble around for days feeling empty and not knowing how to fill emptiness. Unwilling to occupy the hollowness with alcohol. Slowly, painfully, the ache fades and I forget—until the next time.

The fear that I was inviting more heartache by immersing myself in a world filled with babies accompanied me on my walk. I knew that fear would shadow my movements, threatening to crash down on me with a power I couldn't survive without drinking. By the time I reached the clinic, I was frightened. Not for Judith—for myself.

Expecting to find the high-tech clinic in an equally modern building, I walked past the staid brownstone on the corner of Eighty-first Street without giving it a second glance. After a few blocks, I realized I'd gone too far and retraced my steps, carefully checking the numbers on the buildings. I found the Metropolitan Fertility Clinic in an old brownstone on a side street near the Metropolitan Museum of Art. I climbed the wide granite stairs and let myself in.

The receptionist watched me. Suspicion darkened her face. I wasn't a regular; I didn't have an appointment. My brightest smile didn't soften her.

"May I help you?" The woman was lying. She didn't want to help me; she wanted me out of her exclusive domain.

Regretting the blue jeans I'd donned that morning—she would have been impressed by one of my expensive suits—I said, "I'm here to see Dr. Nelson."

Frostina, the Snow Receptionist, didn't blink. "I'm sorry, the doctor is with a patient. Would you like to schedule a meeting?" She reluctantly opened her appointment book and pretended to study it. "Dr. Nelson has time available for new patients on the fourteenth and fifteenth of next month. Would you prefer a morning or afternoon appointment?"

"Neither." I leaned over her desk so my eyes were level with hers. "I want to see him now. My name is Blaine Stewart. Judith Marsden sent me."

"Has Mrs. Marsden recommended you as a new patient?"

I flashed my investigator's license and let her form her own opinion about the reason for my visit. "Dr. Nelson is expecting me. I want to see him—now."

We glared at each other. I won; I get more practice. Frostina dragged the telephone to her face and whispered into the mouthpiece. She listened, frowned, and dropped the receiver in the cradle. Without looking at me, she said, "Please have a seat. The doctor will be with you shortly."

Distaste dripped from her mouth. I smiled and walked back to the waiting room; juvenile battles with receptionists always brighten my spirits. After draping my coat on the brass rack near the door, I looked around.

Every chair was occupied by an impatient mother-, or father-, to-be. The tension in the air encouraged stereotypic behavior. The would-be mothers read *Parents* magazine; the daddies scanned the *Wall Street Journal*. I watched them and felt a strong urge to have a cigarette. The tiny signs on the wall warned me to think about something else.

I prowled around, examining the decorations. The walls of the waiting room and lobby were covered with paintings of hunters, men rowing boats, and a lady with her dog. They were good reproductions of Thomas Eakins's works, but I'd rather stroll across the street and see the real thing.

A large bulletin board near the entrance caught my eye. The bold headline proclaimed: "Our Newest Patients!" Testimonials to the clinic's good works crowded the board.

Pictures of babies cradled in the arms of smiling parents. Birth announcements. Letters praising doctors and staff. Holiday greeting cards signed with a school child's primitive scrawl. Proof the clinic's magic worked. Proof it was worthwhile to spend thousands of dollars a month to grow a baby.

A man's soft voice interrupted my reverie. "Ms. Stewart, I'm Dr. Nelson. Mrs. Marsden called and said you would be coming to see me. She also said it was urgent. Let's go to my office. Perhaps you can explain Mrs. Marsden's emergency."

The doctor was tall, lean, and blond, with the ruddy complexion of a man who spends too much time on a golf course. Since all the greens within commuting distance were buried under a foot and a half of snow, he was spending too much time in a tanning booth. I offered my hand. The doctor ignored it and turned away. "My office is this way."

The people in the waiting room watched me with resentful looks on their faces. They weren't happy; I'd been bumped to the head of the line. Frostina shuffled her papers, building a defense to repel angry patients. I shrugged and followed the doctor through a set of heavy oak doors into a narrow corridor.

I stepped into another world. The restful atmosphere of the waiting room was gone. Harried technicians rushed up and down the hallway, ducking in and out rooms that were identified by only a number. Some were carrying specimen jars; others carried racks of test tubes. I began to ask Nelson if the tubes were filled with babies, but caught myself in time. The doctor's stiff back cautioned me to hold my jokes.

Nelson's office was furnished with a set of chairs for visitors, a gleaming oak desk, and the doctor's oversized leather chair. Diplomas and pictures of infants covered the walls. I nodded at the photos. "More products of your labors?"

"We have one of the highest success rates in the country." Nelson made a show of looking at the gold watch on his wrist. "I have an appointment in five minutes. I suggest you skip the small talk and explain the nature of your urgent business."

I disliked Nelson almost as much as he disliked me, but I managed to control it. I slipped a notebook and pen from my jacket pocket. Nelson's eyes followed my hands as I flipped the notebook open to a blank page.

"When was the last time you saw Hannah Wyrick?"

"I can't answer that question. You may have heard of patient confidentiality. If not, I'll be happy to explain the concept to you."

"Dr. Nelson, let me explain a concept to you. Hannah Wyrick has run away. I'm trying to locate her. Mrs. Marsden expects you to cooperate with my efforts to find Hannah. When did you last see her?"

"Are you positive your information is correct?"

His smug attitude angered me. I snapped, "Yes. I'm sure."

The doctor removed his glasses and rubbed his eyes. When he resettled the glasses on his face, the lenses magnified the red streaks in his eyes. "Who are you?"

I recited, "My name is Blaine Stewart. I'm a private investigator. You know I'm working for Mrs. Marsden."

"Isn't this where I'm supposed to ask to see a license or some other type of identification?"

"You've been watching too much television. But if it'll make you happy, I'll dig it out and wave it under your nose—isn't that how it's done on TV? Would you like to see my gun too?"

He consulted his watch again. "Three minutes. You have exactly three minutes before my next patients arrive. I suggest you get to the point."

"The point is this: Hannah Wyrick, your surrogate, is missing. Judith Marsden hired me to locate her."

"Our expectant parents are often quite anxious in the months preceding the baby's birth. Because of the unfortunate circumstances, Mrs. Marsden has been more anxious than most. Hannah missed yesterday's appointment—hardly a cause for alarm." He blinked. "Are you quite sure she's missing?"

"Quite."

My answer floated over Nelson's desk. He shook his head. "I don't believe it. Our testing showed Hannah is quite capable of fulfilling her obligations under the surrogacy agreement."

Quite. That word was beginning to annoy me. "My testing shows that your surrogate has run off. She's not at home—I checked." I'd pulled two of the six investigators on my staff off their assignments and had them watching her apartment, but I wasn't going to give that information to the doctor. "Hannah also sent a letter to Mrs. Marsden telling of her intention to keep the baby. Doctor, it's obvious your surrogate changed her mind."

Nelson removed his glasses for another polishing. He pursed his lips and asked, "What do you want from me?"

I launched into a quick series of questions. Nelson grudgingly answered, wiping his glasses with a tissue as he spoke.

I learned that Hannah had been born in New Jersey, attended one semester at Rutgers University, and then moved to Manhattan to pursue an acting career. After a million unsuccessful auditions, Hannah's thespian dreams faded and she decided to satisfy another dream. She would help a less fortunate woman give birth.

Hannah's life story was a fairy tale. The perfect girl grew up to be an unselfish woman determined to give anything, even her body, to help another. I nearly gagged.

Since Nelson wouldn't give me any specific information on Hannah, I tried another approach. "How do you locate your surrogates? And how do you decide if the woman should be allowed to act as a surrogate?"

The doctor ignored my first question, which made me curious, and made believe he was answering the second. "We are not like other clinics. We don't automatically approve every applicant. Our screening process is the most rigorous one used in the field today. We are positive the surrogate is capable of abiding by the contract before we ever introduce her to the genetic parents."

"It sounds so easy. How can you be sure the woman won't change her mind at the last minute?" I wanted to add: just like Hannah did.

The doctor peeked at his watch. "We administer a number of tests to identify any psychological or psychosocial traits which would cause emotional difficulties with the surrogate agreement."

I wanted to see Hannah's test results, but knew Nelson would give me another lecture on confidentiality if I asked for them. I'd have to find another way. Quickly, before he ended the interview, I asked, "What are the warning signs of potential trouble?"

"Family background is one of the most important indicators. More than half the candidates we see have a history of abusive and/or alcoholic parents or other childhood traumas. These women want to be surrogates to compensate for their awful parents. Or they want to raise their self-esteem by doing something noble.

"Hannah isn't like that. She comes from a good, stable family. I'm convinced Hannah is simply taking a break from Mrs. Marsden's constant attention. Hannah will be back after she's had some quiet time alone." He stood up. "Now, if you don't have any more questions . . ."

I wasn't ready to leave. I crossed my legs and said, "Just one more question. How much is Hannah being paid to carry this baby?"

"This clinic does not practice commercial surrogacy. A woman who volunteers to act as a surrogate does so because of a firm desire to help a less fortunate sister. Surrogates, who are family members or close friends of the family, are reimbursed for expenses. Nothing more."

"Wait a second. Judith and Hannah aren't related. They aren't close friends. They never met before you introduced them. What happened to your policy?"

Nelson lost his temper. "Substantial start-up costs were incurred during the clinic's development. The Marsdens were among our major backers. Given the unusual circumstances of Mr. Marsden's untimely death, our directors made an exception."

Chapter 4

Nelson tried to cover his miscue. "I've kept my patients waiting long enough. I'll see you out." The doctor silently waited for me to uncross my legs and follow him out the door. Without speaking, he escorted me to the lobby.

Before we entered the crowded waiting room, Dr. Nelson stopped and turned to me. His smile was sincere; his eyes weren't.

"I trust I've put your mind at ease. Mrs. Marsden is simply overwrought. I trust you'll convince her to relax. We don't want any trouble."

"Dr. Nelson, you can't brush Judith Marsden off as nothing but a hysterical woman. Hannah Wyrick has run away. She intends to keep the baby. Doesn't your clinic have an obligation to Judith?"

"We are fulfilling all our obligations. Unless I see definite proof that Hannah has indeed run away—"

"I'm tired of repeating myself. Your surrogate is missing. I'm not going to waste time trying to convince you. I'm going to find her—with or without your help." I gave him a business card and said, "Call me if you hear from Hannah or if you decide to co-operate."

The doctor slipped the card in his pocket without looking at it. "I have nothing more to say to you. I have to see my patients now. They've waited long enough."

He rudely pushed me aside and walked into the waiting room. My temper flared, but I let him go without fighting. At least he hadn't called the security guards to throw me out.

Three messages, all of them from Judith, were waiting on my desk when I arrived at my office. Cursing Judith's impatience, I shredded the message slips and dropped the pieces in the garbage.

Brad, my childhood friend and assistant, strolled in as the confetti fluttered to the bottom of the trash can. He grinned. "Somebody make you mad, Babe?"

I smiled. No one else on my staff is brave enough to call me Babe. I let Brad get away with it because we have known each other since kindergarten. On the first day of school, I nearly broke his nose in a fight over arts and crafts supplies. We've been friends ever since. We even tried dating once but gave that up before we ruined our friendship. When a knee injury ruined Brad's promising pro-football career he came to work for me.

"Yeah, Brad, my newest client is making me mad. I hate clients who call every ten minutes, expecting to hear you've solved their dirty little problem." I looked at the pile of paper flakes in the bottom of the garbage can and said, "It's going to have to wait until tomorrow. I'm not talking to another client today."

"Giving up early, aren't you? It's only four o'clock." Brad settled his two hundred and seventy-five pounds into a chair and swung his feet to the top of my desk. I leaned forward and pushed his feet to the floor.

"Go scuff up your own desk. I've got work to do."

Brad ignored me. He stretched his legs out and settled in the chair for a long visit. "What are you working on? I hope it's something good. I'm tired of checking out bogus insurance claims."

"Don't complain, Brad. Those bogus claims pay the rent *and* your salary. Insurance work might not be exciting enough for you, but it beats unemployment."

Brad raised his hands and surrendered. "Please, stop the lecture. I give up. I love insurance fraud. I don't want to do anything else. Are *you* working on something interesting? Why is your client so anxious; didn't you give the 'you're in good hands' lecture?"

"It's a missing person." I paused and thought of a more accurate description. "It's a runaway and a missing person. A woman who's about to give birth disappeared yesterday. My client wants me to find her."

"Poor guy. He must be out of his mind worrying about his wife."

"Sexist—my client isn't the husband. My client is the baby's mother."

Brad raised his eyebrows. I sat back and started telling him Judith's story. My partner, Eileen, who's also my older sister, walked in midway through my narrative. Motioning for me to continue, she dropped into the seat next to Brad's and lit a cigarette. I quickly recapped what she'd missed, then finished my story.

Brad shook his head. "We're looking for a lady who's pregnant with another lady's baby. This is some weird shit, Babe."

Eileen frowned her agreement. Before she repeated the misgivings I'd heard earlier when I told her about our newest client, I quickly said, "As I said before: It pays the rent, Bubba."

Eileen stubbed her cigarette out in my battered ashtray and casually asked, "Blaine, where have you been? I was looking for you. I had a telephone call . . ."

Brad has sensitive ears. Claiming the urgent need to make a phone call, he jumped to his feet and bolted from the room. I watched Brad leave, then turned to Eileen. Feeling like an unruly student about to be reprimanded by the principal, I asked, "Who called? And why are they mad at me?"

"Frazier, Maxell, and O'Keefe called about twenty minutes ago. I talked to Mr. O'Keefe." Eileen laughed, I relaxed. "I should say I listened to Mr. O'Keefe. He carried on at great length about how you slandered and harassed his client. He promised to take legal action if you persist."

I've been threatened too many times by too many people to be intimidated by a lawsuit. I yawned. "Who's his client?"

"The Metropolitan Fertility Clinic."

"That was fast. The clinic director must have called O'Keefe as soon as I walked out the door. What did you tell him?"

Eileen has a lot of experience dealing with angry calls from people like O'Keefe. When we first started working together, she always jumped on the side of the complainers. I spent as much time battling her as I did uncooperative subjects. Now, after nearly a decade of working together, Eileen is less willing to believe the irate callers.

Eileen couldn't hide her amusement. A broad smile covered

her face. "I said, 'So sue us.' He told me I was being unprofessional and hung up."

I put my head back and laughed. "It's about time you started being unprofessional. I was beginning to think you were hopelessly serious."

"You're a bad influence." Eileen stopped grinning and tried to look serious; her eyes sparkled with laughter. She blinked and the merriment disappeared. "Do me a favor, will you? Don't harass the clinic too much. O'Keefe has a bad reputation. He'll do everything he can to make your life miserable. You'll ignore him and he'll make mine miserable."

I frowned. Eileen noticed and shook her head. "Don't complain that I'm not supporting you. Wait until you hear the rest of my story. O'Keefe's call set me to wondering. I wondered why an awfully big gun was firing so soon into the battle. I made a few calls."

Eileen took a sheet of yellow paper from her pocket and laid it on my desk. Eileen has a great memory. Without glancing at the notes, she said, "I talked to a staff attorney on the New York State Judiciary Committee." She looked at me to be sure I was listening. Her eyes were bright with excitement—Eileen loves a chase almost as much as I do.

"Is Judith paying the surrogate?"

"I don't know. Dr. Nelson said they don't pay their surrogates. He also said the Marsdens were different because they were major investors in the clinic. He caught himself before any figures slipped out. When I see Judith tomorrow I'll ask her."

"It's important. Surrogates can be reimbursed for expenses. They aren't supposed to receive payment for carrying the baby. Commercial surrogacy is illegal in New York. Of course, there are ways around the law, but—"

"That's why their lawyers called minutes after I left the clinic. Dr. Nelson is afraid I'll find out too much about his financial arrangements with his surrogates."

Eileen nodded. "I think you're right. The fertility business is incredibly profitable. The entire industry generates over two billion dollars a year in gross revenues. I don't know how much of that two billion goes to the Metropolitan Clinic, but I guarantee they don't want to lose any of it."

"It also means Nelson won't volunteer any information about Hannah. I'll have to try something else."

"What . . . never mind." Eileen shook her head. "I don't want to know. It'll be easier on my stomach if you don't tell me. Just try to stay out of jail. If you get yourself arrested again, please do it during the daytime. I hate being woken up in the middle of the night to bail you out."

It's been a long time since I've been arrested. I looked at Eileen, ready to argue. She was grinning and waiting to see my reaction.

My secretary, Jona, chose that moment to interrupt. She pushed the door open and said, "Blaine, sorry to bother you. You have a call. It's Dennis."

Dennis Halstead. FBI agent. Lover. The man who introduced me to my husband. Ex-lover. Lover again. We're always confused. We don't know from one day to another if we're friends, lovers, or enemies.

Jona leaned against the doorjamb and tried to warn me. "He sounds angry. Something about lunch."

A faint memory of a late-night promise to meet Dennis for lunch stirred. It was four o'clock—much too late for lunch. "Lunch—I completely forgot."

Jona discreetly backed out of the room. I ignored Eileen's giggles, grabbed the telephone, and tried to apologize. Dennis wasn't in a forgiving mood.

"You left me sitting in the restaurant like a fool, waiting for you to show up. Why didn't you call? What the hell is going on with you?"

I swiveled my chair around to look out the windows and avoid the smirk on Eileen's face. "Dennis, I'm really sorry about lunch. I got wrapped up in a new case and couldn't get away. I'm sorry . . ."

The words sounded flat to my ears. They didn't sound any better to Dennis. He didn't answer.

I rushed on, trying to recover, knowing everything I said was wrong. "Dennis, you know I don't have predictable hours. You should understand better than anyone. Your job isn't nine to five either. You've canceled lots of dates on me. I always manage to get over it." Dennis responded with an icy silence. I quickly said, "That's the stupidest thing I've ever said. Can I try again?"

Dennis's voice was deliberately calm. "Maybe I don't want to get over this. Have you noticed a pattern? I get mad at you. You say you're sorry. You get mad at me. I say I'm sorry. Then we do it all over again. Do you want to know what I really think—"

We were on the verge of saying unforgivable things, something I didn't want to happen. I interrupted. "Dennis, I don't want to argue. Let's take a break and calm down. I'll call you tonight."

"Blaine, you're right about one thing: we need a break. A long break. Don't bother to call me tonight. Call me when you figure out what you want."

"Dennis, I—"

He hung up. I dropped the receiver in my lap and stared at it.

Eileen politely coughed to remind me she was still in the room. "What was that all about? It sounded serious."

"I'm not sure. I think I've just been dumped. . . ."

Chapter 5

• • • • • • • • • •

Pleading a headache, I brushed aside Eileen's concern and left the office. Despite the cold, I walked down Sixth Avenue to my house in Greenwich Village. I wanted to be alone. I wanted to think.

Dennis and I met in the middle of my first year of my partnership with Eileen. We often describe that time as a whirlwind of activity. It wasn't; the years have gentled our memories.

Our office, three closet-sized rooms on the fourteenth floor of a Wall Street skyscraper, had been open for five months. Three names were on our client roster: an elderly couple suing their broker because he gambled their retirement savings away on oil futures; a drugstore owner being robbed by his employees; a bank wanting a discreet check on an employee before promoting him.

Business was bad. Eileen and I were wondering if giving up our jobs—Eileen had been on the fast track at a fancy law firm, I was a staff investigator for an insurance company—had been a mistake. We were wondering, but we weren't talking about it.

I was worrying about the rent. It was due in two days and we didn't have enough money in the corporate account to pay it. Eileen and I were taking turns paying the rent until the business paid its own way. It was my turn that month. My mortgage was also due in two days. I sighed and thought about my shrinking savings account. Two days and two big checks to write.

Sighing again, I dabbed correcting fluid on the report in the typewriter and hoped it wouldn't dry in a white glob that makes the paper look like it had developed pimples. Our part-time secretary was out to lunch. Eileen was also out, using her credit card to buy an expensive lunch for a pair of stuffy potential clients who were hesitant about hiring "two girls." Fearing my temper would get away from me, I agreed to stay behind.

I was sitting at the secretary's desk, cursing at the typewriter and smoking a cigarette, when the door opened. Grateful for the interruption and hoping it was a paying client, I stopped typing. One of the most attractive men I'd ever seen walked through the door.

I always look to see how tall a man is before I look at anything else. I'm five-eleven—height is important. I smiled. This guy was tall, at least six-two. He had brown hair, brown eyes, and an early five o'clock shadow creeping across his jaw. I was trying to decide which designer made his suit when he cleared his throat to get my attention. He asked for my boss.

I bristled at the official tone of his voice. I took a drag on my cigarette and slowly blew the smoke out. "Who are you looking for?"

"Mr. Blaine—"

"I'm Blaine. It's Miz, not Mister. Who are you?"

The man's face and neck reddened. He told me he didn't like my attitude. I smiled and waited for an answer to my question. His name was Dennis Halstead, an FBI agent with questions about our banker client. I refused to answer them; he got angry. It was our first argument.

Eileen returned in time to break up that fight. Two weeks later, Dennis walked into my office again and invited me to lunch. I agreed.

Weekly lunches became long romantic dinners. Quiet dinners became sexy evenings and lazy weekends. We were falling in love.

What began at lunch ended at lunch. One day, Dennis invited an associate, Jeff Stewart, to join us. Six months later, Jeff and I married.

Shortly before the wedding ceremony, Dennis and I argued. We said bitter hateful things that ended with me slamming out of Dennis's apartment. After that evening, we saw each other only on the rare occasions when our jobs threw us together.

After Jeff was killed, Dennis tried to offer sympathy. I pushed him away, as I did everyone else, preferring the comfort of alcohol. Dennis never went away; he hovered around the edges of my life, sporadically dropping in.

Recently, my twin barriers of liquor and grief cracked slightly, leaving a gap wide enough to allow Dennis inside. And now, what? It was a long walk home, I had plenty of time to think about Dennis. When I got home I didn't have any answers.

The lights were on, ruining my plans to spend the evening alone. I unlocked the door and stepped inside. Michael Jackson's voice blasted from the stereo, an unmistakable sign that my cleaning lady was at work.

A cheerful voice called from the kitchen, "Blaine, is that you?"

A brainstorm hit; my sulky mood lightened. If Nikki was busy in my house, I'd spend the evening in her house. I started up the stairs to get my tools.

I was halfway up the stairs to my bedroom when Nikki called again. I leaned over the bannister and shouted over the music. "Hi, Nikki. How are you today?"

"Fine." She came out of the kitchen and looked up at me, wiping her hands on a tattered green towel as she spoke. "You're home early. Hope you don't mind the racket, I got a late start to-day. I've got at least another hour of work before I'm done."

"That's okay." Better than okay, it was perfect. I smiled. "I'm just running upstairs to get some papers, then I'm gone again. Did you see the check on the table?"

Nikki sounded preoccupied and anxious to get out of my way. "Yeah, thanks. Maybe I'll see you later."

She waved and went back to the kitchen. I ran up to my bed-room, grabbed my SuperPick from its hiding place in the back of my closet, and ran down the stairs. I shouted good-bye and hur-ried out before Nikki responded.

The Wyrick sisters lived in a burglar's paradise near China-town. The lobby door was unlocked, the foyer was empty, and the hallways were deserted. No one noticed me.

The apartment was on the fifth floor—no elevator. Telling my-self it would make up for the exercise sessions I'd been missing, I ran up the five flights. The corridor was deserted, I made it to 5J without seeing another person.

There are two groups of locks. The standard locks found in every doorknob make up group one. Those are the easy ones to open. A strip of celluloid, a cheap pick, or even a screwdriver, and the lock pops open. Group two are high-security/high-priced locks sold to the insecure. They're good, but they can't stop a skilled locksmith.

Nikki and Hannah were definitely insecure. The bottom lock was one of the cheap ones; but the top lock was one of the best. I looked at them and smiled. I'm not a good locksmith, but I buy excellent tools. After a final glance over my shoulder to be sure the hallway was still empty, I took my SuperPick from my pock-etbook and started working.

The SuperPick is an irreplaceable tool for clumsy fingers like mine that never mastered the art of using a pick to align the lock's pins, one by one, until it opens. I don't have the patience to coax a lock open. If my fingers don't defeat me, my temper does. My impulse is to blast a stubborn lock open with my gun.

My toy looks like an electric toothbrush with a thin, flat blade instead of a brush at its tip. You stick the correct pick in the holder, insert it in the lock, and flip the switch. Pros can open a lock in just a few seconds. I was out of practice—it took ten seconds to open the top lock. Twenty seconds before the lower security lock clicked free.

Thirty seconds is a long time to be standing in a hallway picking a lock in plain sight of inquisitive neighbors. Sweat poured down my forehead before the door swung open.

The apartment was spotless and much bigger than I expected. There was a living room, a kitchen large enough to fit a dining room table and a half dozen chairs, two bedrooms, and a bathroom. My brief conversations with Nikki always gave me the impression she was struggling to get by. Working two jobs to pay the rent and tuition at NYU, hoping for a scholarship to lighten the bills. Was Judith paying the rent?

The apartment may have been expensive, but the furniture wasn't. The living room was furnished with a futon, three mismatched chairs, a tarnished brass pole lamp capped with a yellowing shade, and a rickety coffee table. The nineteen-inch television and stereo were the only expensive items in the room. Plants—spider plants, ivy, miniature palm trees, and other things I couldn't identify—took up every inch of free space.

Someone was spending a lot of time reading and watching television. A stack of well-thumbed magazines sat on top of the table, the TV's remote control anchored the pile. I riffled through the stack. Running, fashion, and parenting magazines, soap opera roundups, and astrology guides made up the collection.

The mailing labels made me laugh. They were all addressed to the Metropolitan Fertility Clinic—Hannah was stealing magazines from the waiting room.

There wasn't anything useful in the living room, so I moved down the hallway to the first bedroom. I flipped the light switch and looked around.

Another futon, no bed. I'd stumbled across the only people in New York City who actually slept on a futon. A down sleeping bag was stretched across the cotton pad, acting as sheets and blanket. Baseball bats and mitts, weights, running shoes, and sweat socks were scattered across the floor. Dirty blue jeans and sweat suits were mixed in to make it interesting. Posters of athletes with the caption "Just Do It" covered the walls.

I'd heard enough lectures about vitamins, exercise, taking care of my body, and not smoking to know this was Nikki's room. I was happy to see she couldn't keep it clean.

I rummaged through the dresser, desk, and closet and didn't find anything. No address book. No letters from friends or relatives. No mysterious scraps of paper with phone numbers. The corner of a paperback book stuck out from beneath the sleeping bag. Interested in Nikki's choice of bedtime reading, I pulled it out.

Good pill? Bad pill? "What you don't know about the drugs your doctor prescribes can kill you!" The glossy cover featured a picture of a medicine bottle tipped over on its side, multicolored pills spilled out. A bookmark was stuck in the middle of a chapter on allergies. I replaced the marker in the book, stuck it under the sleeping bag, and went to the next bedroom.

Nikki and Hannah may have been identical twins, but their decorating ideas weren't even close to being similar. Nikki's room reminded me of a rebellious teenager's, stocked with posters and music that would offend a strict parent. Neat and frilly, Hannah's was the bedroom of a little girl yearning to be a ballerina or princess.

The bedspread and curtains were cut from the same lacy pink material, the rug was a deeper hue of pink. Teddy bears, giraffes, and other stuffed animals occupied the bed, the tabletops, and the bookshelves.

An empty crib stood in the corner inches from the bed so Hannah could reach its occupant without getting up. An embroidered picture hanging over the crib labeled it "Joshua's Home."

Two boxes sat on the floor next to the crib. One was filled with diapers and tiny blue sleepers. Rattles, toys, and pacifiers spilled out of the second box. Not the things you'd expect to find in the bedroom of a woman planning to give the baby away moments after its birth.

I quickly checked the drawers, closet, and garbage cans. I looked under the mattress, then the bed, and didn't find a thing.

No photo album. No childhood treasures. No vacation souvenirs. No diary. No typewriter.

The bathroom was a waste of time. After quickly poking through the containers of baby powder, shampoo, and toothpaste, I went to the kitchen.

Kitchens are a popular spot for hiding valuables. People stick the jewelry in the freezer, extra car keys in the flour canisters, and the cash in the refrigerator. If this had been my lucky day, the address and phone number of Hannah's hideout would have been taped to the refrigerator door. It wasn't my lucky day—a shopping list (tofu, broccoli, decaffeinated coffee) was the only thing hanging on the gleaming white surface.

The kitchen was a health food haven—organic this, whole wheat that. The refrigerator held a pitcher of orange juice, fruit, a bowl of leftover brown rice, milk, and a jar of sprouts. No meat. No ice cream in the freezer. No junk food in the cabinets. Nothing to satisfy a pregnant woman's cravings.

I went back to the living room, sat on the lumpy futon, and frowned. The apartment was lifeless. It had no character, none of the individual touches that make our living quarters home. This apartment had the charm and personality of a shabby furniture showroom or a seedy motel.

Where were the photos, the mementos, the correspondence, the clues to the lives of the people who occupied the space? Why were they missing?

The hissing and clanking of the radiators as the heat worked its way up from the basement were my only answers. I pushed myself to my feet and left. The hallway was still empty. I pulled the door closed, used the SuperPick to lock the locks, and got out of the building before anyone saw me.

I treated myself to a cab ride home and was blessed with a driver who didn't ask directions, didn't drive like a demolition-derby contestant, and didn't have an opinion on anything. The car turned the corner to Barrow Street and I saw light shining from the windows of my house. I smiled. Nikki was still working; I'd have another chance to talk to her.

Michael Jackson was still blaring from the stereo. My callous ears couldn't tell if it was the same song or a different one. The vacuum cleaner was humming upstairs, its wheels scraping across the wood floor. I kicked my damp running shoes into the corner near the door and hurried to the living room to snap the stereo off. The vacuuming stopped before Michael's voice faded away.

Nikki ran down the stairs. She was two or three inches shorter than me. Her hair was blond, her eyes blue, and skin tan. Nikki looked like one of the California girls immortalized by the Beach Boys. She carried the vacuum in one hand, the hose and attachments in the other.

Nikki smiled. "Hi, Blaine. I'm done. Let me dump this monster and I'm out of here. You'll have peace and quiet; I'm taking Michael with me." Nikki went to the kitchen to hide the vacuum in the pantry. It would stay there until her next visit.

I followed, making inane conversation about the weather. "It's cold out. I think it's going to snow again."

Nikki smiled again. She always smiled. "Good. I just love all this snow. I hope we get another foot. Cross-country skiing in Central Park was a blast. I want to do it again."

"Don't rush out just because I'm home. If you have more work to do, do it. Take your time. You won't bother me."

"Nope, I'm really done. This is my last job tonight; I'm going home. What about you? Are you home for the evening, or do you have to go back to work?"

"No more work for me tonight. I'm going to make some hot chocolate and relax." I casually invited her to join me. Nikki shifted her weight from one foot to the other, looking for an opportunity to escape.

"No, thanks. It's late. I've bothered you enough tonight. I know you really didn't have to go out before. You were just too polite to hang around and make me feel rushed."

Laughing, I filled a kettle with water and put it on the stove. "It's been a long time since anyone accused me of being polite. Hey, Nikki, don't worry, you didn't push me out into the cold. I had to go back to my office and drop off some papers for my sister. I insist. It's too cold to go out without something warm inside you."

I kept a straight face as I repeated the lectures my mother used to give. I took two mugs and hot chocolate mix from a cabinet. The box was empty. I tossed it in the garbage and said, "Time to go shopping again. How about tea?"

"Is it decaffeinated?"

"No. How about coffee?"

"Decaf?"

I was prepared. "Yes. A well-meaning aunt gave it to me for Christmas. I've been trying to get rid of it ever since."

"Skim milk?"

I laughed. "How about no milk? You've seen inside the refrigerator—that stuff in the milk carton isn't fit to drink."

Nikki sat and watched me make the coffee. While we waited for the water to boil, I entertained her with fictitious stories about how my mother made hot cocoa on cold winter nights, read a story, then sent us off to bed. Mom would forgive my lies; I wanted Nikki to relax.

I did all the talking. Nikki nodded her head and smiled. She didn't reciprocate with any stories from her childhood.

When our drinks were ready, I carried the cups to the table and sat down next to her. "Nikki, did you grow up in the city?"

"No. No, I didn't."

"When I was a kid, I always wondered what it was like to live in the suburbs. Eileen and I used to make up little plays about growing up in Connecticut. For some reason, we decided Connecticut was the place to be. What was it like?" Nikki's face was expressionless. I said, "The suburbs—was it like *Leave It to Beaver?*"

"What were the suburbs like?" She hesitated. "I don't know. The country. I grew up in the country."

"Oh, really? Where?"

"Where did I grow up?" Nikki bit her lip and stared at the coffee mug. "Out West. I grew up out West. I hated it. I couldn't wait to leave."

I started another question. Nikki stopped me. "Blaine, I gotta ask you something." She hesitated. I told her to go ahead and ask her question. "I went down in your basement for a mop—it's a mess down there. Do you want me to put in a few extra hours next week to get it in shape? You're gonna have a fire if you leave those boxes too close to the furnace."

Agreeing would give me more access to Nikki, more time to pump her for information about her sister. Nikki misinterpreted my silence. Her personality changed; my good-natured cleaning lady disappeared. Anger poured from Nikki's eyes, a crimson flush spread across her face. She rolled her hands into fists and clenched them at her side.

In a tightly controlled voice she asked, "What's wrong? Don't you believe me? I'm not trying to rip you off. Go down and look around; the work needs to be done."

Hoping my calm would be contagious, I said, "You're doing a great job. My house hasn't been this clean since the day it was built. You caught me by surprise; I didn't realize the downstairs had gotten out of control. If the work needs to be done, do it. When can you start?"

The flush on Nikki's face receded; her hands relaxed. "My schedule is tight, but I'll come back in a few days. I'll come twice a week until it's done." After another slight hesitation, she said, "There's gonna be a lot of heavy cleaning. I'll have to charge extra. Is that okay?"

"It's fine." I didn't care how much it cost. My basement would be clean and I might get a hint about Hannah's whereabouts. Judith's fee would be high enough to cover the added expense. "It'll be worth it."

"I'm gonna have to come at night. I can't do it during the day. I have too many other jobs. I can't afford to dump any one of them."

"Nights are fine. I may be around, but I'll try to keep out of your way." With Dennis gone, I'd be home every night—alone. Hanging out with Nikki and pumping her for information would be a good diversion.

After settling on a fair wage for the increased work, Nikki escaped. I watched her leave before making a quick inspection tour of the house. My suspicious nerves were jumping.

Nikki had been busy. She'd cleaned the place, and tossed it too. Her cleaning was professional; her snooping was sloppy. Papers in the desk were out of order, clothes in my closets were hanging askew, a slight scratch on the filing cabinet betrayed a clumsy attempt to pick the lock.

Nikki didn't find anything that would connect me to Judith Marsden because there wasn't anything. I never brought information on current cases home from the office—just in case someone decided to snoop.

I talked myself into believing it was coincidence that Nikki had chosen that evening to become curious about my work. My theory held until I noticed the blinking light on my answering machine.

I punched the button to play the message and heard a breathless voice. "Blaine, this is Judith Marsden. I called your office, but you were gone. I'll be in your office at nine tomorrow morning. Don't do anything about locating Hannah until I talk to you . . ."

I snapped the machine off. Had Nikki listened to the message? I went to bed with the disquieting thought that the enemy had a key to my front door. When the morning came around again, I was happy to get out of bed.

Chapter 6

In less than a day, Judith had changed from an overanxious client who called every two minutes for updates to a sullen, uncooperative stranger. From the moment she walked into my office—twenty-three minutes late—I knew I was going to have a difficult time.

Judith didn't apologize for being late. She didn't even say hello. She dropped into a chair and curtly asked, "Have you found her yet?"

"Did I guarantee overnight results?" Quickly, because I didn't want to argue, I asked, "Did you bring a copy of Hannah's surrogate application and the contract?"

"I've been thinking. I'm not sure it's a good idea to give them to you. That's why I called you last night."

Judith stared at me, defying me to challenge her. I accepted the challenge. "How do you expect me to find Hannah if you won't tell me anything but her name and address?" Judith shrugged, her perfectly made-up face remained impassive. "Do you want to fire me? It's no problem. I'll have the bookkeeper draw up a check. We'll refund the entire retainer. Consider yesterday's work a gift."

If Nelson called his attorneys after my visit, wouldn't he also call his patient? Bastard. He called Judith, yanked on every fearful nerve, and convinced her to drop the search. For the good of the baby.

Stifling a curse, I gently asked, "Did Dr. Nelson talk to you? Did he tell you to stop your silly worrying? That Hannah will come back if you leave her alone for a few days? That you should get rid of me before I cause trouble between you and Hannah?"

Judith trusted Nelson because he was going to give her a baby. He was using that faith to protect his clinic. *Bastard.*

I tried to shake Judith's confidence in the doctor. "Nelson may be a genius in his field, but he doesn't know anything about missing people. I do. Hannah is not going to wander back after a few days' vacation. Her note made that clear to me. I think it's clear to you too. Do you want to find your son? Or are you going to let him disappear forever because you're too afraid to do anything?"

Tears were running down Judith's cheeks by the time I finished. Feeling guilty for being so brutal, I sat back and watched. Nelson and I were in a tug of war, using Judith's love for her unborn child as the rope, not caring if we stretched her past her limits. Judith quivered and slid closer to my side.

"I don't know what I should do. Dr. Nelson was trying to help. I . . ." She closed her eyes and repeated the words she used the day before. "I want you to find my son."

Before Judith had second thoughts, I asked, "Do you remember the name of the town where Hannah grew up?"

"It's in New Jersey. Somewhere near Pennsylvania. Hannah

talked about it the first time we met. The name is . . . I don't remember."

"If you were pregnant, frightened, and alone, wouldn't you
want to be in a familiar place? A place where everyone is on your
side? Hannah may have gone back home to be with her family
and friends."

The blank look on Judith's face destroyed my patience. I
tossed my pencil on the desk and snapped, "This is ridiculous.
You're wasting my time. I can't find your son if you won't give
me anything to go on."

Judith ignored my outburst. She closed her eyes. "The name
of the town has animals in it. Animals that live in the forest."

"Lions, tigers, bears, deer." I was born in Manhattan. I don't
have much experience with animals that live in the forest. I
stopped. My animal list was almost exhausted. "Eagles?"

"Beavers."

"Beavers. Beavers what? There's got to be more to the name
than beavers. Beavers Hollow? Beavers Lake? Beavers Dam?
Beavers Falls?"

Judith opened her eyes. They were bright with triumph. "Beaver Ridge. Beaver Ridge, New Jersey."

Progress, no matter how small it is, makes me happy. I smiled
my encouragement. "Are Hannah's parents still alive?"

"Yes, they are. I wanted to know about Hannah's childhood; I
asked a lot of questions about her parents. They're in their late
sixties, early seventies. Hannah said she grew up on a farm. Do
you really think she went home?"

Hope wiped the worry lines from Judith's forehead. "It's possible. People who are running away tend to go back to comfortable surroundings."

"What are we going to do? Should we call them?"

"*We're* not going to do anything." The lines reappeared on
Judith's face, wrinkling her makeup. "You'll go home and put together a packet of the papers you have on Hannah. I'm going to
get up early tomorrow morning and visit the Wyricks."

I know how anxious minds work, so I added a warning:
"Don't do anything stupid like calling Beaver Ridge. If Hannah
is there, she'll be gone before you hang up the phone. This is our

first good lead. Don't blow it." Judith promised. I crossed my fingers and hoped she wasn't lying.

I walked Judith to the elevators, offering encouragement along the way. As the doors closed on her, I hoped her resolve would last. The office gradually quieted down as five o'clock came and went. By six, almost everyone was gone. I didn't leave, I was afraid to go home. I was in the restless, uncertain mood that used to lead to an evening of drinking. I decided to stay in the office and work on my neglected paperwork. Dull, but better than going home and pretending I didn't want to get drunk. I buried myself in the papers on my desk.

Eileen wandered in around six-thirty. She was wearing her coat and carrying a briefcase. It's a tradition. No matter how late we are, or how busy the day has been, we always take a few minutes at the end of the day to visit with each other—as sisters, not partners.

"I'm on my way out. Everyone else is gone. What about you, are you staying?"

"Yeah." I brushed hair from my eyes. "I'm going to be here at least another hour. Maybe longer." Maybe all night.

Eileen dropped her briefcase on a chair and walked around the desk to look over my shoulder. "What's keeping you here so late? Anything I can do to help?"

"Thanks, but there isn't anything you can do. I'm reading reports and writing reports. Making notes to Jona about things I need done tomorrow." I lit a cigarette, balanced it on the lip of the ashtray, and turned my chair to face Eileen. "I won't be in tomorrow. I got a lead on the missing surrogate. I'm going to Jersey to check it out."

Eileen sat on the edge of my desk. She took a cigarette and absentmindedly tapped it on my desk. "I was going to ask about that project. I heard from Mr. O'Keefe again today."

"What was he complaining about? I haven't had time to do anything to make him mad."

"Mr. O'Keefe sent a letter as a follow-up to our telephone conversation. He threatened to get a restraining order to keep you away from the clinic. You know, Blaine, if he gets it and you violate the order, you could wind up in jail."

I shrugged. "That's a chance we'll have to take. Next time I go visit Dr. Nelson, I'll take a quarter along. When the cops bust me, I'll call you."

"Blaine—"

"Eileen."

Sometimes our sisterly chats quickly slip into an argument. Eileen would accuse me of being flippant. I would call her humorless. It's our standard fight. We've been having it since I was old enough to talk back to her. This time Eileen surprised me; she laughed.

"Forget it, do what you want. I'm getting out of here. My daughter's waiting for me to take her out to dinner. Don's out of town again. Sandy really misses him when he's gone. It's difficult for her to understand that her Daddy's a pilot and he has to be gone a lot."

Eileen sighed. "I can sympathize. I have trouble with it myself. Why don't you come with us? Sandy would love to see you. It's been weeks since you visited. But I have to warn you, she's still on her Chinese food kick. We're going out for moo shu beef."

I looked at my half-written report, then I looked at Eileen. Six months earlier, Eileen almost died when a letter bomb exploded in her office. Since then, the worrying tables had subtly turned. Now I was the worrier.

I've learned to rant and rave and let my problems fly; Eileen still holds her problems inside, letting them ferment. I took a closer look at Eileen. Her smile didn't carry to her eyes. The dark circles under her eyes were only partially hidden by makeup.

I put the cap on my pen and tossed it on the desk. "You win. I'll go—as long as I can order something else. Give me a minute to put this stuff in a pile."

We stopped at the nursery where Sandy spends her after-kindergarten hours. My niece was making believe that she was playing with Play-Doh, but she kept glancing at the door. It was time for her special evening out with Mom. And Mom was late.

When we walked in, Sandy rushed across the room and flung

herself at her mother's knees. The hugging and kissing commotion lasted until she realized I was standing behind her mother. While Sandy hugged and kissed me, Eileen gathered up boots, mittens, and coat. I watched the struggle to get the garments on and expected to see Eileen lose her patience as Sandy flailed her arms and legs. Instead, mother and daughter collapsed into giggles.

We went to a typical Upper East Side Chinese restaurant. The pink tablecloths on the oval tables were protected by glass tops. A squat votive candle, its flame sputtering as the wick burned close to the pool of wax, a drooping carnation in a Perrier bottle, a bottle of soy sauce, and an ashtray sat in the center of each table.

I shrugged out of my coat and dropped it on an empty chair. While Eileen and Sandy went through a reverse struggle to get the warm clothes off, a waiter silently placed a teapot, cups, and menus on the table. I poured tea and watched.

Even though she was only five years old, Sandy had the stubborn jaw and disposition of her mother's family, the green eyes and quick smile of her father's. Her hair was curly blond. If Sandy followed her mother, her hair wouldn't get much darker. If she followed her dad, her hair would gradually deepen and turn black.

After we ordered, I sat back and lit a cigarette. The flickering candlelight highlighted the deep furrows in Eileen's forehead; those lines always appeared when Don was out on an extended trip. We let Sandy talk about her day, drank tea, and avoided any talk of business or those lines.

The light conversation lasted until midway through the meal. That's when I made the mistake of yawning and saying, "I'm tired. How about you? You look beat."

On cue, Eileen dropped her chopsticks and sighed. "I don't know how much longer I can put up with this. I'm tired of being a single mother. Don's been doing an international route. He flies in, stays for a day, then he flies out. He's never around to deal with the measles, teacher's conferences, and getting the kid into bed. It's hard to do all that and still win in court in the morning."

The kid rolled pancakes around pieces of beef. She didn't pay attention to the dull conversation going on around her. I poked around in the pile of vegetables on the platter in the center of the table and speared a shrimp that was hiding under a snow pea. Before popping it into my mouth, I casually asked, "What are you going to do?"

"I'll put the kid to bed tonight. I'll go to the teacher's conference next week. I'll deal with the measles when she gets them. I'll go to court tomorrow—and I'll win."

"Always the good soldier . . ."

Eileen's temper flared. "I'm so sick of hearing that. Let me use one of your favorite lines: I'm only doing my job. I said I'm tired. I didn't say I was quitting. You're not the only stubborn one in this family. What about you?"

Turning the conversation around to question the questioner is a favorite family trick. I searched for another shrimp. When I couldn't find one, I laid my chopsticks across my plate and sat back.

"This discussion isn't about me, Eileen. It's about you."

Sandy's fragile grip on her moo shu beef faltered. The mess dropped into her plate with a soggy plop. She impatiently jerked on Eileen's arm for help and ended our conversation. As Eileen made a child-sized bundle out of the pancake and meat, she cautiously said, "There's something else I want to talk to you about. People who go to fertility clinics are usually pretty desperate. They're not as selfish as you think . . ."

Eileen stopped talking and stared at the fork in her hand. I didn't intrude on her thoughts; I refilled the teacups and waited.

"Sandy never would have been born if we didn't go to a clinic."

My sister and I had been working side by side for the past ten years. Forty, fifty, sixty hours a week. I thought I knew everything about her. I was wrong.

I put my teacup down and stared across the table at this sudden stranger. I remembered the times when Eileen or Don abruptly ended any discussion about children by saying, *When we decide to have a baby, you'll know.* "Why didn't you say something? Did you think we wouldn't understand?"

"We considered the clinic an extension of our bedroom. It wasn't a subject we wanted to open up for debate by our family and friends. We were feeling enough pressure. We didn't want to add to it by talking about what we were trying to do. We had nothing but faith. 'Faith may be defined briefly as an illogical belief in the occurrence of the impossible.' "

Knowing Eileen's penchant for quoting Greek philosophers, I asked, "Plato?"

Eileen looked at me like I was an idiot. "H. L. Mencken. Going to the clinic was a leap of faith. Faith in the doctors. Faith that our marriage would last through the dehumanizing tests and procedures. It was a decision Don and I had to make on our own. There were times I didn't think we'd survive. But whenever I look at Sandy, I'm so thrilled that our faith was rewarded. There's one more thing you should know: We'd do it again."

A sudden thought struck. I leaned forward for a closer look at Eileen's eyes. "Does the Marsden case make you feel uncomfortable? Would you like me to find a graceful way to withdraw from it?"

She laughed, a loud, deep laugh that made two other couples in the restaurant turn to look at us. "Graceful? You? Don't worry, Blaine, we used a different clinic. There's no conflict of interest here."

I wanted to ask about emotional conflicts of interest, but never got the chance. Sandy decided it was time to go home.

The rebundling efforts took another ten minutes. In that time, I paid the bill and left a tip. When Sandy was securely wrapped in her coat, hat, and mittens, I led them outside and stopped a cab. Before Eileen climbed inside, she stopped, put her hand on my arm, and issued her standard warning.

"Blaine, be careful tomorrow. Call me when you get back so I know everything's okay."

As always, I promised to be careful and promised to call. Sometimes I even keep my promises.

Chapter 7

A cheerful voice blared in the darkness. "Good morning, New York City. It's six-thirty in the a.m. and a chilly thirty-six degrees on the outside. Clear and cold is the forecast for the day. Stay home if you can. And now for the news—"

Without opening my eyes, I slapped the snooze button. I didn't want to hear the news. I didn't want to get out of bed. It was cold outside and I was warm under my down comforter. Getting up and driving to New Jersey didn't seem like a good idea. I decided to wait until the sun came up . . .

Then I remembered the stack of unfinished work on my desk. If I got up, I could go to the office, get through the mess of papers that needed my attention, and be on my way with a clear conscience. Regretting the lost sleep, I rolled out of bed.

I thought I'd be the first person in the office. I was wrong. Judith Marsden beat me. She sprang from the chair that's next to the door and clutched my arm. Even through the heavy sleeves of my coat, I felt the panic in her grasp.

"Your receptionist isn't here yet."

"That's because it's only seven-thirty. She usually doesn't get here until nine. Judith, what are you doing here?"

"I hope you don't mind. The man who let me in said I could wait here. He said he had work to do, but it was okay to sit here."

Brad chose that moment to pop his curly head around the corner to investigate the noise. I nodded at him. He saluted and disappeared.

"Judith . . ." I pried her fingers from my arm and stepped back to take a close look at her. No makeup this morning. Judith's face was pale and drawn with the slack look of a person in shock. The frayed hems of black sweatpants hung below her long overcoat. "What's wrong?"

"Hannah sent me a letter. Blaine, she calls my son Joshua. How can she do that? He's Jerry Junior, not Joshua."

"Let me see the letter. Come on, let's go sit down while I read it."

Judith held out a wrinkled, and I think tear-stained, envelope. I took it and guided her to the leather sofa that fills a small recessed nook at the far end of our small reception area. After pushing Judith down onto it, I sat beside her and took the note from the envelope.

The note was written by hand in black ink. It didn't have any greeting.

"You aren't having this baby, I am. If you knew what we've been through, you'd leave us alone. You'd understand why we left.

"They took me to the room and told me to lay down. No one explained anything to me. No one paid attention to me. The room filled with people, doctors I think. They made me spread my legs and make jokes about the weather while they stuck things inside me. To them I was nothing.

"I closed my eyes and tried to imagine that I was far, far away. But even with my eyes closed, I knew I was in a hospital room. The same room where I was before. And the time before that and the time before that.

"Five times. 'Hannah, this is your last chance,' they said. Your last chance to make this work. The doctors didn't care that it hurt. They didn't care that I was afraid.

" 'Keep still. Don't move or you'll jar the embryo loose before it has a chance to root.' Like it was my fault it didn't work the other times.

"I was so afraid. I kept my legs pressed together as tight as I could. I concentrated on not moving. I was afraid to move. Afraid the the slightest motion would spill the egg from my body. It would bounce across the tile floor. The janitor would find it in a dusty corner of the room.

"I prayed, 'Be still. Give him time. Give him life. Be still. Give him time. Give him life.'

"It worked. I felt Joshua grab hold and begin growing. He was safe. Every morning, before I do anything, I pat my belly just to be sure he's safe. He'll be safe with me forever.

"Joshua is my child. It was wrong to say I'd sell him to you. Stop trying to find us. If you don't, we'll go away forever."

The handwriting was difficult to read, but the message was clear: Forget the search or forget the son.

"What *she's* been through!" Judith's voice hit a loud, shrill note. "What about what I went through? I had my own set of tubes and pain and fears and prayers. What gives her the right to take my son away from me?"

My attempts to calm Judith were inadequate. The door opened. I looked over, hoping for salvation. Eileen walked in, wrapped in her warmest coat and carrying her biggest briefcase. I waved. She walked over to us.

"Blaine, I didn't expect to see you this morning. What's going on?"

"Eileen, this is Judith Marsden." Judith acknowledged the introduction with a shaky bob of her head. Eileen's eyes narrowed as she studied Judith's face.

I held the note out to Eileen. "Take a look at this. Judith received it . . ." I looked at Judith and asked, "When did this come?"

After dropping her briefcase on the floor and stripping her coat off, Eileen took the note from my outstretched hand and sat on the arm of the sofa. Judith talked about finding the note while Eileen read it.

"I found it this morning. Someone slipped it into my newspaper. I get the *Times* delivered. When I opened the front page, the envelope fell out on the floor. I thought it was an ad. I almost threw it away unopened."

Eileen finished reading the note and gave it back to me. She looked at Judith. "I can understand this woman's feelings but—" Judith moaned a protest. Eileen held up a hand and motioned for her to wait. "—this is emotional blackmail. Who delivered it?"

I answered. "Nikki. Who else has access to the house?"

"She doesn't have access anymore. I fired her two nights ago. Under the circumstances, I thought it best to keep Nikki out of my sight and my house. I paid Nikki off and told her I'd make other arrangements."

Eileen and Judith looked at me. In unison they asked, "Blaine, what are you going to do?"

I smoothed the paper on my lap, hoping knowledge of Hannah's whereabouts would seep in through my fingertips. "There's nothing here that can help me find Hannah. The plan remains the same: I'm going to Beaver Ridge to see if Hannah is hiding out with her mom and dad. Judith, let me hang on to this letter. If you get any more, bring them to me. If I'm not here, ask for Eileen."

"Can't I keep the letter? You just said you don't need it."

Visions of Judith spending her entire day and most of the night sitting in a chair and staring at the letter guided my answer. "No, it's best if I keep it here in your file."

Eileen guessed the reason for my answer and added her support. "Judith, that note could become evidence. It's very important for us to have the original in our possession. Now, why don't you go home and try to get some rest? Let Blaine do her job."

That seemed to work. Judith sniffed and agreed to go home. Eileen and I walked Judith to the elevator and stood on either side of her as we waited. Judith bit down on her quivering lower lip and sighed. Eileen patted her arm reassuringly. "Judith, Blaine's doing everything she can. Just hang in there. If something comes up while Blaine's out of town, call me."

Judith tried to smile. After the elevator disappeared, Eileen followed me back inside our office. "Do you think she'll hold up?"

"I don't know. Nelson's putting a lot of pressure on her. This note only makes it worse."

I sat on the sofa and read the note out loud. The words sounded worse when they floated in the quiet air of our reception room.

"Do you think the surrogate put this letter together on her own? Or do you think she had some help?"

"From someone like Dr. Nelson?" I smoothed the paper again and felt a blanket of depression fall over me. "This is a wonderfully effective threat. Hannah jabs all of Judith's tender spots: You're a failure because you can't have a child. You made me go through endless cycles of fear and failure. I'm only trying to do what's best for the child and you're hounding me." I shook my head. "No wonder Judith's a mess."

I believe in bad luck, and this day reeked of bad luck. I wiped beads of sweat from my forehead and realized I was still wearing my coat. Rather than taking it off and going to my office, I decided to leave before another interruption walked through the door.

Eileen had other ideas. Before I could get away, she said, "I hate to bring up business, but I will. Can you delay your trip for fifteen or twenty minutes? I need your advice."

Advice on an upcoming court case led to a discussion of other matters. Before I knew it, an hour had passed and I was still in Manhattan. Without going to my office to confront the stack of papers, I said a hurried good-bye to Eileen and rushed out.

Chapter 8

· · · · · · · · · ·

It should have been an easy trip to drive to Riverside Drive and up to the George Washington Bridge, but it wasn't. I got caught in a traffic jam caused by New York City's perpetual road repair program and crept along the potholed asphalt to the bridge.

Forty-five minutes later, I was driving across the George Washington Bridge. If I hadn't been so annoyed about the traffic, I would have enjoyed the view. I glanced at a cruise ship slowly making its way to the piers and fantasized about a trip to a warmer climate. Even through the protective lenses of my sunglasses, the glare of the sun on the Hudson made me squint. I gave up thinking about sailing away and concentrated on driving.

Once I was safely across the bridge, I stopped at a gas station to fill my tank—gas is a lot cheaper in New Jersey. I also bought a cup of coffee and, since my maps end a few miles outside New York City, a map. I parked near the highway to look at the map and drink my coffee.

After a lot of searching, I found my destination. Beaver Ridge was a few miles south of the Delaware Water Gap, not far from Route 80. I folded the map, bought a second cup of coffee, and drove west through the backyards of the bedroom communities and the factories that inspired generations of New Jersey jokes. The suburban ugliness was gradually replaced by snow-covered fields, woodlands, and hills.

The trip took over two hours; it would have been less if I'd given into temptation and driven faster. My bright red Porsche always attracts attention from cops anxious to make their ticket quota or stop a big-time drug dealer. I ignored the lure of the empty highway and kept the speedometer at a steady fifty-five.

The urge to speed disappeared when I left the interstate and hit the first pothole on Route 46. The road, which was once the main thoroughfare between New York City and the Pocono resorts, was dotted with ruts and poorly repaired ruts. I eased up on the gas pedal and watched for a phone booth. My plan was simple: find a telephone book and match the phone number given to me by New Jersey Bell information. "We don't do that," was the response to my request for an address.

My head told me it was time to find that telephone book; my stomach told me it was lunchtime. Since I'd never eaten breakfast, I couldn't ignore the rumblings.

A few miles down the road, I came to a truck stop called Bobo's Diner. The two signs hanging from the awning cheered me. The first sign proclaimed that the diner was open. The second promised a telephone. I swung the car into the empty parking lot and stopped a few feet from the door. Leaving my coat behind, I grabbed my cigarettes, matches, and wallet, and hurried inside.

Gleaming aluminum covered the inside and outside of the long, narrow diner. A row of empty booths lined the wall near the entrance; four steps beyond was a long counter with stools for solitary patrons. The grill, steam tables, and refrigerators were all behind the counter.

The diner had only one occupant. A woman sat on a high barstool behind the counter, smoking a cigarette and reading a book. She was big and her uniform was small. The buttons of her pink blouse strained to stay closed.

The woman held up an index finger. Without looking up from the page, she said, "Make yourself comfortable. I'll be with you in just a sec—I can't stop in the middle of a paragraph. I lose my place, then I get pissed off."

I sat at the counter and used her lighter to get a cigarette going. The woman closed the book and tossed it on the counter. I glanced at the title. Anne Tyler's *The Accidental Tourist.*

The woman behind the counter pointed at the book. In a slightly embarrassed voice she said, "That's the only kind of tourist we get around here these days. Are you lost, honey?"

"No, I'm hungry." I looked at the clock hanging over the grill. One-thirty. "Is it too late for breakfast?"

"Honey, people around here usually get around to eating their breakfast a bit earlier in the day. But it don't matter to me. Long as you have the money to pay the tab, you can order anything your stomach needs to make it happy. I don't care. I can cook breakfast just as easy as I can cook lunch."

She slid to her feet and waddled to the coffee urn. "Name's Doreen. You want coffee? It's fresh, I just brewed it."

"Coffee's fine. How about scrambled eggs, bacon, and rye toast to go with it?" Cholesterol be damned; I wanted to eat. As atonement, I'd run five miles tomorrow morning. I sneezed and added a large orange juice to the order.

"Sure thing, honey. The eggs are the freshest you'll find in the county. They were laid 'bout twenty minutes ago. We have our own hens out back. They're in a fertile period right now, laying two, three times a day. I say they're freaks. Bobo says they're gifted and we should be thankful. Here's your coffee."

She put a thick white mug down in front of me and placed a carton of half and half next to it. The coffee was strong and hot. After taking a sip, I finished smoking my cigarette and watched Doreen throw bacon on the grill and crack eggs into a bowl.

Doreen weighed at least three hundred pounds. Her beehive hairdo, which was anchored by a black hair net, was at least six inches high, making it difficult to judge her height. The hair net matched the dark roots growing in her dyed blond hair. She wheezed and chattered as she worked.

"Where are you from, honey? I haven't seen you around here

before. I certainly would have remembered you. Is that red hair real?" She laughed. "If it isn't, your hairdresser deserves a big tip. Anyway, I would have remembered you. We don't get much out of town business during the winter."

She laughed again and fought off an attack of wheezing before continuing. "Hell, we don't get much business during the summer. But we can always count on the weekend canoeists to put in and come in for a helping of real food. By the time they get this far on the river, they're sick of the stuff they've been burning over their campfires. We put a sign up about a mile or two upstream advertising a canoe special. Free parking. Free refills of coffee thermoses. Free ice for their coolers. It always works. On a good weekend we make enough money to pay the mortgage."

Doreen put a fresh mug of coffee in front of me and repeated her question. "Where are you from, honey?"

I said, "Manhattan," and braced for the usual flurry of questions about how I could live in such a dirty, violent, expensive place. Sometimes I lie and tell people I'm from Vermont or Colorado.

Doreen sighed. "I just adore Manhattan. We couldn't live without the museums and the theater." She patted her thighs and laughed again. "We love the restaurants too. It's a shame, we only get there a few times a year. We'd go more often except we don't have anybody to run this place when we're gone."

I was surprised and told her. Doreen laughed and put a dish, covered with towering piles of food, on the counter. While I ate, we talked about plays, restaurants, and shopping. Every time I was close to finishing the coffee, Doreen filled the mug.

I ate until I couldn't swallow another bite and reluctantly pushed the plate away. Doreen snatched the plate, scraped it clean, and quickly stuck it in the dishwasher. She refilled my coffee mug and emptied the ashtray. Then she resumed her perch on the barstool and lit a cigarette. Plop, plop—her shoes dropped to the floor.

She sighed and watched me light another cigarette. "My feet are killing me. So, if you aren't lost, why are you up here in the middle of winter?"

I answered her question by asking, "Do you have a telephone book? I have to find an address."

"Help yourself." Doreen leaned back and pulled a phone directory from the shelf behind her. She tossed it on the counter. "Who are you looking for?"

I found an address: Brunswick Road. Disappointed, I closed the book. I was hoping for a clearer address. Doreen waited for an answer. I didn't feel comfortable with the truth, so I lied. "I'm looking for a place to stay, in case I decide to stay over tonight. Do you know any place that would be open this time of year?"

"Sure. Cecilia Hoffman runs a bed and breakfast in town, on Main Street. It's not fancy, but it's clean. You can't miss it. It's a big white house with red shutters." I ignored the little voice which was telling me to be careful and asked another question. "Do you know Ethel Wyrick?"

The friendliness disappeared from Doreen's eyes and voice. "Sure, I know Ethel. I know her husband Ronald, too." She uncrossed her legs and leaned forward. "Honey, if you drove up here just to drop in on Ethel Wyrick, you've wasted your time. If Ethel wanted to see you, she would have told you how to find her. I don't know what you're after, but I won't help you. Those poor souls have had enough trouble in their lives."

I protested mildly. "Hey, it's no big deal. I know their daughters. I just wanted to say hello."

Doreen scribbled a figure on the check and dropped it in front of me. "I despise liars. Pay for your meal and get on out of here. I don't put up with troublemakers. And I think you're trying to make trouble."

It would have been useless to apologize, so I didn't. I picked the check up and looked at it. $3.99. A bargain, even if the meal ended on a heartburn-producing note. I pulled a ten dollar bill from the pocket of my jeans and put it on the counter. "I'm not trying to cause trouble. Maybe I'm thinking of the wrong family."

She took the bill and made change. I left a good tip and ran out to the car. A light snow was falling, and the Porsche was covered with a thin white layer. I brushed snow from the windows and shook my head.

Small towns. I'll never understand them. I looked over my shoulder at the diner. Doreen stood in the doorway, watching me. I started the car and drove away before she got nervous enough to call the police or write my license plate number down on the back of one of her checks.

I was born and raised in Manhattan. I'm used to streets and avenues with clearly marked addresses. After an hour of driving around what was supposed to be Brunswick Road, peering at mailboxes and fighting to keep the Porsche on slick roads, I gave up. My hunt would land me in a ditch before it led to the Wyricks. I slowly backtracked to the highway. By the time I found the village of Beaver Ridge it was nearly dark.

Main Street ran through the middle of town, neatly dividing it into two equal sections. An old-fashioned town square, complete with band shell and gazebo, sat in the center of the town. The courthouse, library, post office, and police station anchored the corners surrounding the square. I parked in front of the post office and shuffled through the snow to the brick building.

I was following a brilliantly simple plan. If you're looking for an address, ask at the post office. They know where everyone lives; sometimes they can be convinced to be helpful. Before going inside, I stamped the snow from my feet and cautioned myself to be more tactful than I'd been with Doreen.

Another bit of good advice I couldn't follow. Within minutes of stepping inside the post office, I was arguing. "All I want is directions. Is it too difficult for you to tell me how to get there?"

The man behind the counter was not amused, impressed, or frightened. He said, "You want stamps, I'll sell them to you. You want directions, go to a gas station." When I tried to argue, he looked past me and called out, "Next!"

Chapter 9

The short, cold walk from the post office to the bed and breakfast sent me off on fantasies of living in tropical climates. For the thousandth time that winter, I decided to move to a place where the temperature never goes below sixty-five.

According to the brass plaque screwed into one of the pillars, Hoffman's Inn was an authentic historical landmark built in 1875. I read the marker and prayed that the furnace was built in this century.

The door was unlocked. I walked into the foyer and rubbed my cold hands together as I looked around. A gleaming mahogany desk, with nothing but an old-fashioned black rotary telephone on it, sat in the corner. Beyond the desk, I saw a narrow corridor ending in a dining room. To my left was a sitting room; a small fire burned in the fireplace inviting me to sit down and warm my cold feet. I called, "Hello. Is anybody here?"

A faint voice told me to wait in the lobby. I did as ordered and patiently waited until an elderly woman hurried down the hallway, wiping her hands on her apron as she walked. "I'm sorry, I didn't hear you come in. I'm Cecilia Hoffman. May I help you?"

"I hope so." I introduced myself and smiled. "I'm looking for a place to stay tonight. Doreen from the diner recommended your bed and breakfast."

"Well . . ." The woman forced a stray lock of her silver hair back into the neat bun at the back of her head and examined me. I tried to look respectable. "I wasn't expecting guests. It's my off-season. But I do have a room available. I always keep one ready. It's twenty-five dollars a night. It has a private bath."

She spoke rapidly, afraid the price was too high. "It includes breakfast. And a light dinner too—if you don't have other plans. Would you like to see the room before you decide?"

Relieved the sales pitch was over, I quickly said, "That won't be necessary. I'll take the room. My car's in front of the post office. I don't think it's a good idea to leave it there overnight. Where can I safely park it?"

Cecilia briskly answered. "By all means, use the driveway. I'm not going out again today. And if it does snow, your car will be safely out of reach of the plows. That's important. Otis tends to sideswipe cars parked at the curb. He hasn't attacked any in the driveway yet."

"Thanks. I don't want to give Otis an opportunity to add another trophy to his collection." Praying the snow wouldn't be deep enough to strand me in the town, I sprinted to my car and moved it to safety. I grabbed the overnight bag that's always on the floor behind the driver's seat and hurried back inside the house.

The innkeeper was waiting. She took me upstairs and led me to the back of the house, then stood in the hallway while I inspected the room. It didn't take me long. I dropped my bag on the floor and glanced around.

The room was clean. It was warm. The antiques filling the room didn't interest me, but the canopied bed looked soft and comfortable—I was sold. If Cecilia had immediately gone away and let me crawl under the fluffy comforter, I would have paid fifty dollars for the room.

"This is the most quiet room in the house, not that Beaver Ridge is noisy. But Otis makes a racket when he gets his snowplow going. You won't hear a sound."

After showing me the bathroom and the light switches, Cecilia explained the rules. "If you smoke, please use the sitting room. Smoking is prohibited on this floor. I lock the doors at ten-thirty. If you're going to be out past that time, I'll be happy to give you a key."

After telling her I wouldn't be going out, I asked permission to use the phone on the desk. I wanted to tell Eileen I'd be out for another day. Cecilia reluctantly granted me permission—if I used a credit card or made it a collect call—and disappeared.

The bed was inviting, but I resisted; I wasn't finished working. After splashing cold water on my face and trying to comb my hair, I went downstairs and called Eileen. It was a brief conversation. Brief because I didn't have anything to report.

Cecilia was waiting in the living room. Queen Anne furniture filled the room. The simple lines and worn upholstery told me it was the real thing, not a cheap department store knock-off. Cecilia sat on a stiff and obviously uncomfortable sofa. I chose a plush chair to the left of the sofa and glanced at the bottle on the table.

"Would you care for a glass of sherry? I find it a relaxing way to end a day. If you'd prefer something else, I have wine and beer."

I hesitated until I was sure I'd refuse, then said, "No, thank you. I don't drink."

"How about tea? It will only take a few minutes to boil the water." Cecilia bounced to her feet. "Sit here and relax. I'll be back as soon as the water boils."

I waited until she was gone, then prowled around the room, examining the pictures on the walls and the books on the shelves. My hostess was an avid reader. Her bookshelves were crammed with lurid, but true, stories of murder, betrayal, and deception. Hardcover editions of *Helter Skelter, Till Death Do Us Part,* and Vincent Bugliosi's other books filled one shelf. Most of them were first editions, signed by the author.

Another shelf was filled with books by Ann Rule, Joe McGinniss, and other authors whose names I didn't recognize, but the stories were the same. Children killing parents, parents killing children, serial killers, lovers killing lovers, strangers killing for kicks.

I've seen too many murder victims to get pleasure from reading about their murderers. I shuddered and turned away to look at something else. When Cecilia returned, I was staring at a class photo that hung on the wall next to the fireplace.

"You found my little darlings. Aren't they adorable? They're third-graders." Cecilia carried a tray which held a silver tea service, a plate of sandwiches, and two delicate china cups and saucers. She put the tray down on the low table in front of the sofa and poured tea.

Despite the huge meal I'd eaten a few hours earlier, my stomach rumbled. I ignored it and asked, "Are you a teacher?"

"I used to be. For forty-two years I taught third grade. When I started to have students who were the children of the children I taught in the fifties and sixties, I knew it was time to retire. It's not quite two years since I taught my last class."

I stopped patrolling the room and sat next to Cecilia. I sampled the tea. "After a day of driving around, this tastes good. Did you teach here in town?"

"Oh no, Beaver Ridge isn't large enough to have a school of its own. I taught in the regional school that's a few miles outside of town. Students are bused in from all over the county."

"Did you run this bed and breakfast while you were teaching? Or is this a new venture?"

Cecilia laughed. "You make it sound like it's a big business. It isn't. When I retired, I decided to open my house up as an inn. The income stretches my pension. That's nice, but it's the people I enjoy. The most interesting people stay here." She sipped her tea and studied me over the rim of the cup. "What is your occupation?"

I thought of the books on her shelves and made an unusual decision: I told the truth. "I'm a private investigator."

Curiosity brightened her eyes. "My goodness, that's an unusual occupation. Especially for a woman. I've never met a private investigator. How did you ever become involved in that type of work?"

I told her an abbreviated version of my professional life. Studying criminal justice in college, a brief stint with New York City's police department, and bouncing from an insurance company to a private agency before forming my partnership with Eileen. Cecilia was fascinated. Every time I paused to drink tea, or nibble on one of the sandwiches, she eagerly, but politely, waited for me to continue.

After three cups of tea, I stood to stretch my legs and check the weather. Snowflakes as large as my fist were falling, hiding the ground under a white blanket. Hannah's trail was getting cold and snow-covered while I enjoyed a tea party. I turned away from the window to nudge the conversation closer to the reason for my visit to Beaver Ridge.

Cecilia made it easy. "That's quite enough. I've been making you do all the talking while I sit here, drinking tea and eating. Give me a minute to warm the tea and put together another tray of sandwiches, then we'll talk about other things. I promise."

Half a cigarette later, Cecilia was back carrying the tray. Roast beef sandwiches made with thick slices of rye bread and homemade mayonnaise replaced the delicate tea sandwiches. "You've been such a patient and charming guest. I thought you'd like something a bit more substantial." She refilled my teacup and passed a plate of sandwiches to me.

Patient and charming? I was so busy thinking about a way to bring up the Wyrick family that I almost missed the compliment. I smiled, bit into a sandwich, and chewed without tasting. I was so engrossed in my thoughts that I missed the question my hostess asked. I hastily swallowed and apologized. "I'm sorry . . ."

Cecilia smiled. "Woolgathering. You don't teach school for over four decades without recognizing the signs. You're a guest. Don't be afraid to tell me I'm being a nosy old lady. If you'd prefer a bit of peace and quiet, just say so. I'll leave you alone."

Cecilia held her breath, afraid I'd send her away before her curiosity was satisfied. I put the sandwich down and smiled reassuringly. "You're not nosy compared to most people. You wouldn't believe the questions I get asked. I was too busy enjoying the sandwich to hear your question. If you want to try again, I promise to pay attention."

Nauseating, but it worked. Relief flickered across Cecilia's face. "I asked if you were in town for business or pleasure. I assume it's business that brought you here. I can't imagine anyone coming to Beaver Ridge in the middle of February for anything but business."

I took a deep breath and reconsidered my plan to tell the truth. The little voice inside my head told me to go ahead. Telling the truth was such a novel idea—it might just work.

I sighed. "It's business, unfortunately."

"Oh?" Cecilia dropped her sandwich on her plate and leaned closer. "Can you talk about it? Is it murder?"

This was too easy. I stretched my legs out and started talking. If Cecilia Hoffman wanted a thrill, I'd do my best to give her one.

"It's not murder—thank God. I'm looking for a woman who's missing. I think she grew up in Beaver Ridge."

"I can help you. I taught almost every child who grew up in this town. If I didn't teach the child, I taught her brother or sister."

I hesitated and frowned as if I was considering Cecilia's offer to help. She quickly said, "I am discreet. I promise you, I won't be on the telephone gossiping about your business."

"Well . . ." I paused again. The thought of Cecilia making calls sent a jolt of doubt along my back. I shook it off and asked, "Do you know the Wyricks?"

"Yes. The twins were in my class." She spoke slowly, dragging the words out. "I don't understand how the Wyricks could possibly be involved in your case."

Cecilia's mood shifted to uncooperative. Before I lost her, I quickly asked, "Have you seen Hannah Wyrick recently? She's not in trouble, but it's very important that I find her."

Using a teacher's stern voice, Cecilia said, "Young lady, is this a perverted joke? Who put you up to this?"

I was baffled and I admitted it. "I don't understand. My client hired me to locate Hannah Wyrick for reasons I can't discuss. However, let me reassure you, Hannah is not in trouble. I'd appreciate any help you can give me."

She shook her head. "No one can help you. Hannah Wyrick died eight years ago."

Chapter 10

• • • • • • • • • • • •

The chill that hit me wasn't caused by the weather. Hardly believing what I'd heard, I sat back and stared at Cecilia. Her eyes shone with unshed tears. She blinked and struggled to keep them from spilling out. Either Cecilia Hoffman was telling the truth, or she was an excellent actress.

My stomach churned. Mistaken identity was my first thought. Wyrick isn't a common name, but it was possible Judith gave me the wrong town and coincidence led me to a dead Wyrick. A slim hope, but I didn't want to abandon it. Chance had led me to stranger places. "Did Hannah have a sister?"

"Yes, Hannah had a sister—a twin sister. Nicole. Everyone called her Nikki. The girls were inseparable." My stomach twisted into a tight knot.

Cecilia pulled a lace handkerchief from the pocket of her skirt and wiped her eyes. She apologized. "I'm sorry. After all these years, it's still a shock. The girls died together. In an accident . . ."

My stomach rolled. This was worse than I had imagined. I was searching for a missing person who was dead but pregnant with another woman's child.

Cecilia's eyes focused on the logs in the fireplace. The crackling sounds and smoky fragrance of the burning wood added to the gloomy atmosphere of her story.

"Hannah and Nikki were bright, attractive, athletic girls. They were seniors when they died. They'd been accepted to Princeton." Cecilia dabbed at the tears and pushed them back. "Hannah and Nikki would have been the first students from Beaver Ridge to go to an Ivy League school. Hannah wanted to be a political science major. Nicole was thinking about journalism."

I lit a cigarette and inhaled greedily. The smoke relaxed my taut nerves. I exhaled. "You said there was an accident. What happened?"

"It was the night of the senior prom. I heard the sirens and prayed that none of my students were hurt. It's the same prayer I say every time I hear sirens in the middle of the night. God didn't hear my prayers that night."

I didn't comment. I've said too many prayers that weren't answered to offer any argument.

Kids killed on the night of their prom. It was easy to guess the cause. "They were drinking and never finished the ride home."

Cecilia nodded. "The girls, and their dates, were killed instantly. Their parents never recovered from the shock. Once the funerals were over and the dirt laid on the graves, Ethel locked herself up in her house. She rarely leaves. Ronald . . ." Cecilia shook her head. "Ronald's erratic. You never know if he's going to talk to you or spit on your shoes. He starts fights for no good reason. Someday he's going to get into serious trouble."

"Tell me about the accident. When did it happen?"

"A few weeks before graduation. Everyone in town was shocked, shaken, by the accident. The students wanted to cancel graduation out of respect to their classmates. Ethel convinced them to hold the ceremonies." Cecilia shook her head. "The girls had so much potential. It was such a waste."

"It usually is. Did anyone survive?"

"No. They were speeding. The police said the car was going over eighty miles an hour when the driver lost control and ran off the road. The car hit a tree. All four children died instantly." Cecilia shuddered. "I saw the wreckage. Twisted mangled steel wrapped around a tree trunk. Pieces of plastic and glass strewn along the roadside. The windshield . . . Not even a miracle could have kept those children alive."

Our conversation faded to silence. Cecilia offered to cook dinner, but I wasn't hungry. My appetite disappeared along with my hopes of finding the missing surrogate. Cecilia excused herself to clean up. I sat on the sofa and watched the fire die.

Missing people—I know how to find them. You track them through their past. Old friends, fellow workers, classmates, neighbors, drinking buddies. You talk to all of them. You go back to Girl Scout leaders, kindergarten teachers, and pediatricians, if necessary. Sooner or later—if you're lucky and if you talk to enough people—you get an idea of where to look for your missing person.

How do you find someone who's been dead for eight years? How do you find a person when you know nothing about her past?

Nikki. Nikki was my only link to Hannah's real identity. I slumped on the sofa and morosely lit another cigarette. Nikki was also hiding behind a dead girl's name. She wouldn't willingly divulge her secret and I couldn't think of a way to coax her into talking.

I went to the window and watched the falling snow, fervently praying it would stop. I had to get back to Manhattan.

At ten, I grabbed a book from Cecilia's shelves without looking at the title, tucked it under my arm, and climbed the stairs to my room. The bedside lamp had been turned on, the covers on the wide bed had been turned down, and the pillows fluffed. I settled under the blankets and read about murders on a tropical island until my eyes wouldn't stay open.

When I was a child, about two or three years old, I'd never say good-bye to anyone. When my father went off to work, I wouldn't look at him. I refused to say anything that sounded like good-bye. If Eileen was going to school, I'd turn away when she walked to the door. When my parents tried to make me say good-bye to guests, I'd hide behind the sofa and cry. Leaving meant dying.

As I got older, I stopped making a fuss, but the anxiety lingered. Once I tried explaining my childhood fears—which never completely disappeared—to Jeff. Hugging me tightly against his chest, he promised he'd always come back. Jeff lied. He went to work one evening and didn't return. I never saw him again.

Jeff was a DEA agent. I thought I accepted the dangers of his job with the same understanding and grace he used to accept mine. I was wrong. When the doorbell rang at four in the morning and I was greeted with news of Jeff's death, I raged and cursed and cried and refused to believe it. Until the funeral. The hollow sounds of wet earth hitting the copper coffin convinced me he was gone.

When I went to sleep in the warm bed at Cecilia Hoffman's inn, Jeff and others came to me. Faces of people who heard my good-byes and never came back floated above the bed. Grandparents who died at ninety. Aunts and uncles who died after long illnesses. High school teachers, college coaches. Friends who drifted out of my life and died before we kept those vague promises to get together.

At first the images only interrupted my sleep, making me restlessly toss and turn. They gradually became more sinister. A parade of people, their faces frozen in grotesque death masks, walked through the bedroom. Some were faces I knew, some were inspired by Cecilia's book. Some were people I had killed. The parade of corpses suddenly whirled and formed a tornado. Just like Dorothy's house, my bed flew through the air. It landed in a snowy cemetery. I jumped to my feet and stood next to the bed, helplessly rooted in the snow. The faces danced around me. Lifeless eyes winked, bloody hands waved, then slowly reached out to touch me. I couldn't get away.

Looking for comfort, I rolled over and grabbed the empty mattress. The unoccupied space frightened me more than the ghosts. I almost screamed. Then I realized I wasn't at home. I wasn't in bed with my husband.

I buried my face in the pillow and groaned. The phantoms were a new lead-in to an old nightmare. A dream that always leaves me shaking, crying, and staring at the bodies of my husband and unborn child.

Without turning on the light, I groped in my purse and found my cigarettes. If I managed to fall asleep again, the dream would come back. I wouldn't be able to fight it off; I wasn't strong enough.

It's been years since I hung out a bedroom window and sneaked a smoke, but I was desperate. I quietly opened the window, slowly easing it up to avoid any noisy creaks that would draw the schoolteacher's attention. The window opened without making a sound. I leaned out over the garage roof, cupped my hand around the cigarette, and struck my lighter.

The wind blew the flame out. It took three tries to get a satisfactory glow on the tip of the cigarette. I inhaled, then slowly blew the smoke out. The wind carried it away from the house and up to the snow clouds. None of the telltale smoke leaked back into the house.

I smoked and peered at the sky, hoping to catch a glimpse of a star. The cold air and tobacco calmed my skittish nerves. After two cigarettes, I pulled my head inside and closed the window.

The room was cold, cold enough to drive away the ghosts. But I wasn't going to take any chances. I dove into the bed, pulled the covers up to my shoulders, and started reading again. Justice triumphed as the sky lightened. I was safe; my ghosts never come around in the daylight. I dropped the book on the floor and closed my eyes.

I slept for an hour or two, then hurried to shower and dress. There wasn't time to stay in bed and make up for my sleepless night. I had work to do before I left Beaver Ridge. Overnight bag in hand, I ran down the stairs to find Cecilia and complete any check-out ritual she might have.

The front rooms were empty, so I walked down the narrow corridor, lined with more pictures of schoolchildren, to the kitchen. I went in without warning. Cecilia was standing near the back door, looking out at her snow-covered lawn and talking on the telephone. She glanced over her shoulder as the door swung closed. With a guilty look on her face, she mumbled into the phone and hung up.

My eyes flickered from her face to the telephone and back to her face. Cecilia's eyes darted away. She turned to the refrigerator and pulled the door open. "Let me get you a glass of juice. What would you like for breakfast?"

"Nothing, thanks. I'm in a bit of a hurry." Even more of a hurry now that my business was being discussed by Cecilia and her friends.

"Nonsense. You can't do a good day's work on an empty stomach. Now you just sit and drink your juice while I scramble some eggs. It won't take but a minute. Breakfast is included in the price of the room. No sense wasting your money." She put a glass of orange juice on the table and quickly turned to the coffeemaker on the counter. "Here, let me get you a cup of coffee."

I didn't move; I didn't say a word. I stood in the doorway with my arms folded across my chest. Cecilia casually said, "That was Doreen on the telephone. She called to see if you followed her recommendation."

"Oh?" I leaned against the wall and watched Cecilia fill a mug with coffee. "Does this town keep track of all its visitors? Or am I receiving special attention? Could it be because I asked questions about the Wyrick twins? I've received very strange reactions to my questions."

"Curiosity is a small town vice. Especially in the winter. People have too much time to sit around and watch other people. When a stranger arrives and asks questions about one of our own, it sets people to wondering."

"Just how much wondering are they doing? How many rumors are flying around this peaceful town?"

She spun around; her eyes burned with anger. "No one invited you to slash open old wounds. If you can't take responsibility for your actions, you should consider a different occupation. One which does not cause controversy."

Authoritative lectures always leave me with the same reaction: My lips twitch. I laughed, then apologized. "I'm sorry. I spent many sleepless hours doing just that last night. You're witnessing the short-tempered results."

Cecilia's eyes softened. "And I'll never stop lecturing unruly students. It's hard to retire old habits. One habit I'll never give up is telling the truth. As I told you last night, I don't engage in idle gossip about my guests." After a moment's pause, she smiled and said, "Now, how about that breakfast?"

My stomach wasn't ready for food, but I had questions that needed answers. "Coffee and toast will be fine." Before my hostess suggested that I go to the formal dining room where she usually served meals, I sat at the table and yawned.

Cecilia put a mug of coffee in front of me and started buttering toast. "I didn't tell Doreen anything she didn't already know." I sipped the coffee. Cecilia rushed on, anxious to prove she hadn't been gossiping. "Doreen told me she'd recommended my inn—I think she expects me to send people to her diner every time she sends me a guest. I thanked her and tried to change the subject—"

"Did you?" My question broke Cecilia's concentration. She turned to me, a puzzled look on her face. "The subject—did you change it?"

Cecilia waved the knife in the air. "We didn't talk for more than a minute or two. Doreen asked if you were staying over for another night. I told her I didn't know and that I wouldn't discuss it with her if I did. We didn't talk long after that; Doreen doesn't like to chat on the phone."

Cecilia turned her attention to the toast. I watched her spread butter with quick, efficient strokes and wondered if I could believe her.

After that, our conversation turned to a strained, but polite, discussion about the weather (less than an inch of snow) and road conditions (good). I quickly ate and refused her offers for more toast or coffee. We were both relieved when I left.

The Porsche's engine started without a complaint about being left out all night in the snow; the wipers easily brushed away the thin layer of snow. I drove the half block to the center of town and parked in front of the library.

The inside of the building was as deserted as the streets. A librarian sat in the empty building reading a book. At the sound of my footsteps on the wooden floor, she put the book down and eagerly watched me approach the desk. I explained my mission. Her brow wrinkled.

"Newspapers? That could be difficult. Automation hasn't reached Beaver Ridge yet. If you don't mind waiting, I'll go in the back and see if I can find them."

I scanned the headlines—they confirmed Cecilia's story. I didn't bother to read the stories, I knew how they ended. After carefully making copies, I gave the papers back to the librarian and asked for directions to the cemetery.

"It's the twins you're wanting to see." The man I found sitting in a shed near the gates of the cemetery pulled the wool cap from his head and scratched his greasy hair. He swung his feet down from their warm perch on the side of the electric heater and painfully stood up. He shuffled over to the high counter and rested his elbows on it as he spoke.

"I don't know why you want to, but I don't know why you can't. No good reason to see them. No good reason not to. I'd show you myself, but it's too cold to go tramping around in the snow. I'll draw you a little map. Shouldn't be too hard to follow."

He found a scrap of paper and pencil in the pocket of his flannel shirt and laboriously drew a rough map, apologizing as he worked. Smiling until my mouth hurt, I waited for him to finish. "This should do you. If not, come on back and I'll point you in the right direction. Don't worry about getting lost. The road leads right back here. You can't get lost."

Shaking his head, he gave me the paper. "Every morning and every evening, I get down on my knees and thank God that my children grew up okay." He tapped a crooked index finger against the map and said, "It's a wonder more of our kids aren't buried here. Booze. Drugs. Diseases. Not enough mommies home to watchdog their babies. Kids today, they grow up too soon and die too soon. Not much we can do to stop it."

I looked at the map. Shaky arrows pointed to the center of the cemetery. A dark X marked the Wyrick gravestones. The map sat on the counter. I stared at it. The caretaker stared at me. I didn't want to visit another grave. Before my resolve crumbled, I thanked him, went out to my car, and slowly drove to the Wyrick family plot.

The thin cover of snow lightened the ominous mood of the burial grounds. It transformed the mounds on the graves to miniature ski slopes and left a delicate fringe on top of the tombstones. It hid the footprints and flowers left behind by mourners. But the snow didn't deceive me; I knew what was beneath the coldness.

Tears. Betrayed hopes. Children left without a parent. Parents willing to trade their own lives for the child being buried. Spouses crying over the coffins of their mates. The list went on forever, endless as the tears shed at the funerals.

The plot was at the rear of the cemetery, on top of a small rise, set off from the other tombs by a row of low bushes. I parked at the curb and followed a set of narrow footprints to the graves.

Two blood-red carnations, gently dusted by the snow, were nestled against the tombstone. The inscription was stark: HAN-NAH & NICOLE WYRICK. 1967–1984. BELOVED DAUGHTERS OF ETHEL AND RONALD. GOD'S LOVE CARE FOR THOSE TAKEN BEFORE THEIR TIME.

What better proof than to stand at their graves? Hannah and Nikki Wyrick were dead.

Chapter 11

A chip of granite flew off the corner of the tombstone and landed at my feet. Reacting instinctively, I dove to the ground and landed face-down in the snow, sprawled across the graves. Then I heard the report of a hunting rifle.

After wiping the snow from my face, I cautiously peered out from behind the marker. Two more rapid shots spurted into the snow. The second hit less than twelve inches away. Too close. I dropped my head, pulled my legs up to my chest, and huddled in the tomb's shadow.

At least two hundred yards of empty corn field separated me from the shooter's hiding place in a stand of trees. Weekend hunters forget about the laws of gravity and friction that drag a bullet down or the vagaries of wind and humidity that cause it to rise. Telescopic sights help, but they can't compensate for a lack of practice. This rifle was wielded by an experienced hand.

Every time I moved from the monument's protective cover, a shot flew out of the woods. Each one landed uncomfortably close.

My options were limited: I could run the short distance to my car and hope I wouldn't get shot in the back as I ran. Or I could wait until the thrill of shooting at a tombstone wore off, or until the cold drove my hunter home.

The rifleman helped me make my decision. He, or maybe she, fired a half dozen shots. Not one missed the tombstone. Small chips of granite flew off and stung my cheeks.

I decided to sit and wait. And think. I thought about my coat, hat, and gloves, sitting on the passenger's seat in the car. I thought about my gun, safely locked away at home. I thought about Cecilia Hoffman and Doreen. Most of the time, I thought about the girls buried beneath me.

★ ★ ★

Kids may enjoy rolling around in the snow, but at my age, it's not much fun—especially when someone is shooting at you. The snow melted beneath me. The denim of my blue jeans soaked up the icy water better than any sponge could have. I shivered.

Unrolling the turtleneck of my sweater, I pulled it up until my ears were covered. I pulled the cuffs down over my hands and tried to close the makeshift mittens around my fingers.

Anger kept me from freezing. My impatience probably prolonged the fun. No matter how many times I advised myself to be patient, every few minutes I'd turn and try to look around the monument. Each time, my movements set off another round of shots.

I gave up, wrapped my arms around my chest, and rocked back and forth, trying to get warm. A cemetery is a cold, lonely place on an early winter afternoon, especially this cemetery. The citizens of Beaver Ridge were living long lives, there weren't any funeral processions. The caretaker hadn't budged from his warm shack. No one drove up to place flowers on a loved one's grave. My gunman and I were the only ones out.

When the snow started again, I groaned. The storm began with fine, gentle flakes and quickly intensified. Large, wet snowflakes covered me and obscured the landscape, making it difficult to see more than a few yards ahead. Visibility would also be bad for the guy with the hunting rifle.

I stretched my legs out and bounced them on the ground to wake the sleeping muscles. Then I scrambled to my feet and slipped and slid down the snowy embankment to the car. I dove inside, started the engine, and put the car in gear. The tires spun on the wet pavement, then grabbed hold. A bullet shattered the rear side window as I drove away, a good-bye present from Beaver Ridge.

Chapter 12

• • • • • • • • • • • •

The note on my desk said Eileen needed to see me. As soon as I came in. I filled a mug with strong, hot coffee and went to her office. Eileen was on the telephone, arguing about something legal. She pointed to a chair and mouthed that she'd be done in a minute. I made myself comfortable and gulped my coffee—I was still trying to get warm.

The conversation ended when Eileen slammed the receiver down. She smiled at me and said, "I think he'll get the message and come around to my way of thinking. How was your trip to Jersey?" Her smile fell into a frown. "What's wrong with you? You look—"

"Try frozen. I spent the morning sitting on a snow-covered grave, hiding from a sniper. My jeans are still damp." I sneezed. "It was like a carnival game. You know, the type where you shoot at the ducks floating past. Except I wasn't having any fun. Every time I lifted my head, he—or she—took a few shots."

"What did you do?"

"Nothing. I sat there until it started snowing again and he couldn't get a clear shot when I ran for the car. Did you ever sit in the snow for an hour? The snow melts. Your clothes get soaked. Then they freeze. Go home and sit on a bag of ice cubes—that will give you a good idea of the fun I had."

"I can't believe you just sat there."

"You can't be serious. What did you expect me to do? I'm not Superwoman and I don't wear bulletproof lingerie. Bullets don't bounce off me."

Eileen muttered, "I'm glad you finally learned that lesson."

We were silent. Images of Eileen's bedside vigils floated through my mind. I shook my head to clear them away. "I went back to the caretaker's office. He was asleep. 'You still here?' was what he said when I woke him."

"Did you call the police?" Eileen always asks that question. She has much more faith in the powers of the police than I do. "I thought about it. The caretaker was convinced a hunter mistook me for a deer." Eileen snorted. I nodded. "No nearsighted hunter was shooting at me. It was someone with an accurate sight on a high-powered rifle. What could the cops do? Take a report and laugh about the city slicker who thought someone was taking potshots at her? I got in my car, turned the heater up as high as it would go, and drove back here."

"What were you doing in a cemetery? I thought you were trying to find Hannah Wyrick."

"I found her, and her sister Nikki. They're both buried in that cemetery."

Eileen's mouth dropped open. She leaned forward and rested her head in her hands and concentrated on listening to the story of my visit to Beaver Ridge. When I finished, she shook her head and asked, "What's next?"

I yawned. "I'm freezing and I didn't get much sleep last night. I'm going home to take a hot bath and a nap before I see Judith tonight. She's anxious for a report on my trip to Beaver Ridge. I'm anxious to get her copy of the surrogate contract and Hannah's application." I also wanted my pistol—my morning in the cemetery had left me feeling vulnerable.

"Are you going to tell Judith about the dead twins? Will she believe you?"

"I stopped at a local library. I have copies of the newspaper stories and the obituaries. That, and my visit to the cemetery, should be enough to convince her."

"Don't go just yet. We have a big problem." Eileen shuffled through the papers on her desk and grabbed a file that was slipping off the edge. "Blaine, we lost a big client this morning."

Groaning, I lit a cigarette and inhaled. I hate losing clients. I blew the smoke out and asked, "Who and why?"

"Franklynn Equity—the investment bankers." Eileen removed her glasses and rubbed her eyes. "We did contracts for their limited partnerships and other investments, real estate work, and provided general legal counsel. They were steady and profitable."

"What—"

Eileen snapped, "I don't know. A messenger delivered a letter this morning instructing us to immediately sever our working relationship and return all pertinent documents. Of course, I called them. I'm still waiting for someone to return my call."

I shrugged. Eileen wasn't accustomed to having her calls ignored. She could fume about the lost client. I'd write it off as bad luck on a bad day. Offering sage advice isn't my usual role, but I tried. "There's always another client coming through the door. We've survived threats, bullets, and bombs. We'll survive a renegade client."

Eileen sighed and agreed. Satisfied that my advice was sound, I went home to make arrangements to get the Porsche's window replaced and to take a nap before meeting Judith.

We thought we'd be okay—we were wrong. By the end of the following week, my optimism would be gone. Most of my business would also be gone.

Chapter 13

I leaned on the bell and slowly counted to twenty. No one answered, just as no one had answered the first two times. I jabbed the buzzer again and waited, trying to hang on to my temper. No one came to the door. I looked at the light filtering through the windows and twisted the door knob. It was locked.

Judith wouldn't have gone out. She had been too eager to hear my report. I remembered her attempts to talk me into seeing her earlier and pressed the bell again. I heard the faint sound of the chimes through the door, then silence.

A sinking feeling in the bottom of my stomach—the one that always signals trouble—sent me running down the steps and around to the side of the house, searching for another door. One that might be unlocked.

A wrought-iron fence, more decorative than protective, blocked the entrance to the side alley. The crisscrossed bars made it easy. I scrambled to the top, swung over the scalloped edges, and lowered myself to the ground.

The courtyard I landed in was large enough for three garbage cans, a few recycling bins, and a small patch of ground—the garden. There was a door next to the trash cans; it was also locked. Using the butt of my pistol, I broke a windowpane in the door. Carefully avoiding the jagged glass, I stuck my arm in and twisted the locks.

I stepped inside the dark kitchen and waited. No one came rushing in to investigate the noise of the glass hitting the floor. The house was silent—and spooky. My nerves tingled, confirming my sinking stomach. Gun in hand, I walked from the kitchen to the dining room, following the light.

I found Judith in the living room, sprawled across the sofa. The hideous green and orange afghan wrapped around her shoulders tinted her face pea-soup green. Sweat beaded on her forehead. Crouching in front of the sofa, I gently touched Judith's shoulder. Heat radiated through the blanket. She opened her eyes; they were bright and glassy. I pressed the back of my hand against her forehead. My hands were cold; her skin was hot.

"You're burning up. Let me help you to bed. You'll be more comfortable."

She whispered, "Don't make me move. My head hurts too much to move. Let me sleep . . ."

I rocked back on my heels and tried to remember my mother's fever remedies. Aspirin, fluids, cool cloths. I stood up. Judith grabbed my leg. "Don't . . ."

"I'll be right back. I'm going to find aspirin and a few other things. Don't worry, I won't leave you."

Judith released my leg. I scurried around the house gathering supplies, ignoring the feeling of wasting time. When I returned to the living room, my patient was barely conscious.

Trying to sound cheerful, I said, "Come on, Judith, open your mouth. I have to take your temperature. Let's see how sick you are."

Without opening her eyes, Judith let me place the thermometer in her mouth. I knelt in front of the sofa and watched. Anxiety tightened my chest.

I've had measles, mumps, chicken pox, and all the other diseases kids catch. I've had flu bugs that kept me in bed for a week. I've spent time in the hospital recovering from bullet wounds and other injuries. I've never seen anyone as sick as Judith.

Perspiration soaked her hair. Tiny purple blotches dotted her face and neck. I took the thermometer from her mouth and squinted at it. The silver thread of mercury wavered at 106, then stopped.

Fear shot through me. I walked across the room and grabbed the phone. With shaking fingers, I dialed a number and asked to speak with my doctor.

I received a snippy answer. "She's with a patient. May I take a message?"

"No, you may not. This is Blaine Stewart. I have to speak to Dr. Mabe immediately. It's an emergency."

The woman chuckled. "Get in line. Do you know how many people try that ploy? Tell me what's wrong. I'll decide if it's an emergency."

"I'm with a friend. She has spots all over her face—"

"Measles. I'll make an appointment. How about tomorrow morning?"

I wanted to reach through the phone and strangle her. "She has a hundred-and-six-degree temperature and is semiconscious. Get the doctor." *Get her before Judith dies.*

She punched the hold button and left me fuming. Judith stirred. I helplessly watched her labored breathing. I didn't know what to do. I squeezed Judith's hand and waited.

"Ms. Stewart?" A brisk professional voice, different from the first, came on the line. "Doctor's on her way to the emergency room. She'll meet you there. Do you want me to call an ambulance for you?"

The hospital was less than two miles away. Given the light early-evening traffic and the scandals about EMS delays, I decided to use my car. Judith was barely aware of my efforts, but I managed to drape the afghan around her and get her into the car.

I double-parked the Porsche in front of the emergency-room entrance and ran inside. Dr. Mabe met me in the lobby.

"Where is she?"

I pointed to the car. We trotted out; a nurse and resident followed. Dr. Mabe yanked the door open, bent down and looked at Judith. She quickly stood up and snapped orders to the waiting aides.

Dr. Mabe's been my doctor for years. Until that moment, I'd never seen her look afraid. Fear twisted my stomach. I stepped aside and watched the medical team engulf Judith.

They loaded her on a stretcher and wheeled it inside. I parked the Porsche and ran back to the hospital. A beefy security guard stopped me as I headed to the waiting room.

"I'm sorry, ma'am. You can't go in there."

Under normal circumstances, my temper is hard to control. Under normal circumstances, I try to rein it in. This time I didn't. I exploded. "I don't know what the fuck you think you're doing and I don't care. Get out of my way."

"No, ma'am." The guard folded his arms across his chest; thick muscles strained against his khaki shirt. "Doctor's orders." He pointed to a door behind his podium. "You stay there. You want coffee, you see me. You want to pee, you see me. You stay there until the doctor says you can go."

I stared at him, too angry to argue. I turned to walk out. The guard grabbed my arm. "I'm sorry, ma'am. I can't let you leave. The doctor said you got to stay. Please don't make a fuss, 'cause you ain't getting past me and you ain't getting away from me."

The guard's fingers clamped around my arm like iron bands. His resolve was stronger than my anger. I gave up. He led me into exile.

The room was furnished with a vinyl-covered sofa that tried to look like leather but failed miserably, a metal trash can, and a shaky table piled high with outdated magazines. I sat, smoked cigarette after cigarette, and worried.

Quarantined. Why?

Suddenly claustrophobic, I jumped to my feet and paced around the room, which wasn't much larger than my bathroom. I reached in my pocket for another cigarette and discovered they were gone. An entire pack gone and I didn't remember smoking a single cigarette. I crumpled the pack and threw it against the wall.

Dr. Mabe walked in as the package hit the floor. I stopped pacing and stared at her. Her hair was disheveled; her clothes wrinkled. The doctor slumped down on the sofa and sighed. "I'm sorry about having you locked up. It's just a precaution."

"Precaution—that's a frightening word. Precaution against what?"

"The high fever worried me. We've gotten it down, but it's still too high. I'm waiting for the lab tests to identify the specific problem. In the meantime, all I can do is give her antibiotics and try to get that fever down. I have to ask you a few questions."

Fear gave way to anger. "Not until you answer a few of mine. What's wrong with Judith? And why am I in this isolation booth? Isn't this a little dramatic? What's wrong, does Judith have the plague?"

"I don't know what's wrong." She waved her hand in the air. "This may seem melodramatic to you, but it makes good sense to me. Sudden fever, headache, vomiting, rash—those are symptomatic of a highly contagious disease that can quickly become fatal. I'm waiting for the results of the tests on the cerebrospinal fluid."

Blood pounded inside my head. My fear returned; it was so strong I could hardly breathe. I swallowed and tried to steady my voice. "Does this mystery disease have a name?"

"Meningitis."

The doctor sent in cigarettes and coffee. They didn't help. The walls shrank until I was sitting in a telephone booth. A hot, airless telephone booth. One without windows.

When Dr. Mabe walked in, three hours later, she didn't have to speak. The dark smudges under her eyes, the sweat glistening in her hair, told me everything I didn't want to know. My harsh voice sounded foreign to my ears. "She's dead."

Chapter 14

Dead.

I buried my head in my hands. A vision of Judith, sitting in my office and crying, appeared. Dr. Mabe's words barely pierced the vision.

"I'm sorry. The fever did too much damage to her heart and her brain. She never regained consciousness."

Without lifting my head or opening my eyes, I asked, "What killed her? Was it meningitis?"

"Every test was negative. It wasn't meningitis, Rocky Mountain spotted fever, or Legionnaire's disease. You can go home." I didn't move. Dr. Mabe touched my shoulder. "Are you okay?"

"I don't understand. I talked to Judith around five o'clock. She didn't sound sick. She was looking forward to seeing me. What caused an illness that sudden, that violent?"

The doctor shrugged. "I don't know yet. It could be a rare viral infection, a drug overdose, an allergic reaction to something. We'll have to wait for the autopsy." She yawned. "It's been a long night. Go home and try to sleep."

"Yeah." I agreed, but didn't move. Fatigue and shock anchored me to the seat cushions. "Do you think it was natural, accidental, or intentional?"

Dr. Mabe looked at her watch and sighed. "Blaine, it's quarter after two. I'm too tired to think about anything except my bed. That's what you should be thinking about too. Take my advice. Go home, sleep, and wait for the autopsy."

I said good night to the doctor and went out to my car, but I didn't go home. Sleeping would have to wait until after I made another visit to Judith's house. I wanted the files Judith had promised me before well-meaning relatives showed up.

This time I used the front door. The keys I'd grabbed on the way out easily opened the locks. I went inside and turned on the lights. The house was as quiet as it had been earlier in the evening.

I resisted the obvious comparison to a silent graveyard and quickly checked the tables in the living room where I had found Judith. The tables were empty. No magazines, newspapers, or dust. How much cleaning had Nikki done?

I tried the other rooms. As I searched, the question *What about the child?* kept me company. When I finished, I had nothing. No files, no contracts. Nothing relating to the surrogate. I fixed the broken glass in the kitchen door with cardboard and packing tape, locked all the doors, and went to my office. Maybe I'd find an answer in Eileen's law books.

I've spent so many late nights in my office that I can find my way around in the dark. Without turning on a single light, I made my way back to our conference room/law library. After squinting at the fine print in an index, I pulled a dozen thick books from the shelves and started reading. It didn't take me long to discover a new cure for insomnia: law journals.

Eileen's ungentle hand shook me awake. I lifted my head from the book I'd been using as a pillow and blinked until I focused on her face. It didn't look happy. I stretched and yawned. "What time is it?"

"Seven-thirty." Eileen's an early-bird workaholic; she's usually the first person in the office. Since I don't straggle in until later in the morning, I understood Eileen's surprise at finding me. I blinked and looked again. There was more than surprise in Eileen's eyes, there was suspicion.

During the worst of my drinking nights, when I was tired of hanging out in bars, but not drunk enough to face my empty bed, I'd go to the office. Eileen would find me asleep at my desk. She'd wake me and send me home to shower, change clothes, and sober up.

Finding me sleeping in the conference room stirred unpleasant memories in Eileen's mind. Old suspicions can linger forever; I ignored hers and yawned again.

"It's early for you. What are you doing here?"

"Working."

Eileen examined me carefully. She checked for bloodshot eyes, beer breath, and other signs of a night of drinking. I waited patiently; I'd earned her suspicions. When Eileen didn't find any traces of a binge, she smiled. "Sorry partner, you were snoring—not working. Have you been here all night? You look like shit."

"Thanks. You look good too." Eileen was wearing a dark blue courtroom suit. Knowing my red curls were flying in every direction, I ran my fingers through my hair. My throat felt raw and scratchy from the cigarettes I'd smoked at the hospital. "Is there coffee?"

"Not yet. I started a pot, it should be done soon." She sat next to me and glanced at the books scattered across the table. "Why are you sleeping on my books?"

"Judith Marsden died last night." Eileen gasped. I went on, "I'm trying to find out what happens to her son." I yawned, rubbed the crick in my neck, and wished for a cup of coffee. It didn't appear, so I told Eileen about Judith.

While I talked, Eileen flipped through the books and took notes. Her precise handwriting irritated me. After two sleepless nights everything irritated me.

I pushed my chair back from the table and stood up. "I'm going to see if the coffee is finished. I'll be right back."

Eileen nodded absentmindedly. "Bring me a cup. Bring my cigarettes too. They're in my briefcase." After a quick trip to Eileen's office and the kitchen, I returned with the coffee and cigarettes. Without looking up, Eileen said, "This is going to take a while. I'll find you when I'm done."

Dismissed.

I went to my office, ordered bagels from the deli, and skimmed the newspapers I'd snatched from Eileen's briefcase. Before I finished drinking my coffee, Eileen walked in with a legal pad, coffee mug, and a paper bag in her hands. She sat, put everything on top of my desk, and opened the bag. After passing me a bagel and cream cheese, she said, "I intercepted the delivery boy. You owe me for this. Five bucks."

"Five bucks?"

Eileen laughed. "I knew you were paying, so I gave the kid a big tip."

"You should be so generous with your own money." I unwrapped the bagel and took a bite. "That was fast."

Eileen thought I was talking about her research, not the deli's speedy delivery. She smiled. "There wasn't much to read. Very few cases concerning gestational surrogates have come before the courts. I didn't find any cases involving the death of what the courts call the genetic parents."

"I didn't get very far with my reading." I yawned and took another sip of coffee. The hot liquid burned my raw throat. "What do the courts say about gestational surrogates?"

"Are you going to stay awake for this? I don't want to waste my breath talking to a zombie." After I promised to keep my eyes open to the end, Eileen put her glasses on and read her notes.

"In 1990, a California gestational surrogate went to court to gain custody of the baby she had given birth to. The case was remarkably similar to Judith's story. The genetic mother had had a hysterectomy. Her uterus, but not her ovaries, had been removed. Therefore, she couldn't carry a baby, but she could produce eggs. One of those eggs was fertilized with her husband's sperm and implanted in the surrogate.

"After the child was born, the surrogate petitioned the court for parental rights. She claimed that even though the child didn't grow from her egg, she spent nine months bonding with the child and should be granted the same rights as any parent."

Eileen didn't have to worry about me falling asleep. I hung on every word. "What did the court decide?"

"The Superior Court denied her request. The judge said the surrogate acted as nothing more than a foster home for the embryo and wasn't entitled to any rights to the child."

"Rent-a-womb?"

"Something like that. Bizarre, isn't it? Doctors are making babies in laboratories and judges in courts are deciding who the parents are."

"What else did the ruling say?"

"The judge said the surrogate was a genetic stranger who didn't have a claim to the baby. He said having two mothers wasn't in the best interests of the child. In the war between nature and nurture, he chose Mother Nature.

"The judge also said that surrogacy 'invites an emotional and financial extortion situation.' The ruling ended with the suggestion that legislators start issuing guidelines."

I repeated Eileen's words. "Emotional and financial extortion . . ."

Eileen nodded. She knew what I was thinking. "Kidnapping. The surrogate ran off with the child—I could make a good case for kidnapping."

"All I have to do is find her."

Chapter 15
• • • • • • • • • • • •

At ten o'clock, I admitted defeat and went home to sleep. After dumping the mail on the kitchen table, I went to my bedroom, pulled the curtains tight to keep out any glimmers of light, and plunged into bed. I was asleep before my eyes closed.

Twenty hours later, I woke up smiling. Not a single telephone call or knock at the door had interrupted my sleep. Before my lucky streak ended, I pulled on a sweat suit, grabbed my gym bag, and headed to the Y for an early-morning swim.

Two days without exercise left my body feeling sluggish—not good for someone who needs to move fast. I swam until I was fully awake, stopped at a coffee shop for a quick breakfast, went home to dress in work clothes, and was in the office by eleven.

My attempt to lead a normal life ended moments after I walked into the office. My secretary, Jona, was at her usual station outside my office. She cradled the telephone against her shoulder with one hand and frantically scribbled on a message pad with the other. A thick pile of message slips waited for me next to the phone. I absentmindedly flipped through them and listened to Jona end the call.

Jona hung up and finished writing the message before handing it to me. "Here's another one for your collection. I'm sure you don't want to talk to any of these turkeys—"

"—Turkeys. That's strong language for you. What's going on around here? You look frazzled."

Jona is our original employee. Newly divorced and left to raise two children without reliable child support, she appeared in our office to apply for the part-time secretarial position we'd advertised. That happened ten years ago. Today, the kids have graduated from college and Jona makes jokes about retiring. I'm retiring when she does; I'd rather quit than try to find a replacement for her.

She patted her graying hair back into place and rubbed her hands. "I'm getting writer's cramp. You're quite famous this morning. Everybody wants an exclusive interview with you."

Famous isn't good when you're a private investigator. I frowned. "Why am I famous? Did I win the Nobel peace prize?"

"If you had, no one would call. That's too dull. No, Blaine, they're calling about Judith Marsden. Her death is big news."

"Why? Because of Judith's money?"

Jona smiled and patiently explained. "It's not only the money. The Marsdens are old-time New Yorkers. They made their fortune during the Depression. Joe Kennedy did it by buying stocks. Joe Marsden bought real estate. They've been society folks ever since."

"The next time we're looking for a staff investigator, remind me to hire you. Have you been keeping a file on Judith Marsden and her family? Or did you spend all of yesterday collecting information?"

"I've been reading the newspapers. The same newspapers that want to talk to you. You're the mystery woman who brought Judith to the hospital and then disappeared. Everyone wants to know why Judith hired a private investigator. That's why the reporters are calling."

I grimaced. I was going to have to search for the missing surrogate while in the glare of New York City's media spotlight. I shuffled the messages again. WCBS, WABC, WNBC, the *Daily News,* the *Post* . . . Every television station and most of the newspapers had called.

The great thing about New York is that another scandal would erupt during the day and drag the cameras elsewhere. The best way to survive the storm was to ignore it. I dropped the stack on Jona's desk.

"Throw these away. Don't waste your time writing any of the names or numbers down. I'm not returning calls, I'm not talking to reporters, and I certainly don't have any comment."

Jona shook her head. "It won't work. That's what I told them the first time they called. They keep calling back to see if you've changed your mind. Some of them are on their fourth round. I left the newspapers on your desk so you can see what they're writing."

I thanked Jona and started to my office. She stopped me. "There's more. A few people that you probably want to talk to called. I left those messages on your desk. On top of the papers so you can't miss them." A faint smile came to her face. "Two more things before you get away from me. Eileen's looking for you. And Dennis called. He wants you to call him back."

Jona bit her tongue before any words encouraging me to call Dennis slipped out of her mouth. She approved of Dennis, everyone does, and couldn't understand why I was letting him slip away. I got away before Jona broke her long-standing rule to never meddle.

I always start with the easy items. For once, Eileen was the easiest. I went down the hallway to her office, composing a list for the rest of the day as I walked.

Eileen. Newspapers. Dennis—I pushed his name to the bottom of the roster and stuck my head in Eileen's office. She was on the phone. I waved and kept on walking to the kitchen for coffee. She was still talking on the telephone when I walked past again. I waved a second time and went to my office.

I read the newspapers while I waited. The tabloids prominently displayed Judith's story on the opening pages. The stories were similar: Society matron stricken by unknown illness. Rushed to the hospital by private eye who mysteriously disappeared. Autopsy suggests suicide.

Suicide? I dropped the paper and leaned back in my chair, hands laced behind my head. Closing my eyes, I reviewed my last conversation with Judith. She'd been waiting for my call and eagerly agreed to see me.

Nothing in Judith's message or voice had suggested thoughts of suicide. She was upset about Hannah, but not depressed to the point of taking her life. Judith ended our conversation by describing the wallpaper she'd picked out for the baby's nursery. What happened in the five-hour span between our talk and her death?

"Napping already? I thought you spent the past day and a half in bed, catching up on your sleep. Wasn't it enough?"

I opened my eyes. Eileen stood in the doorway, laughing at me. "Thinking—not napping. You must learn to recognize the difference. What's up? I heard you were looking for me."

"Imagine the results we'd get if you worked with your eyes open." Eileen settled into a chair and crossed her legs. After kicking off her shoes and rubbing her feet, she pointed to the newspapers. "I see you're catching up on current events. Any conclusions?"

I lit a cigarette and slid the pack across the desk to Eileen. "My client did not commit suicide. I want to see the autopsy that says she did."

I took a drag on the cigarette and watched the smoke curl to the ceiling. "The baby's still missing. The surrogate is using a dead girl's identity. I'm stumped. My client is dead. I'm unemployed. I don't have any choice but to drop the case. What else can I do? I don't have a reason to keep it going. I don't have a client. And what would I do if I found the kid? Keep him?"

Eileen rubbed her feet again and complained about corns and high heels. "You sound miserable. Do you really want to keep this investigation going?"

Without hesitation, I answered, "Yes."

"I guessed you might be feeling that way. So I made a phone call. I talked to Charlie Spragge."

"Who's he?"

"I saw his name in a newspaper article. He's Judith's attorney. Charlie and I went to law school together. We suffered through a few miserable courses. Charlie knew about Judith and the baby. He didn't know about you. He didn't know the baby's missing."

"What does he know?"

"Judith inherited a lot of money when her husband died. Conservative estimates value the estate at twenty million dollars. The baby is the only heir. Charlie wants you to find the child. He's going to be a very rich baby. You're back in business. You have a new client.''

Chapter 16

• • • • • • • • • • • •

One of the things I did find in Judith's study was a picture, a Polaroid snapshot of a sonogram screen. The shadowy blob didn't look like a baby, but Judith had proudly assured me it was the first portrait of her son. I propped the photograph against my coffee mug and stared at it. I'd never had a client who was a month away from being born. The historic first didn't cheer me.

I rested my head in my hands and ordered my frozen brain to think. There were only two places to go for information: Nikki and the clinic. Neither would be cooperative. I sighed and picked up the telephone. Before I started asking questions, I wanted to know how Judith died. I dialed and made arrangements to see my doctor.

We ate lunch in the hospital cafeteria, I treated. After we finished eating our tuna fish sandwiches, we took our sodas and moved to the steps at the hospital's rear entrance to talk about Judith. We sat in the lee of the brick walls surrounding the doors and basked in the warmth of the sun.

Dr. Mabe took a cigarette from the pack, cupped her hands around the tip, and let me light it. She took a long, slow drag and leaned back against the stairs, turning her face up to the sun.

"Feels good. Almost good enough to make me forget we're in the deepest, darkest part of winter." She shook her head. "February in Manhattan. This has to be one of the most hellish spots on earth when winter jumps on it. The wind. The snow. Everything is gray. God, it's so depressing."

"So many people say that. Do you think the suicide rate goes up in February?"

Dr. Mabe opened an eye and looked at me. "Do you think it went up the other night?"

"That's why I grabbed the check for the tuna fish. I was hoping you'd tell me. I don't like the stories I've been reading in the papers. What happened?"

The doctor opened both eyes and sat upright. She scanned the faces of the other smokers to be sure no one was paying attention to our conversation. Then Dr. Mabe grinned sheepishly and said, "We've had too many people sniffing around this hospital looking for stories. I want to be sure my name isn't on the front page of tomorrow's *Post*. The hospital doesn't need more publicity."

I dropped the cigarette butt on the sidewalk and ground it out with the heel of my boot. "What did the autopsy say? Do you think Judith committed suicide?"

"The preliminary reports say drug overdose. There was a lethal amount of a common tranquilizer in her blood. That alone would have been enough to kill her, but there was more. The high fever couldn't be attributed to the tranquilizer, so we ran a few more tests. We also found fairly high levels of a beta-adrenergic blocking agent in her blood."

I had just struck a match to light a cigarette. Holding the flaming match in midair, I asked, "What's a beta whatever?" and dropped the match as it burned my fingers.

"It's prescribed for high blood pressure. A high fever is one of the adverse side effects. The combination of drugs and the fever caused too much harm to the internal organs. We couldn't do anything to counteract it."

Did Judith have high blood pressure? Another question added to the list. Wishing I'd examined Judith's medicine cabinet during my search of her house, I asked, "How are these drugs administered?"

"Tablets. Capsules. I think there's a liquid form too. An overdose doesn't necessarily mean it was intentional. Accidental overdoses happen more frequently than you might think. People get confused and forget what they've taken, or they take two or three different medications at a time without realizing the combination can be fatal. Mixing prescription drugs is a big problem, especially with the elderly."

"Could the drugs have been administered without Judith's knowledge?"

Dr. Mabe ran her fingers through her hair and thought about my question. "Are you asking if Mrs. Marsden could have been murdered? It's possible—I've seen millions of crazier things. Would I testify to that in court? No. I'd be more inclined to go with the suicide theory."

"I'm not ready to jump on your suicide bandwagon. Judith and I talked earlier that day. She didn't sound suicidal—"

"How much experience do you have dealing with people who are about to kill themselves?"

"Not much. None. Why?"

"Umm. Were you and Judith close?"

"No."

"How often did you see her? Was it frequent enough to know her emotional state? Would you have caught the changes that might have foretold a suicide?"

The sharpness of the doctor's voice astonished me. I raised my hand to cut her off. "Give me a break. I'm not a psychologist."

"Exactly. I'm not attacking you. Suicide seems to be the cause of death. If you're going to disagree, prepare to get hammered by people who'll say you're not a psychologist. You don't know anything about suicide."

The wind shifted direction and blew into our cove. I shivered and zipped my jacket. "So make me an expert."

My challenge drew a request for another cigarette. Dr. Mabe took a cigarette and tapped it against her knee while she waited for me to find my matches. "In twenty-five words or less. If you want to be an expert, go to the library and check out a dozen books. Then take a dozen courses."

She paused while I lit her cigarette, then said, "Suicide is a depressive reaction. The depressed mood seems to be out of proportion to the loss or injury suffered. There are a variety of emotional and physical symptoms: withdrawal from social activities, lack of ambition, pessimism, fatigue, insomnia are a few. Was Judith despondent about anything?"

It was my turn to scan the half-dozen smokers sharing our perch for overeager ears. "Does this conversation fall under doctor/patient privileged communications?"

She shrugged. "I'm a doctor. You are my patient. Your mental health is also an unspoken part of this discussion."

I raised an eyebrow. Dr. Mabe noticed and nodded. "Fatal suicidal acts cause grief for those left behind. They also cause a great deal of guilt in people who felt they could have prevented the act."

The muffled sound of a beeper in Dr. Mabe's pocket didn't give me a chance to respond. She dug it out from beneath her coat and looked at the display. Before getting to her feet, she patted my knee. "Sorry, I have to go. *If only I'd done more.* That's your motto. Don't push it because you feel guilty."

Chapter 17

• • • • • • • • • • •

I avoid the subways during the winter months. Whenever I get in a train, I have ugly visions of tuberculosis germs hovering around my nose, waiting for me to inhale. Without fail, I get wedged in a crowded car filled with hacking, sniffling riders, each one trying to infect me. I close my eyes and try to hold my breath until the end of my ride—it's easier to take a taxi.

I walked over to Lexington Avenue and hailed a cab. I climbed inside, waited for the driver to stop coughing, and gave him the address of the clinic. It was the dirtiest, smokiest cab I've seen. I kicked aside the litter on the floor and lit a cigarette—self-defense.

The driver, whose cigarette had burned down to his fingers, didn't complain. He looked in the mirror and tossed the butt out the window. "You got another one? I stopped buying 'em. I'm trying to cut down."

I took a few cigarettes from my pack and passed them forward. I'd take them off the tip. "Now you just bum them off your riders."

"You got that right. I'm still smoking a pack a day, but I am saving money." The driver's laugh tailed off into a deep cough. Fearful of the evil germs spewing from his mouth, I leaned back and sent a cloud of smoke forward to kill them.

The cabby rattled on about the Knicks and their newest center, and the Rangers and their newest goalie. I looked out the grimy window and thought about suicide.

After Jeff died, I had fits of rage and I drank, which some called a suicide attempt. While drinking I entertained myself by concocting plans to kill the person responsible for my husband's death. During all my bloody dreams, the thought of killing myself never came to mind.

I understood the urge to murder. Could I understand self-murder?

The atmosphere surrounding Frostina's desk was colder than the air outside. I didn't need to introduce myself; she remembered me. "I'm sorry. You won't be able to see Dr. Nelson today. I'm sure he's busy."

Some people never learn. I shook my head and walked past her desk. Before she punched the intercom to call a security guard, I was through the door and inside the lab.

Nelson intercepted me before I got to his office. His face flushed, his eyes blazed with fury. "How dare you bully your way in here? My patients need my attention. I have neither the time nor the desire to cater to your juvenile need to play Dick Tracy."

My temper flared. "Judith Marsden needed your attention. You were too convinced of your infallibility to give it to her. Maybe she'd be alive today if you were doing your job instead of worrying about bad publicity."

"Now you're a one-woman morality committee. Don't presume to lecture me about my practice."

I bit down on my lip. A shouting match in the corridor would get me nothing but the door slamming against my butt as they threw me out. I lowered my voice and tried to bring the hostility level down. "Dr. Nelson, I'm not questioning your expertise. But I do have questions about Judith Marsden's surrogate."

I watched his eyes, looking for a flicker of guilt or apprehension. I saw annoyance. He blinked. "I suggest you worry about your business, not mine. In this economy . . ."

Now we were on familiar ground. I grinned. Shaking my head, I said, "Threats, threats, threats. Doctor, you should understand something. Threats don't frighten me. They make me curious. Let's try another approach. I have information that might interest you. You have some that definitely interests me. Let's trade."

Dr. Nelson's face twisted into a sardonic grin. "Ms. Stewart, you could never say anything which I would find interesting. Amusing, yes. Interesting, no."

Nelson flourished his chunky gold watch; the interview was over. Maybe it was the cold that was beginning to attack me, or maybe I was getting too old to fight with everyone—I left without an argument. Maybe I'd find another way to examine the doctor's files.

I planned to spend the rest of the day on mundane tasks: reading reports on our other ongoing cases, separating the bundle of receipts in my briefcase for an expense report, and updating Judith's file. My plan ended the moment I stepped inside our office lobby.

Marcella, our receptionist, battled with the ringing telephones. Her French accent becomes more pronounced when she's pressured. I listened and found it almost impossible to understand her. She hung up and mumbled French obscenities under her breath.

I patted her shoulder. "Bad day?"

Marcella cursed. "*Connard. Abruti.* Imbeciles. The newspapers. They don't understand English. They don't understand French. I tell them you are not in. I tell them you have nothing to say. They keep calling. Imbeciles."

I cursed; it sounded better in French. "I thought they would have given up by now. It's been a day and a half."

Marcella's usual optimism wasn't in sight. She frowned. "I

have seen these types before. They will never give up. Every day they will be calling."

I laughed. "Come on now, it's not that bad. Give it another day, those nasty reporters will forget all about us. You'll be complaining that you miss the excitement."

"I will never miss this tumult. I will welcome the peace when we are forgotten. Your sister, she is looking for you again."

"Good mood or bad?" Marcella was a co-conspirator in my frequent attempts to dodge Eileen on the days when her mood wasn't good.

Marcella's mournful expression deepened. "It is not good. She has received her own intrusive calls today. She asked to see you as soon as you stepped into this office. It is very, very urgent that you do so immediately."

I grinned. Marcella's flair for melodrama frequently turns routine communications to life-or-death emergencies. Instead of reacting to Marcella's interpretation of a message, I've learned to hold my temper, or excitement, until after talking to the caller.

"Thanks. I'll see Eileen as soon as I check in with Jona. I'm sure she's been looking for me too."

Frazzled nerves were widespread. I found Jona sitting at her desk staring at the telephone with an evil glare. She watched me walk down the corridor. Her face didn't soften.

I tried my brightest smile. "Asking if you're having a bad day would be a waste of breath. It's obvious."

"I'm too old for this." Jona picked up a stack of messages and held them out to me. "Take these. Everyone wants you to call them—immediately."

I shook my head. "If those are reporters, I don't want them. Throw 'em away."

"The reporters are already in the garbage. These are clients."

Eileen didn't knock even though we usually knock on closed doors. She strode into my office carrying a wad of message slips in her hand. I hated those pink papers. Each one represented another lost client.

Eileen tossed the bundle on my desk. "These calls are from

yesterday afternoon and today. If you care to count, there are twenty-seven. How many did you get?"

I mumbled, "Thirteen."

"Forty. Did yours fire us too?"

I nodded miserably. Eileen collapsed in a chair. "We lost forty clients in two days. Were your calls from big accounts?"

"Yeah—my biggest." I pulled a list from beneath my blotter and read the names. The last was the most difficult to say out loud. "Stan Adams called a few minutes ago. CIG dumped us too. I don't know who was more upset, me or Stan. He said it was a board decision and that he fought it as hard as he dared."

The Canfield Insurance Group had been our first corporate client. CIG, thanks to Stan's support, had stayed with us through some tough moments. Pressure strong enough to cut through a senior vice-president's objections severed the relationship.

"After Stan called, I checked the books. We were on track to bill over a million dollars with them this year. We used to be their primary investigator on fraud claims."

Turning away from Eileen, I punched a few keys on my computer keyboard. "Read me your clients again." While Eileen spoke, I entered the names and pulled up accounts.

Her voice was a death chant accompanying my calculations. When she finally stopped talking I stared at the computer screen, too drained to move.

Without turning my head from the monitor, I groped around on the top of my desk, found my cigarettes, and lit one. "Do you remember the financial projections I did last month? The ones that showed we'd have gross revenues of twelve million dollars this year—a thirty-five percent increase over last year?"

Three years ago, we broke through the million-dollar mark and had a wild celebration. The blood-red Porsche parked in a garage near my house was my trophy. Since then, our rapid growth surprised no one—no one except me and Eileen. Success attracts clients like no advertising campaign can. We were hot, everyone wanted to do business with us—until this week.

Eileen's voice was calm; she'd already guessed the answer. "What does your computer say? How bad is it?"

I thought of the investigators and attorneys we just hired to handle the extra business, our recently expanded offices, and the new car I'd been looking at, and sighed. "Sixty-five percent—gone. It's only Tuesday. If this keeps up, we'll be out of business by Friday."

Eileen, the optimist, looked for a bright side. "It's not that bad. We have money in the bank. We have a credit line. That will carry us until—"

"Until what? Until a mad scramble for clients replaces some of the lost business? It's going to be difficult—maybe impossible—to make up for those clients. We'll have to lay people off."

Eileen snapped, "In ten years we've never laid anyone off. We're not going to start now. No layoffs."

I turned the computer off and swung around to face her. "Are we going to fight?"

Eileen forced a smile. "With each other? I don't think so. Let's save it for the bad guys. Do you have any ideas?"

"You play nice. Soothe the clients who want to jump and reassure the ones who decide to stay. I'll twist a few arms. I want to find out who's trying to put us out of business."

"A conspiracy." Eileen didn't call me crazy. She spread the message slips out on the desk and studied the names written on them. "Not a single individual. These are corporations, other law firms, investment firms, insurance companies . . ."

"Money. It's the only thing that could scare these clients away from us. Money—and the fear of losing it. Follow the money. It'll lead to—"

"Who? And why?"

I shrugged, then laughed. "How many people ended last week mad at you? Three, four, five, ten? I could double that number and not be close to the number of people mad at me. Tracking down all our enemies could take forever. It'll be faster to find the common bond among those who fired us."

"Blaine, you're wrong. There's an easier way. Try following my instinct for a change. Of all these people who are mad at us, the fertility clinic is the most irate. Look at them first."

Eileen picked up a handful of message slips and let them flutter back to the top of the desk. "Do they have the connections to make this work? What about a motive? I can't believe this is happening because the clinic is worried you'll stir up bad publicity about their missing surrogate."

I thought of Dr. Nelson's poorly veiled threat. Had his mocking smile meant he'd already put in motion the process which led to the stack of pink slips on my desk?

Chapter 18

By the time I dragged myself home that night, I barely had the strength to collapse on the sofa and turn the television set on. I got up twice: once to change clothes, once to get a container of yogurt from the refrigerator. TV numbs my brain; I willingly sat back and let it happen.

The doorbell rang moments after the eleven o'clock news ended. I stabbed the power button on the remote control to shut the TV off and pulled on my slippers. When I opened the door, one of the faces I'd just been watching greeted me.

He smiled and wedged his foot in the door before I could close it. "Are you Blaine Stewart?"

"I don't have anything to say—"

"Then you can listen. Can I come in? I'd really like to talk with you." He smiled again. When I didn't swoon and fall back to let him inside, he said, "This is off the record. I don't even have my tape recorder with me. Please, it's about the Marsden case."

"The millionaire baby?"

"You watched my piece." Johnnie Bramble smiled with genuine delight. "That was a good story. It would have been better if I'd managed to get a camera inside the clinic. I tried. They threw me out."

The cold air whipped around the newscaster and hit my face. I let him in; arguing on the doorstep would only raise my heat bill. I took his reporter's trench coat, tossed it over the bannister, and pointed to the living room. Bramble sat on the sofa, taking care to not crumple his fancy suit. I wasn't impressed. Dennis wore better clothes and didn't worry about wrinkles.

I pulled the rocking chair closer to the sofa, sat down, and looked at my guest. Johnnie Bramble was new in town, called up from Washington to replace a heavy-drinking anchor who showed up drunk to host the Thanksgiving parade. Neither Macy's nor the network thought his description of Charlie Brown's balloon peering up Olive Oil's skirt was amusing. So far, Bramble had managed to keep his vices hidden.

I lit a cigarette—only because he looked like the type who would be annoyed. He was. Bramble frowned, but didn't complain or lecture me.

"Your co-anchor said you were on special assignment tonight. Did you skip the eleven o'clock news just to visit me? I'm honored. I try to keep my home address a secret. How did you find me?"

Johnnie leaned back away from the smoke. "You PI's don't have a monopoly on informants. We newsmen have our own sources. Don't ask for a name. I have to protect my source."

The self-satisfied grin on his face warned that I was in for an evening of clichés from the Nordic god. I stifled a groan, took another drag on the cigarette, and blew a huge cloud of smoke in his direction. Maybe I could smoke him out.

Bramble didn't twitch, but my silence made him nervous. I waited. He crossed his legs and tugged at the crease of his slacks. "Beneath these anchor duds, I'm an investigative reporter. Back home in DC there was plenty of good material. You know, Congress. The President. Ted Kennedy. I never ran out of ideas. It's tougher here. Political scandals aren't good enough. Too routine, is what my producer says." Bramble shook his head. "If it's not bizarre, you people don't pay attention."

"Mr. Bramble, I watched your report on the news tonight. Your people back home in DC might consider a dead woman and a missing baby bizarre; I don't. If you've come to enlist me in your ratings battle, forget it. The only thing I have to say to you is *No Fucking Comment.*" I tapped ashes into the empty yogurt container and smiled. "If you quote me, please be accurate."

"Did Judith Marsden hire you to find the missing surrogate?

Do you think the surrogate killed Marsden? You know, like a Mary Beth Whitehead gone mad?"

"I thought I made it clear that I wasn't answering questions. I didn't let you in here to conduct an interview. You said you wanted to talk. Talk or get out. It's late and I want to go to bed."

"Look, Miss Stewart, Blaine—can I call you Blaine?" I nodded, anything to speed him to the point. "Bizarre was a poor choice of words. This story is compelling, not bizarre." His voice dropped to a sincere level. "I want to tell the story from both sides. What drove Mrs. Marsden to hire a surrogate? Did it ultimately force her to commit suicide? What drove the surrogate to run away and possibly murder the woman whose child she's carrying?"

I shifted on the rocker, an uncomfortable audience to his rehearsal. It was easy to visualize him looking into the camera introducing his story. I've seen this powerful charisma turned on by politicians and movie stars—a personality so powerful it overwhelms skeptics seated in the far corners of an auditorium. Power that reaches through the television and convinces the viewer this person will step out into the room, put an arm around your shoulder, and whisper in your ear, "Try it my way. You know I'm right."

Bramble's seductive voice wrapped around my misgivings, pulling me to his side. I stood and shattered the mood. He stopped talking and blinked. His mouth hung open as he scrambled for the words to lure me back inside his trap.

"Sorry, Johnnie, my legs were falling asleep. Why don't you skip the dramatic introduction to your video and get to the point before the rest of me falls asleep too?"

"I'm proposing we work together. Friends, not enemies. We can help each other. I'll feed you information. After this situation is cleared up, you'll let me wrap it up with an exclusive." Bramble made a show of pushing his jacket sleeves up over his elbows. "That's it. No tricks up my sleeve."

Bramble, unwilling to give me quiet time to think of reasons to turn him down, pushed. "What do you say? Do we have a deal?"

I tossed my cigarette butt into the fireplace. "How about a

good-faith deposit? Tell me something I don't know. Something to convince me that your sources are worthy of an exclusive."

"How about this: Marsden studied journalism in college. She freelanced for radical right magazines under her maiden name, L'Ameillaud. The clinic made discreet inquiries about the contents of her desk and computer. Someone is afraid she was working on a story that would have blown the roof off the building." Bramble didn't wait for his information to settle. He snapped, "Deal?"

"On my terms?"

"Any terms you want—as long as they end with an exclusive for me." To seal the pact, he slid a business card from his breast pocket to my hand in one smooth movement. Two handwritten telephone numbers were on the back.

"Don't go through my secretary; I don't want your name added to the rumor treadmill. If you need anything—research assistance, rumor checking, anything—call the numbers on the back. Just don't forget to call when I can run with a story. If you want glory, I'll give it to you. If you want anonymity, I'll protect you. Deal?"

"Your information is provocative, but I'm not doing business with you until I check this journalism story out. Where did you get it from?"

"Cops talk to me. I hang out in cop bars, buy a few rounds of drinks, and listen. They tell me wild stories, hoping I'll get them on the evening news." Bramble laughed. "Most of it's too filthy or too bloody for anything but a porn movie. Sometimes I put the word out that I'm interested in a particular case."

"So someone whispered in your ear." I didn't bother to ask for a name. "Is he reliable?"

"Don't be insulting. I wouldn't be sitting here if I was uncertain about my facts. Regardless of what you may think, I earned my reputation. I'm not a dumb blond talking head reading from a monitor with everyone in the control booth praying I'll pronounce the words properly. I get down in the trenches and pull my stories out from where it's happening."

"Cutting-edge journalism?"

Bramble missed the sarcasm in my voice. "Exactly. Cutting-edge journalism—I like that."

"Before you get carried away with your new advertising slogan, answer this: You have unimpeachable connections and your station's magnificent resources. Why do you need me?"

"Can I be honest with you?"

In a dry voice, I said, "Does that mean you've been less than honest so far? And here I was believing you, just like your viewers do." I shook my head. "How disappointing."

He blushed and ignored my ridicule. "I've been asked—ordered—to pull back. The clinic is threatening libel suits and my bosses are nervous. It's common knowledge that you were working for Marsden. I figured I could feed you information. I help you. You help me."

I stared at my guest and tried to decide how much was truth and how much was crafted to get me on his side. Bramble was comfortable on my sofa, as comfortable as he would be sitting in his plush anchor seat reporting the story. He had nothing to lose; I could find myself working in a dull agency again. I squinted at Bramble. Could I use him to my advantage?

"Johnnie, I don't take partners on until I know they're good. How about an audition? Put your staff to work and send me a package of information on the fertility clinic. Film clips, background information, everything. Send it to my office."

The professional smile returned to Bramble's face. "Then we have a deal? I can count on you?"

"Maybe. Let's see how you do with this assignment. We'll talk again after I look into Judith's writing career and review the material you send me. Send the info. I'll call you."

With mutual distrust, we shook hands and agreed to talk in a few days. I gave Bramble his coat and let him out. Peeking out from behind the curtain, I watched him walk down the street, vainly looking for a taxi. After he was out of sight, I went back to my rocker, sat down, and lit another cigarette. Minutes later, the doorbell rang again.

Cursing my life which didn't allow for five minutes at midnight to enjoy a quiet cigarette, I rocked to my feet and went to the door expecting to see Johnnie Bramble's smiling face. I was wrong—and surprised. The man pushing my doorbell was Dennis.

Chapter 19

I turned the locks and let Dennis in. He hung his coat in the closet and said, "I would have come sooner, but I saw another gentleman caller ringing your bell. Have you already found a replacement for me? That was quick work."

I sat on the stairs and looked at Dennis. His face and voice were carefully balanced between jealous and joking. "Dennis, it was business. I'm amazed. What did you do, hang around on the snowy street until he left?"

"I went to the View and drank beer until I thought he'd be gone. If he was still here, I was going to throw him out."

"Dennis, please . . . I'm tired. It's been a long day. I don't feel like fighting." I yawned. "I don't even feel like talking. If you want a heart-to-heart discussion, it's going to have to wait until I'm awake." I yawned again. "Try me in a day or two."

Sometimes the man can't take a hint. Dennis squeezed in next to me on the stair. He put his hand on my knee. "I couldn't sleep. The last few times we talked, I've been—"

"Rude and nasty."

"I came to apologize. Will you forgive me?"

He smiled. Some, not all, of my fatigue and anger disappeared; tiny remnants of it rattled around inside me. I pushed the doubts aside and kissed his cheek. "I'm never too tired to listen to an apology. It's a nice change to be getting one rather than giving one."

Before Dennis answered, I took his hand. "Sometimes it's better to just shut up. Come on, don't say another word." I pulled him to his feet and led him up the stairs to my bedroom.

Every time Dennis attempted to talk, I kissed him quiet. I was tired of words. I distrusted every word I heard. I didn't want to apply the same standards to the man in bed with me.

Wrapping my arms around Dennis's shoulders, I pulled him to me, welding his body to mine. Dennis didn't speak. He held me and stroked my skin until it vibrated. We made love and fell asleep on the rumpled sheets.

I woke near dawn, fighting off a recurring nightmare. I rolled over and crashed into a body. Startled, because the dream always ends with me groping the empty space at my side, I opened my eyes and looked into Dennis's brown eyes and the great big smile on his face.

"Sorry . . ."

I started to move back to my part of the bed. Dennis rolled on his side and put an arm over me, keeping me close to him. "You've been thrashing around hard enough to make me think about waking you up. Are you okay?"

"Yeah . . . sorry. You should have kicked me; I would have settled down and let you sleep."

Dennis didn't believe me. Leaving his arm draped over me, he said, "You know, Jeff was one of my closest friends. I miss him too."

Mornings are a vulnerable time for me; I'm sleepy and slow to raise the guards. If the sun had been up, I would have pushed Dennis away. But I didn't.

I pushed my hair from my eyes and said, "I vividly remember Jeff's laugh, the way he smelled when he came out of the shower, the notes he'd leave on the refrigerator—without any trouble. But sometimes I have trouble remembering his face. I pinch my eyes closed and try to conjure up his image. His features aren't sharp anymore. They're fuzzy. Like a picture slowly fading in the sun."

"You're not being disloyal. You can't dedicate your life as a memorial to Jeff."

A flash of anger ran through me. "Don't tell me it's not what Jeff would have wanted . . ."

Dennis resisted my attempt to slip from beneath his arm. "I'm not going to say you should forget Jeff and get on with your life. Jeff was my friend, but I can't presume the right to speak for him. No one can speak for the dead."

We stared at the ceiling, stirring our private memories of my husband. Dennis broke the stillness. "Blaine, I don't want to force Jeff out of your life, or make you choose between us. There's room for both of us. Keep your memories of Jeff, but let me in. Let's build something new."

"What are you suggesting?"

"I'm not suggesting. I'm proposing."

I giggled. "Blaine Stewart and her two husbands. One's a ghost and the other isn't. That would make a great play."

"It's been done. Blaine, this isn't the romantic scene I had in mind—"

"You don't think lying here naked in bed is romantic? Would you like me to find some candles and soft music?"

Dennis tossed the covers aside and got out of the bed. I sat up and watched him walk to the closet. "Are you leaving? What did I say that was wrong?"

He stuck his hand in his jacket pocket, took out a ring box, and came back to the bed. "If you stop laughing for a second, I'd like to propose."

He opened the box. A ring, its diamond cut in a marquis shape, was nestled inside. Dennis took the ring out, then snapped the box closed and tossed it to the floor. It was a simple, impossible to misunderstand, proposal: "Blaine, I love you. Will you marry me?"

Without stopping to think, the answer jumped from my mouth: "No."

Chapter 20

• • • • • • • • • • •

Dennis flinched. "You're joking, aren't you?"

"No."

Dennis pulled his hand away and rolled out of the bed before I could stop him. He dropped the ring on the bed, grabbed his clothes and began dressing.

I sat up and pulled the blanket over my shoulders. "Dennis, please let me explain."

"Don't. Don't say a word. Let's follow the same rules as last night. You didn't want to hear it last night. I don't want to hear it this morning." Dennis grabbed the ring and stuffed it in his pocket. Shoes and jacket in hand, he walked out.

After I heard the front door slam, Dennis's unmistakable sign of anger, I slumped down and folded my hands under my head. When my personal life is great, business is bad. When business is good, my personal life . . . I always thought that someday I'd get both lives in synch and I'd be happy. I never imagined they'd mesh and leave me in hell.

I loved Dennis. A fear I couldn't face had pushed the refusal from my mouth. I said no because of a grown-up version of never saying good-bye. If I didn't marry Dennis, I couldn't be the widow standing at the grave of another dead hero.

I rolled over on my stomach and smashed my fist into the pillows. I was a coward.

Chapter 21

I had staff following Nikki, hoping she'd lead us to Hannah's hideout. I had staff watching the clinic in case Hannah showed up for an unscheduled prenatal visit. I used my contacts to get copies of Nikki's telephone records to see if I could find calls that would lead to her sister.

I could have joined one of the surveillance crews and wasted hours drinking coffee, freezing, and praying for a glimpse of Hannah. I could have joined Eileen's battle to keep our clients on board. I could have found Dennis and tried to explain my cowardice to him. I didn't. I did what any good coward would do: I got out of town.

I decided to make another visit to Beaver Ridge. Without stopping to think, I got out of bed and left a message for Eileen. After a fast shower, I dressed, filled a thermos bottle with coffee, and hurried out of the house. This time, I took my gun.

By nine, I was rolling down the steep hill on the outskirts of Hackettstown, half way through New Jersey, well past the shopping malls and condo developments, into cow country. The ride gave me time to think about Beaver Ridge, and by the time I pulled off Route 80, I had a plan.

This time I didn't charge into town, loudly announcing my presence. A few miles outside of Beaver Ridge I pulled into an Exxon station and stopped at the pumps. A tall, gawky boy ran out from the garage. The acne on his face made me wonder if the term "pizza face" was still popular with high school students. In seconds, I learned that owning a Porsche was the only ambition he'd developed in his short life.

I popped the hood. He spent five minutes admiring the machinery, then carefully closed the lid and gently wiped away the spots his greasy hands left on the finish. A twenty-dollar contribution to his Porsche fund purchased directions to the Wyrick house. When I drove out of the station, I glanced in the rearview mirror. The boy's eyes stayed locked onto the car until I disappeared around a bend in the road.

Following his directions, I clocked three and a half miles on the odometer, then turned right onto an unpaved road marked by a large boulder which had been painted red. If the boy's directions were accurate, I should see the Wyrick house after five more miles of twisting road.

I almost drove past the tiny sign on the mailbox that marked the Wyrick house. I took the turn too fast and hit the ice-covered gravel at fifteen miles an hour. The Porsche's wheels spun on the ice. The car fish-tailed and slid toward the snowbank lining the side of the driveway. I took my foot off the gas pedal and the car straightened out as the wheels gained traction on the slippery surface. I down-shifted to first and slowly drove to the house.

An old two-story farmhouse sat on top of a small rise. The white siding had faded to a dull gray. The shutters on the ground-floor windows were bright green, but the ones on the second floor were faded and peeling. A project abandoned halfway to completion?

A curtain in a second-floor window moved. I saw the dark shadow of a person watching my arrival; the glass was too streaked for me to tell if it was a man or woman. Keeping an alert eye on the shadow, I drove up to the house. The figure disappeared when I reached the end of the drive.

I parked next to a barn that had collapsed inward like a fallen soufflé and cautiously walked up the icy steps. An unopened bag of salt sat on the top step next to the door; no one had bothered to brush off the thin layer of snow covering it. I rang the bell and stamped my feet to get rid of any loose snow or ice. And waited.

I would have stood on that doorstep all day long, ringing the bell until someone answered, but I didn't have to. The door opened slightly. A woman's voice spoke through the tiny opening between the door and frame. "Go away. I don't allow strangers in my home."

I leaned against the door to keep it open. "Please don't send me away. I understand your reluctance to entertain visitors, but I hope you'll make an exception. I've driven a long distance to see you. Mrs. Wyrick, please let me in. It's very important." I sneezed. "I can stand out here and talk, but it's cold. Please let me in so we can talk." I sneezed again and tried to look pathetic.

Maybe I was catching a cold; my sneezing changed her mind. The door opened. I rushed inside before she changed her mind. A short, white-haired woman closed the door and looked me over, an uncertain expression on her face. Ethel Wyrick. I recognized her from the newspaper article I'd read on my previous visit to town. The photos showed a much younger woman; grief had added premature age lines to her face.

Without speaking, Ethel led me through a short hallway to the back of the house. While the outside of the house was rundown and neglected, the inside shone from meticulous cleaning. The furniture polish and ceramic jars of potpourri on the tables couldn't disguise the musty smell of decaying wood.

One long room ran along the entire length of the house. It was filled with a dining room table and chairs, sofa and recliner, television set and stereo. A large Franklin stove sat in the center of the floor.

The walls were bare. I could see faint outlines of the places where pictures once hung. I wondered if they were pictures of her daughters.

Ethel nodded at the table and chairs near the stove. "It will be warmer there. In the wintertime, we close up most of the house and spend all our time in here. The stove heats the downstairs . . ." She stopped; her voice abruptly changed from friendly hostess to someone who was thinking about calling the police. "Who are you?"

Little old ladies have trouble throwing you out when you're comfortably seated at their dining room table. Without waiting for an invitation, I took my coat off, draped it over one of the oak chairs, and sat. I took a fresh notebook from my pocket and flipped it open.

I tried to sound official. "My name is Blaine Stewart. I came to ask you a few questions about your daughters."

Ethel fell into a chair opposite me. The color drained from her face, leaving it as white as the snow covering her yard. "My daughters? I don't understand. My daughters are . . ."

"I know. I'm sorry. I read the newspaper articles about the accident. I can't imagine the pain you must have suffered. However, there's a situation . . ." I searched for a tactful way to deliver my news.

Ethel's shoulders sagged. "I've spent every day of the past two years dreading the day when the police knocked on my door and asked about the girls."

If Ethel wanted to think I was with the police, I wouldn't stop her. "Mrs. Wyrick, do you know that two women in New York City are representing themselves as Hannah and Nikki Wyrick?"

She whispered, "Yes."

"And you approve?"

"Yes. I helped arrange it."

I thought I'd lost the ability to be surprised by the things people tell me—until my meeting with Judith Marsden. Since then, I'd been rocked by the casual admissions made by all involved. Ethel Wyrick was an unlikely candidate for inclusion on my list of people with strange stories, but her disclosure earned her the number two spot. Judith still held on to number one.

"Mrs. Wyrick, this is a very serious situation. How and why did you agree to let these women masquerade as your daughters?"

The relief of the confessional brightened Ethel's face. "It started during the war—Vietnam. Ronald and I took in people, boys, who were making their way to Canada. They'd come in the middle of the night. The boys would stay here for a day or two, then we'd pass them on to the next stop. Sort of an underground railroad, if you will."

"How did you become a way station on that railroad?"

"My brother, Timmy, got us started. Timmy's a priest."

"Where?"

"St. Timothy's. It's in Brooklyn. Father Timothy preaches at St. Timothy's. The kids in the school think it's funny. Timmy didn't think it was funny that his high school seniors were being shipped to the jungles. He followed God's instructions and undertook a Crusade to save as many young men as he could. Timmy believes that to save souls he sometimes has to break man-made laws. When man's laws are in conflict with God's teachings, those laws are invalid. I'll never forget the first boy."

Ethel stared at the tablecloth, lost in her memories. I quietly said, "Tell me about him."

"Timmy showed up at the door with a young boy. He was so scared, he couldn't eat for two days. His father called him a traitor and threw him out of the house. The boy didn't know where to go. Timmy found him sleeping in the vestibule. The youngster had some half-baked idea that he could claim sanctuary in the church.

"Timmy pleaded with us to help him. Ronald and I were horrified, but we couldn't send the poor boy away. After that, Timmy came once or twice a month. He'd always bring a boy with him, sometimes two. They'd stay two, three days, then move on to Canada. We never heard from any of them again."

"Did anyone in town know what you were doing? They must have noticed your parade of visitors. How many times could you say your guest was a visiting nephew?"

Ethel smiled. "Beaver Ridge lost its 'America, Love It Or Leave It' attitude soon after two of our boys died. They were killed in the same week, during the Tet offensive. Those deaths set people to thinking. I thought our guests went unnoticed, but I was mistaken. Many people knew about our boys. The town protected us and our visitors."

Decades after the war, those protective attitudes were still intact. I wondered which of the watchful townspeople had used me for target practice.

"And after the war, what happened?"

"Nothing for awhile. Timmy stopped asking for favors. Until . . ." Ethel's voice faded. She traced the tablecloth's rose patterns with her index finger.

I hardened my voice. "Until two years ago when your brother asked you to help two girls conceal their identities. You agreed to let them pretend to be your daughters. Why?"

Ethel raised her eyes from the table and stared at me. Her gaze was defiant. "The railroad didn't die after the war. It simply took different passengers. That's what Timmy said when he started bringing the women and their children. They'd stay longer. Ten days, two weeks. However long it took Timmy to find a place where they could stay forever and become new people."

"Abused women?"

"And their children. The stories." Ethel shuddered. "I could hardly bear to listen to the stories. Beaten wives. Children abused by their fathers, or even their grandfathers. I was happy to help them get a new life."

"Tell me about the girls, Mrs. Wyrick. What happened?"

"Timmy dropped in one afternoon. He was alone, which surprised me because he always brought a guest. As luck would have it, I was frying a chicken. Timmy's favorite."

Before she starting telling me about the peas, mashed potatoes, and the rest of the menu, I repeated, "Tell me about the girls."

"Timmy waited until after dinner—he'll never talk business when there's fried chicken on the table. He asked us to give up our daughters so two other girls could be reborn."

Father Timmy sounded adept at twisting doctrine to make convincing arguments. "What else did he tell you about them? Did he tell you their names?"

"Their names?" Ethel shook her head. "No. We never know the names of Timmy's people. It's for protection, in case something goes wrong. In case the police try to find them."

Ethel's restless fingers roamed across the tablecloth, flicking away invisible crumbs. "Timmy told us two girls, two sisters, were in trouble. Bad trouble. We were their only hope."

"What kind of trouble?"

"Faith is difficult, sometimes impossible, to explain. Timmy's requests are never frivolous. When he told me about the girls, I believed him. I did not ask questions."

"What about your husband? Is he also a true believer?"

Ethel frowned. She began to rebuke me for my flippant tone, but stopped midway through it. "Ronald doesn't question anything. He stopped asking questions when the girls . . ." She closed her eyes. ". . . the night the girls were killed."

I cleared my throat. "Mrs. Wyrick?" Ethel started and opened her eyes. They were shiny and filled with tears. "I'm sorry. Just a few more questions and I'll be done."

"Are you planning to arrest me?"

"No." I hesitated and briefly considered telling her the truth. I quickly tossed that idea away; stopping her wouldn't bring me any closer to the baby—and Judith's killer. "Okay, Mrs. Wyrick. Your brother, the priest, comes to you. You give him dinner. He pleads with you to help two lost souls. You agree. What happens next?"

"Timmy took the girls' birth certificates and social security cards. He said that was all he needed to start a new life for his girls. He said if anyone, especially the police, asked questions, I should send them to him." Ethel remembered her brother's advice much too late. She waved her hands in the air, trying to pull the words back.

"Mrs. Wyrick, I appreciate your candor. I—"

A voice spoke from behind my back. "What's going on here?"

I turned. A man stood in the doorway. His features escaped my notice, I was too busy looking at the rifle cradled in his arms. The polished wooden stock, the telescopic sight, and the blue steel barrel gleamed in the sunlight.

Ethel snapped, "Ronald, put that thing away. You know I

won't allow it in the house." Ronald didn't move. Ethel raised her voice to a threatening level. "Ronald! Do as I say."

His hands tightened around the gun. I held my breath and waited, ready to dive under the table if the man lowered the barrel. After several long seconds, he turned and shuffled away.

I watched him disappear down the hallway and calmly said, "I went to the cemetery a few days ago. Does your husband spend a lot of time out there?"

Ethel whispered, "Did you have trouble?"

"Trouble? He shot at me."

"Ronald's harmless—"

"Your husband is dangerous. He tried to kill me."

"Ronald didn't want to kill you, or anyone. He was confused and upset. Doreen called. She said someone was in her diner asking questions about our girls. Ronald listened in on an extension. He got upset—he gets that way sometimes—and walked out of the house."

"You didn't try to stop him, or ask where he was going?"

"I didn't know he went to the cemetery. I thought he went hunting. Ronald spends a lot of time in the woods. I guess he spends a lot of time at the cemetery. The girls were his babies . . . We don't talk about it much anymore."

An unstable man with a Remington rifle. I suggested she disarm him, and left the house. I didn't want to be within shooting distance when Ronald learned I was asking questions about his babies.

Chapter 22

It was a long ride from Beaver Ridge to Brooklyn. While I watched the scenery gradually regress from quiet farmlands to the disorder of the cities, I thought about the Civil War.

Despite the government's efforts to shut it down, as many as a hundred thousand slaves made the trip via the underground railroad to freedom. The conductors couldn't be stopped by threats or legal action. Government attempts to enforce the laws prohibiting giving assistance to fugitive slaves only increased the railroad's activities. The conductors of the new railroad would be just as adamant in protecting their passengers. By the time I drove across the Brooklyn Bridge and made my way to Brooklyn Heights, my hopes of getting useful information from the priest had disappeared.

St. Timothy's church, school, and rectory occupied an entire block overlooking the East River. The brick buildings were blackened from a century's exposure to city soot and pollution. A lone basketball player ignored the frigid air and practiced free throws in the deserted schoolyard.

I parked at the end of the street and walked back to the row of buildings in the center of the block. Freezing wind lashed at me and penetrated my coat with ease. Within seconds, I was shivering. I didn't stop to admire the famous view of lower Manhattan that's on all the postcards. I hurried through the gate and ran up the rectory stairs.

Hoping the priest wasn't out on a call, I pressed the bell and bounced up and down, trying to get warm. The door opened. A middle-aged man dressed in a flannel shirt and black knit slacks greeted me by saying, "I'm sorry, office hours are from one to three. Perhaps you can come back tomorrow."

"I'm sorry, I can't come back tomorrow. I have to see Father Timothy." I stopped—I didn't know his last name. Quickly, before the man tried to send me away, I said, "I have to see him right away. It's urgent."

"I see." The bifocals on top of the man's head slipped. He pushed them back up. "If it's an emergency, we can make an exception to our policy."

A Catholic school education stays with you forever. I wasn't going to lie to a priest, stories of eternal damnation were still too vivid in my mind. "Well . . . I wouldn't call it an emergency. But it is important. Is Father Timothy in?"

He smiled. "An honest soul. Come in, miss. I'm Father Timothy. I don't doubt that your business is important. It must be to bring you out to our riverside perch on such a cold winter's day.

Only fools and people with urgent business come here when the wind blows off the river."

The priest led me to a cramped study in the front of the house and closed the door. The room was brightly lit and cheerfully decorated with Ansel Adams's pictures of Yosemite. A bookshelf near the door held enough Bibles and religious texts to satisfy the more orthodox visitors.

Father Timothy took my coat, hung it on a hook on the back of the door, then settled into the chair behind the desk. "Forgive my civilian garb. The collar intimidates people; I only wear it for official business. I don't recall seeing your face at Mass. You're not from this parish, are you?"

"No, I'm not." My next words would wipe the cordial smile from his face, but I didn't hesitate. "I visited your sister, Ethel, this morning."

The priest's eyes hardened with anger. "So, you're the one. My sister called me. She was very upset. She warned me that the police would be showing up on my doorstep. I didn't expect you so soon. I am quite willing to take responsibility for my actions. But I implore you to not persecute my sister. Ethel's had enough heartache in her life."

"Father, I'm not interested in persecuting anyone. You should also know that I'm not with the police. I'm a private investigator. My client hired me to locate Hannah Wyrick. I don't care about the reasons why she's using your niece's identity. I only want to know Hannah's real name so I can find her." His eyes darted away from mine. I leaned forward. "You know where she is."

"I can't tell you anything. I would be betraying a confidence if I revealed any information about the girls. The church—"

My temper flared. "The church won't protect you when ugly stories appear in the newspapers. Stories about how you used the identity of your dead nieces to provide false ID to two other women. Stories about how you hid draft evaders—"

"That was twenty-five years ago. Do you really think people will care?"

"I think it will make for exciting news coverage. Some reporters might say it establishes a pattern of deception. Do you think your superiors will agree?"

"I've been doing good work. Would you take the chance of destroying it?"

"You're preaching that good works supersede everything else. I'm also trying to do good work; I don't care what I destroy to do it." I crossed my legs and grinned at him. "Father, we're playing a game that doesn't have any rules. I'll do anything to find that woman. How far will you go to protect her? My reputation is already in shreds, I don't have as much to lose as you do."

Showing a remarkable lack of curiosity about me, the priest folded his hands on top of the desk and asked, "What do you think is the worst possible crime?"

"Father Timothy, let's not waste time. Changing the subject won't work."

"Parricide, killing one or both of the people who gave you life, is one of society's most heinous crimes. Can you imagine the abuse that would bring a child to the point of thinking about killing her parents? What horrible acts would make that child carry out those thoughts?"

"It's a terrible thing, but I don't understand how—"

He snapped, "You would understand if you gave me the chance to explain."

I've come a long way since Catholic school, where I never dreamed of talking back to a priest or nun. Sounding as annoyed as the priest, I said, "Then explain. Don't preach."

He touched his gray hair and fingered one of the few strands that remained black. "Twenty-five years ago, when I was a youngster fresh out of seminary, I decided to follow my conscience, even in cases when it went against man's laws. Ethel told you about my wartime activities, so I won't bore you. But I'm proud of what I did. Just as I'm proud of the people who worked with me. Just as I'm proud of the young boys who made the difficult decision to follow their hearts even when it meant leaving their families behind forever."

His voice slid into the rhythm of a sermon. I abruptly cut into the flow of his words. "My friends and enemies agree on one thing: I'm a very impatient woman."

I looked at my watch and stood up. "It's four-thirty. That gives me enough time to call a man I know—Johnnie Bramble. Maybe you've seen him. He's the anchorman on Channel 4. Johnnie's very interested in my case. I promised him an exclusive. Watch the news tonight, Father. You might hear your name."

"You wouldn't."

I yanked my coat from the hook and found a business card in a pocket. Tossing the card in front of him, I said, "Just so you won't think I'm being unreasonable, I'll wait until six-thirty. The early news will be over. Mr. Bramble will be able to pay close attention to me. Maybe your bishop or cardinal goes to bed early and misses the eleven o'clock broadcast."

Father Timothy glared at me. "You are a hard woman, Miss Stewart."

I put my coat on and patted my pockets for my gloves. "Flattery won't stop me."

"Maybe the truth will. Sit down, Miss Stewart. Let me tell you about the Wyrick girls."

Without removing my coat, I sat and watched the priest. If Father Timmy didn't talk, I'd have to walk out. I hoped he was convinced I'd call in the reporters.

"Our church members aren't content with a weekly encounter with God. Coming to church on Sunday and then going home until the following week isn't their mode of worship. We have programs for children and the elderly. We deliver meals to people with AIDS. Women sometimes arrive at our door with their children, carrying their belongings in a suitcase or knapsack. We always help them."

I shifted on the chair. The priest held up a hand. "Please be patient. I'm trying to explain so you'll understand. My mission includes working with runaways. We give them food, shelter, and counseling. Sometimes we convince them to go home or into a foster home."

"Were the girls you turned into Hannah and Nikki runaways?"

Father Timmy nodded. "It was a frosty day, much like today. On the really cold days, we go to the Port Authority and try to get the kids who are faced with either a night on the freezing streets or choking in the bus fumes as they attempt to fight off the hustlers and bums."

"Aren't there enough kids in Brooklyn who need your help? Why do you go all the way to Port Authority?"

"God never said, Thou shall not commute. We go where we're needed. It was almost midnight. The girls were on the corner of Eighth Avenue and Forty-second Street. They were wretched, clutching battered suitcases and trying to ignore the comments of the troublemakers gathered on the corner. The pimps were interested—twins would have been a unique addition to their staff. I didn't have to do much talking; the girls were relieved to come to the rectory with me."

"Excuse me. Do you let male and female runaways stay here? Aren't you afraid? Not afraid of the children, afraid that people might misinterpret your actions?"

The priest grimaced and took the bifocals from the top of his head. He placed them on the desk, in the center of the blotter, and gently twirled them in a circle. "Sexual abuse is what you mean, isn't it? No, I'm not afraid. But the parish council was. This is a big rectory, built in the days when St. Timothy's was a grand church with a dozen priests. There's plenty of room. We have live-in staff, social workers. Both sexes."

"The girls you picked up, what were their names?"

A smile stretched across his face. "Did you think I would forget myself and blurt out an answer? Please . . ." He squinted at my card. "Please, Miss Stewart, I'm a priest. I know how to keep a secret."

"Sorry, Father. If you won't tell me their names, what will you tell me?"

"You *are* an impatient woman. I am going to tell you why I convinced my sister to give these girls a new life. I don't know why you're trying to find them, but I do know they aren't bad girls."

I sat back and incredulously said, "Wait a second. You started to talk about parricide. Are you going to tell me these girls killed their parents, but they aren't bad girls?"

"Have you ever killed another human being?"

"Yes, about ten months ago. I shot a man. He died." I folded my arms across my chest, I wasn't going to add any details.

My answer surprised the clergyman, but he controlled it. "I see. Do you consider yourself a bad person?"

"No. I killed him before he killed me. I'd rather not talk about it."

"You killed in self-defense and you were exonerated. I'm sure even God has forgiven you."

Absolved by everyone except myself. I squirmed in the chair, wanting to be doing anything other than talking about killing people. "Did you get special training in making people uncomfortable?"

"We get training in the truth, that's all. Honesty can make us uneasy at times. You should have compassion for these girls because you have a special understanding of their pain. They took their father's life in order to save their own young lives."

"Who did the killing, Hannah or Nikki?"

The priest shook his head. "That's something I cannot divulge. The confidential nature of the confessional is sacrosanct." A sly grin appeared on his face. "Well, Miss Stewart, I guess we've discovered one rule in our little game."

Our little game was beginning to feel like a championship tennis match played on a hard court. Father Timothy was in control and enjoying himself. All I could do was return his serves and try to stay on the court. "What drove the twins to kill their parents? It must have been serious for the courts to go along with self-defense."

My shot hit its mark. The priest bowed his head and concentrated on his spinning glasses. "The matter never went before the courts. The girls fled before the body was discovered."

Chapter 23

I almost cautioned the priest about the seriousness of what he was telling me. But I didn't. I waited for the details.

Father Timothy demonstrated remarkable psychic powers. He looked up and caught my eyes. "I guess you're wondering why I'm telling you this. After all, you could leave here and go straight to the police."

I nodded. "I could."

"But I don't think you will. I'm a good judge of character."

I played with the zipper on my jacket and counted to ten. Father Timothy was depleting my meager supply of patience and enjoying the process.

The priest feigned politeness. "I'm sorry. You must be getting tired, sitting here all this time while I ramble on in circles."

The smirk on his lips was too much. I snapped, "I'm trying to remember which commandment I'd break if I leaned across this desk and slapped your face." I stood up and zipped my jacket. "Good day, Father. Be sure to watch the news tonight. Don't bother to get up. I can find my way out." I walked out.

It didn't take the priest long to put on a bulky down jacket and rush after me. He called my name, the words sounded feeble as the wind pulled them away. I kept walking. He ran after me and roughly grabbed my shoulder. I twisted away from him.

"Hey." The priest bent over and tried to catch his breath. "Hey, didn't you hear me? I was calling you."

"Yeah, I heard you." I jammed my hands in my pockets and shook my head. "Your act may mystify your parishioners and the scared kids you pick up in the Port Authority, but I'm not impressed. Game's over, Father. I'm not playing anymore."

"Please, come back to the rectory. I'd like to answer some of your questions."

His eyes appeared to be sincere, but I wasn't taken in by his act. "I'll listen to you, but not in your cozy hole. If you want to talk, talk."

Father Timmy glanced at the snow on the sidewalk and the ice forming on the puddles in the street. "Not here, we'll freeze."

"Cold is a remarkable bullshit reducer. Let's take a walk. Walking and talking will warm you up just fine."

We crossed the street and walked along the sidewalk overlooking the East River. The sun had set. The lights of the buildings of Manhattan made it look like a magical Walt Disney kingdom where anything was possible. Anything was possible in Manhattan, including lots of things Disney never thought feasible. I lit a cigarette and listened to Father Timmy's fantastic story.

"The girls were obviously shaken by more than the trash in the bus station. They were in shock. We took them back to the rectory. I fed them while the social worker searched their suitcases."

"You searched their suitcases? That's an unusual way to welcome guests. Do you do that often?"

"Every time. It's standard procedure. We have to be sure no one has guns or drugs. Anyway, the social worker found bloody clothes in one of the cases."

"What kind of clothes?"

"A pair of jeans and a sweatshirt. At first, the girls denied any knowledge of them. They were afraid we'd call the police; even more afraid we'd turn them back out on the street. Of course, we didn't threaten them with any such thing. We never threaten our charges."

"Why did they open up to you? And why were you so convinced they told you the truth?"

The priest stopped walking. The illumination from the streetlights was strong enough to see the sincerity in his eyes. "The power of prayer, Miss Stewart. We prayed for forgiveness and understanding. After days of constant prayer, the girls unburdened their souls."

I stamped my cigarette out and hoped the unburdening hadn't taken place in the confessional. A sudden burst of wind forced us to start walking again. Father Timmy spoke in a low, almost inaudible, voice. I leaned closer to the priest so I wouldn't miss a word. An innocent eye might have mistaken us for young lovers on a chilly but romantic stroll. His words were far from amorous.

"I've heard so many loathsome stories. Some are the result of overactive imaginations and illusory wrongs. Many are true. When they're telling the truth, the details are too vivid. It's the liars who are fuzzy. I'm sure you find the same thing in your line of work."

We were compatriots sharing a search for the truth. I agreed and gently said, "Tell me their story. It must have been—"

He exploded. "Disgusting. When the Lord sends me children who've been so abused I wonder if He's testing my faith.

How . . ." His voice cracked. He gulped and said, "Please, can I have one of your cigarettes?"

"You don't smoke. Finish your story. You'll feel better and you won't need my cigarettes." My nose, ears, and toes were numb from the cold, but I wasn't going to suggest a warmer location. Not while the priest was talking.

We reached the end of the block and turned to retrace our footsteps. I didn't have to prod Father Timmy; he started talking again as soon as we turned around.

"The girls were about twenty at the time, a few years younger than my nieces would have been, but they looked older. Their life aged them."

"Are they really twins? Or was that made up to fit the new identity?"

"No. No, they're twins. No other children in the family. Father physically and sexually abusive. Alcoholic mother who didn't care to notice."

The cold made me more impatient than usual. "Father, quite a few children grow up with alcoholic and abusive parents. Most of them don't kill their parents."

His voice was tightly controlled. "One of the girls was raped by her father. Her mother walked in at the end. She blamed the girl for seducing her father. As you might guess, the father went after both girls. The mother's drinking increased proportionally."

"They were twenty years old, why didn't they leave?"

"They didn't think they could. The abuse had been going on for years. The girls were brainwashed. They worked at menial jobs and went home. No friends, no dating, no calls. They consoled themselves by fantasizing about how their father would die and they'd be free. The fantasies gradually developed into a mutual defense pact. They had to take care of each other. No one else would."

Cold air seeped through my coat, I started to shiver. I stamped my feet and asked, "What finally pushed them over the edge?"

"The father was an auto worker. The company restructured and closed the plant. He was unemployed and home all day— furious about being out of work, hating the company that rewarded his loyalty by firing him, hating every person he saw. The girls were subjected to weeks of round-the-clock abuse." He shuddered. "They were prisoners of war. They never knew when he would burst into the room and torture them.

"One girl was quite athletic. She went running in the morning, early, before the father was awake. One day, she came back from a run and took a shower. When she stepped out of the shower, he was waiting."

The priest stopped walking. He rested his elbows on the fence railing and looked down at the river. "Imagine you're a twenty-year-old girl. You step out of the shower, naked and dripping wet. Imagine your father standing there, licking his lips and telling you you're his special girl. Imagine him putting his arms around you, trying to kiss you. What would you do?"

Very quietly, I said, "I think I'd go nuts."

"Would you kill him?"

We watched the taillights of the cars on the FDR Drive while I tried to think of an honest response. "I don't know. Maybe."

"She tried to fight him off. She pushed him away. He followed her, telling her she'd be punished for being disobedient. A baseball bat found its way into her hands. She beat him again and again and again until he stopped moving. He died."

I closed my eyes and pictured the scene. A frightened girl standing over the body of her father. His head battered, a bloody bat in her hands. Another frightened girl hovering in the background. Neither one knowing if she should be happy or horrified. Blood splattered on the floor and walls.

I opened my eyes. "It must have been a noisy scene. Where was the mother?"

"Sleeping off the night before. Maybe she heard the noise and was hiding in her bedroom, afraid to come out. Maybe she was cheering the girls on."

"What happened after the girls realized he was dead?"

"They ran away. They arrived in Manhattan with nothing but suitcases filled with old clothes and vague hopes of starting a new life."

"Which you so kindly provided. Where are they, Father?"

"I don't know. It's been a year since I last saw the girls." He touched my arm. "Miss Stewart, you think I'm lying. I'm not.

That doesn't matter, because if I knew where the girls were, I wouldn't tell you."

Chapter 24

I folded my arms across my chest to keep myself from shivering, and looked at the priest. He intently watched a Staten Island ferry maneuver. The captain missed his first attempt at docking and backed away to try again.

"That's it?"

"That's it. I've already told you more than I should. You can threaten me. Believe me, I don't take your threats lightly. But I will not repudiate my vows."

It was too cold to fight a battle I couldn't win. I let him go. The priest went back to his warm rectory. I drove back to Manhattan.

Traffic on the Brooklyn-Queens Expressway was barely moving. The traffic jam gave me plenty of time to think about Father Timothy. I couldn't decide which parts of his story were true. By the time I got home, I was convinced he had lied at least once. Father Timmy had seen the girls less than a year ago.

I parked my car in the garage where I keep it hidden from the weather, traffic cops, and thieves, and hurried home. My house is a few doors down from the intersection of Barrow and Bedford streets. When I turned the corner to Barrow I saw lights shining out, making the icy pavement sparkle.

At first I thought it was Nikki, making an unscheduled visit. I glanced around the empty street and didn't see any sign of the surveillance team assigned to her. Hoping they were so well-hidden that even I couldn't spot them, I unlocked the door and stepped inside.

The smell of food greeted me. I flung my coat over the bannister and quietly walked to the kitchen. Dennis, dressed in faded jeans and a blue flannel shirt, was bent over peering into the oven. He straightened up and looked at me.

A few days ago, he would have kissed me. This time, he didn't. He tensely stood in front of the oven and watched me.

I ignored the strain in the air. "Dennis. I didn't expect to see you. I was afraid I had a burglar who forgot to close the curtains. What are you doing?"

"Cooking dinner. I'm making an old-fashioned roast chicken, just like dear old Mom's." He smiled. "Hope you don't mind. I called your office looking for you. You weren't in, so I talked to Eileen. She told me about the problems you guys are having and how you've been running all over New Jersey looking for the surrogate."

"So you came over to check up on me. Was it your idea, or Eileen's?"

Dennis waved a spatula at me. "Take a vacation and give your suspicious mind a rest. Blaine, the world isn't filled with evil people. Some of us are nice. I thought you'd appreciate a home-cooked meal and a sympathetic ear. That's all. No strings. No checking up. Just an evening with an old friend."

I answered his sincerity with laughter. "Where did you come from? You can't be from this planet." I stopped laughing. "How *did* you get in here?"

"With a key. Remember? The key you gave me. Maybe you should be more careful with your keys. Next time you could find something worse than a lunatic cook who came to make dinner." Dennis turned away from me and opened the oven door.

"Maybe I should be more careful—" My mouth dropped open. I ran from the kitchen to the upstairs bedroom I use as an office. Dennis followed behind, pot holders in hand.

I flipped the switches to turn on the computer and monitor and called up the directory listing the files. The listing is simple, three columns. The first column lists the files, a description of the file is in the second column, and the third shows the date of the last time the file was used.

I scanned the directory and cursed. Dennis walked into the room as I pounded my fist on the desk and ran through every obscenity I know. He stood behind me and put his hands on my shoulders. "What's wrong?"

"How could I be so stupid? I design security systems. I'm supposed to be a fucking expert. I lecture my clients about passwords, and security, and unauthorized users. And what do I do? I leave my computer wide open for looting."

"Calm down. You won't solve anything by beating up your computer." Dennis pulled a chair to my side and sat down. "What's missing?"

"Eileen and I are convinced the fertility clinic is behind our runaway clients. We can't prove it yet. I've been driving myself crazy trying to figure out how they got to our clients. Dennis, it was like they were working off a list, crossing one off and going on to the next. I was beginning to think someone in our office supplied them with the list." I shook my head. "I'm the idiot who let it out. I'm so damn stupid. Why didn't I just fax the list to them?"

Dennis caught my hand and squeezed it tight to get my attention. "Blaine, what are you talking about? What did you do?"

I pointed to the list of files on the screen. "See that one? The one called Clients. See the description? Current client roster. That file contains information on our major clients. I don't use it very often. I keep it in case we have a fire or some disaster that destroys the office."

"Okay. So, what's wrong?"

"Look at the date. Five days ago. That's the night I stayed in Beaver Ridge. And left my computer wide open for Nikki. I even clearly labeled the file so she didn't have to waste time searching for it."

I hate making mistakes, especially expensive mistakes. I stared at the monitor and tried to see how many synonyms I could think of for the word *idiot*. Dennis finally convinced me it was pointless to sit in front of the computer and curse my stupidity. We moved back to the kitchen so I could curse my stupidity there.

I sat at the table, fuming and flipping through the mail while Dennis cooked. "A week of mail and it's nothing but bills and junk. Don't people write letters anymore?" Dennis grunted. I continued my monologue. "Only one piece of mail that's personal and it's from my brother."

"It's been a while since I heard his name mentioned. What does he want? Is he in trouble again?"

My brother, Dick, communicates with us only when he needs help. I read the brief message on the postcard. "No trouble this time. He wants me to visit his new house in Key West. He promises eighty degrees and no snow. He says the only ice I'd see would be cubes."

It would be easy to catch a plane and disappear. I stared at the picture of the setting sun; my cowardly heart started beating faster in anticipation. I sighed and stuffed the card between bills from ConEd and NYNEX. Key West would have to wait.

"What's next?" I looked at the envelope on top of the pile. It was addressed by hand with no return address. "Mystery mail. Must be a new fund-raising technique designed to get the envelope opened."

It worked. I ripped open the envelope and pulled out a sheet of loose leaf paper. Cramped handwriting filled the page. I lit a cigarette, put my feet up on a chair, and read aloud:

"Dear Ms. Stewart,

"You don't know what I been through. If you did you'd leave me and him alone. We belong to each other.

"They made me lie on a stretcher with my legs spread open. The doctors stuck things inside me. It hurt. No one told me it would hurt. They told me nothing. Each time it didn't work, they looked at me like I did something bad. Like I made the baby die.

"I prayed for them. As soon as they put one inside me I named him and prayed for him. George. Richard. Matthew. Luke. Kevin.

"Now I know the doctors were right. I did make those babies die. God took them because I had to be punished.

"When they put Joshua inside me I prayed to Our Lord, Jesus Christ. I told Him I knew it was wrong to give Joshua away. That's why He took the other babies to heaven. He took them so I couldn't give them away. I promised Him I'd never give this one away. That's why Joshua didn't die like the others. I can't let him go.

"Please leave us alone."

Chapter 25

• • • • • • • • • • • •

Dennis quietly exhaled. "Wow."

I dropped the letter on the table and carefully examined the envelope. The postmark was smudged, but not illegible. It came from Brooklyn. Somehow, having my name on the letter made it more chilling than the one Judith received.

My forehead throbbed. I rested my head in my hands and watched Dennis mash potatoes.

"I'm glad I'm sober. No one would believe me if I was still drinking. I'm looking for a dead client's unborn baby who is being carried by a dead girl. I have a priest who lies, a cleaning lady who's stealing information from my computer, and a business that's rapidly going out of business. Now I'm getting letters from the surrogate telling me she's following God's will."

I thought: *I also have a man that I'm afraid to marry who sneaks in my house and cooks dinner.* I could hear my friends shouting, "Marry him, you fool!"

Instead of telling Dennis I'd marry him, I reread Hannah's note. It was worse the second time. I closed my eyes and rubbed my head. "What the hell am I doing?"

I didn't realize I'd spoken out loud until Dennis answered. "If murderers got off because they wrote good letters, the jails would be empty. What about Judith? Don't you feel sorry for her?"

The memory of Judith in my car, her eyes closed and her head lolling against her chest as I sped to the hospital, wiped away the sympathy and guilt I felt for the surrogate. Hannah's pain might be real, but Judith was dead.

Enjoying his role of guest chef, Dennis served dinner, then sat next to me. I looked at the plate of food and suspiciously asked, "Where did this come from? It's been years since a chicken was spotted in my refrigerator. And these potatoes, where did you get them?"

"My dear, we're going to have to take a field trip to a grocery store. Have you opened your refrigerator door recently? I'm a good cook, but I can't create miracles from a gallon of orange juice, a carton of cigarettes, a rock-hard bagel, and milk."

"The juice is the only thing that's fresh. Nikki's convinced I smoke too much and need extra vitamin C. She'd give it to me intravenously if she could." I dropped my fork; it clattered against the plate and bounced to the floor.

Dennis watched silently as I took the juice from the refrigerator and poured it down the drain. When I sat down again, with a clean fork, he had one comment: "Paranoid?"

"If Nikki went into my computer, who knows what else she'd do. Judith died from an overdose. I don't think it was an accident or suicide." I waved the fork in the air. "So I'm paranoid. Let me be paranoid in peace. That's it—no more business. Let's eat." Dennis happily agreed.

Dinner was fun—after we relaxed and forgot we were avoiding delicate subjects such as love. When we finished, Dennis scraped dishes and filled the dishwasher while I made coffee. We sat at the kitchen table, drinking coffee and talking. Two old friends.

By ten-thirty, I was yawning and trying to ignore the knot in my stomach that wouldn't disappear until I talked to Eileen. Dennis caught me stifling a yawn and grinned.

"That's one of the clearest signals I've ever received. I'm going home. You'd better get to bed before you fall asleep with your head in your coffee cup."

I yawned again. "It has been a long day. Dennis, don't go home. Why don't you stay?"

He rinsed his mug and left it in the sink. "Nope. I said no strings." Dennis kissed my forehead. "I didn't come here to seduce you with a chicken dinner. Walk me to the door. I'm going home. I'll call you tomorrow."

In the middle of the night I rolled over and touched the empty mattress at my side. Frightened by the empty space, I opened my eyes. Half-asleep, I whispered, "Dennis?"

I threw the covers aside and started from the bed before I realized I was alone. Waking up in the middle of the night and reaching out to hug the unoccupied mattress was nothing new;

I've done it at least once a night since Jeff died. My heart pounded faster. This was the first time I expected to find Dennis, not my husband, at my side. I pulled the covers up to my chin and stared at the dark ceiling. Another message to ponder.

The next morning, I found Eileen sitting at her desk reading a letter. The scowl on her face made me pause and reconsider my plan to tell her about the pilfered records. Before I could change my mind, I hesitantly tapped on the door.

Eileen looked up; her frown didn't go away. "Blaine, you're in awfully early. I like your suit—it matches the circles under your eyes. What an interesting fashion concept. Is *Vogue* going to use you as a cover girl?"

I nervously smoothed my skirt. "It was a rough night." I closed the door and leaned against it. "Eileen, we have to talk."

"Yes, we do. More bad news came in yesterday."

I sat in one of the chairs in front of her desk and asked, "Did we lose another client? I was hoping you'd be able to hold back the stampede."

Without saying a word, Eileen handed me the letter she'd been frowning at. The logo, a tiny golden eagle sitting on top of a globe, was familiar. It belonged to the First Metropolitan Bank of America. Our bank. "You know, I think that little eagle is clutching hundred dollar bills in his talons."

"Just read the letter. I guarantee you won't feel like joking when you get to the end."

The letter didn't mention our spotless record; it ignored our years of loyalty. It mentioned new banking regulations and the reexamination of portfolios. It mentioned their deep regret and the reclassification of our corporation as a high risk. Then, after informing us our credit line had been reduced to zero, it wished us good luck, expressed the hope we would continue to do business with the bank, and told us they would be happy to reevaluate our situation when conditions became more favorable. I tossed the letter on the desk. "Have a nice day."

"You're the financial person. When were we going to start drawing on that credit line?"

I ran my hands through my hair. I felt a frown deeper than Eileen's spreading across my face. "Soon. We're spending over sixty thousand dollars a month to keep this place running. If we don't get money rolling in, we'll slowly bleed to death."

Eileen made a little steeple with her fingers and stared at them. "I'm completely baffled by the speed and accuracy of this attack. They know our major accounts, our bankers, and the pressure points. We don't even have a definite link between the clinic and our clientele."

I took a deep breath and said, "We have a link. You're looking at her." Eileen's eyebrows raised. I rushed on and told her about my previous night's discovery.

When I finished, Eileen smiled gravely. "That's why you look like you haven't slept for a week. Did you stay up all night? Despite your efforts, Blaine, you're not perfect."

"That's it? Aren't you going to call me an idiot or a knothead?"

"Call yourself all the names you like, I'm not going to join in the fun. Charlie Spragge called yesterday. He wanted to know you how were doing with the search."

Chapter 26
• • • • • • • • • • • •

"Father Timothy's been hiding fugitives for almost thirty years; he's an experienced liar. He's lying when he says he hasn't seen the new Wyricks. He was too quick to answer; his voice was too positive. I'm going to have a few of our idle staff members keep an eye on Father Timmy."

"What are you going to do?"

"I'm going to spend some time learning about the Metropolitan Fertility Clinic. I'm also going to sit and think about being pregnant."

"What?" Eileen's eyebrows bounced again. "Is this an announcement?"

"Get real. I'm trying to put myself in Hannah's head. How do you find a pregnant woman? You think like a pregnant woman."

Eileen lit a cigarette and left it sitting in an ashtray. As the smoke curled to the ceiling, she watched it and thought out loud. "How do you find a pregnant woman? We don't know her name. We're pretty sure she's in Brooklyn. We're guessing she doesn't have much money. We know she loves this child she's carrying."

I thought of the March of Dimes ads I'd seen in the subway and came up with the obvious answer. "Prenatal care. I'm eight and a half months pregnant, I don't have any money, and I'm afraid to go to the fertility clinic. What would I do? I'd check out the public hospitals and free clinics closest to my house. Maybe I'd go for check-ups, if I felt secure in my hideout. If I didn't, I'd stay inside until I went into labor. When those contractions start, I'll know where to go."

"Are you planning to visit every public hospital and clinic in Brooklyn?"

"If I have to."

"That's crazy. You'll never be able to cover every clinic in time."

"I'm willing to bet there aren't as many as you think. This city—this country—doesn't have many places that welcome poor pregnant women who don't have health insurance. Give me a day and a half and I'll get to all of them. I'm going to start in the morning." I looked at my watch and stood up. "Before I go to Brooklyn, I have to visit my stockbroker." Eileen wished me luck and promised to try to think of a more efficient way to search for Hannah. I wished her luck and left.

Jona was out of sight, so I scribbled a note and left it on her desk. Feeling like a teenager sneaking in after curfew, I kept glancing over my shoulder to see if anyone was watching me. No one spotted me. I rushed into my office, grabbed my coat and briefcase, and hurried out.

As soon as the elevator doors closed, I sighed with relief—I'd escaped. Eileen could cope with the ringing telephones and the letters from the bank. I was happy to be out in the cold air, channeling my nervous energy into action. If I stayed in motion, I wouldn't have time to worry.

★ ★ ★

Gardner Norvill & Brunett is headquartered in a building directly across the street from the New York Stock Exchange. Long-time members of the exchange, they set up shop across the street and never left. When the cab passed the building, I carefully kept my eyes averted from the building's imposing facade. Pulling up to the curb, the cabbie commented about the market's recent rally and asked if I was a broker; I grunted an answer. I paid him, stepped out into a slushy puddle of water, and hurried through the revolving doors.

The walnut paneling and antique furniture in the cavernous reception area is supposed to reassure potential investors that nothing frivolous ever occurs within the Gardner domain. Making money is serious business.

I wasn't reassured. The dark portraits of scowling founders clutching stubby cigars and staring out with fierce eyes made me think of dead uncles and funeral homes. I couldn't imagine willingly turning my money over to one of those guys on the wall.

My heels clicked against the parqueted floor as I walked to the far end of the room. A woman sat behind an ornately carved wooden table, watching my approach. Her face was frozen in the same artificial smile used by airline stewardesses when you board their plane.

After I told her my name, she consulted the book that covered most of the tabletop. My name wasn't on it, but that didn't upset her. She smiled at me and whispered into her telephone. Minutes later another woman appeared to lead me to Grace's office.

Grace Hudson has been a stockbroker as long as I've been a private investigator. Over the years, I've had good results from her recommendations. Whenever I call, she cheerfully answers my questions without asking any questions of her own.

The firm's stodgy atmosphere hadn't infected Grace. Abstract paintings done in bright primary colors, sleek furniture, and vases of freshly cut roses filled her office. The antique desk and chairs were new additions.

"Blaine. Nice surprise. Sit." Grace rarely completes a sentence; she's too busy to put nouns and verbs together. "You buying?"

I thought of my evaporating business and ruefully smiled. "Nope." Grace's face fell. "Sorry to ruin your day. I need information. Someone else promised to be my supplier, but so far I haven't seen anything. I thought of you. You're faster and more accurate than any library I know."

Grace raised her eyebrows. "In person. Not on the phone. Should I close the door?" Mumbling something about a silly question, Grace closed the door. She came back and sat on the edge of her desk. "Talk. You in trouble?"

"Is it obvious? I thought I was doing a great job at hiding it."

"Okay—not great. Saw your name in the papers. In the stories about McSperm. Read the two-line description. Choose the sperm. One from column A, one from column B. Babies 'R Us. Pay your money, get the baby of your choice. It's a chain. Metropolitan Fertility Clinic—coming to your hometown. No commuting to make babies. Lots of money."

"Lots of influence?"

Grace nodded. "Lots. Been waiting for your call." She stood up to pull a bulky envelope from the top drawer of a filing cabinet and gave it to me. "Read this. Annual reports. Analysts' reports. Press clippings. You need more, you call."

"Tell me more about this chain. McSperm—how many are there? Who owns them?"

"Ten clinics. Private owners. They're offering limited partnerships to outside investors to raise money for twenty more. Big deal. By firms involved in the deal."

I played with the clasp on the envelope. The clinic had more than bad publicity at stake. "Grace, how big is this fertility business? I've heard some wild figures. How much money is at stake?"

Grace smiled at the opportunity to practice a sales pitch. "The first so-called test tube baby was born in 1978. Approximately twenty thousand test-tubers have been born in this country since then. In-vitro fertilization—IVF. The woman takes fertility drugs to stimulate the ovaries. Eggs are harvested. Sperm and eggs are combined—not in test tubes, in petri dishes. The fertilized eggs are implanted in the uterus. Extra fertilized eggs are frozen and stored for future use. You pay the freezer fees."

"I can get biology lessons anywhere. Tell me about the money."

"Don't interrupt. You have to know this before the money makes sense. Each cycle—drugs, monitoring by the doctors, fertilization, implantation—costs between eight and ten thousand dollars. Ten thousand bucks to try for a baby. Most women don't get pregnant on the first try. Next month, you do it again. Another ten thousand bucks. IVF—can't be beat. Big moneymaker. It's the most profitable procedure for a clinic."

"Every investor's dream. Sounds wonderful. What's the downside?"

Grace frowned. "One big problem: success rates. Very low. Lawsuits for misrepresentation. Government rumbles about fraud."

A faint memory of a newspaper article surfaced. "I read about that recently. Something about clinics that don't deliver the babies they promised."

"Some claim success rates of thirty to fifty percent. The Public Health Service says less than fifteen percent of the women going to fertility clinics actually have babies."

I whistled. "Eighty-five percent of the people paying ten thousand dollars a month never get a baby. How do the clinics explain the discrepancy?"

Her efforts to look serious failed; Grace started laughing. "Remember the cliché about you can't be a little bit pregnant? Modern science has changed that. The clinics say you can be a little bit pregnant. And if you are, it's a success for their brochure. No need to have a baby. If your blood and urine tests say you're pregnant, it counts. If the embryo never develops, they don't care—you're still a success.

"If you can't get pregnant, the clinic may forget to count you. It all depends on what you consider a success. Tell me the rate you want, I'll find a definition that gets it."

"And people call me cynical. Grace, how do the clinics get away with it?"

"Little regulation. Insurance companies don't care. Most won't pay for IVF. The government's not interested. There's been some talk about cracking down, but it won't fly. Too many lobbyists.

Too much money. Two point four billion dollars a year in the U.S. Clinics prey on the emotions of infertile couples. Desperate people ignore eighty-five percent failure rates."

Chapter 27

Aware that Grace was using valuable market time to educate me, I stopped asking questions. I thanked her, took my bundle of reports, and went to find a place to read without interruption. I couldn't go to the office; I couldn't go home. I decided to go to a bar.

The View, officially named the RiverView Bar and Grill, was my choice. The bar, which is a half-block from my front door, would be quiet because the crowd doesn't build until late in the evening. I could sit and read without being bothered by telephones or people.

During my drinking days, Bobby and Ryan—the owners— took care of me. They'd cut me off when I was drunk and walk me home when I was too wasted to navigate the half-block alone. I stopped drinking, but I didn't stop going to the View. Bobby and Ryan poured gallons of club soda for me, tried to cheer me up on those days when everything I did was wrong, and never put anything stronger than coffee in front of me.

I usually sit on the barstool that's wedged against the cigarette machine. It gives me easy access to cigarettes, a clear view of the rest of the bar, and only one person to ignore if I didn't feel like talking.

I waved at Bobby and stood at the bar. He took a frosted mug from the freezer beneath the bar and filled it with seltzer. After dropping a thick lemon wedge into the glass, he pushed it across the counter. I grabbed the mug, ignored my empty stool, and settled into a dark booth in the rear of the bar. I ripped open the envelope and dumped its contents out on the table.

Grace was fast, and thorough. Glossy brochures, copies of

newspaper articles, computer printouts, and thick reports tumbled out. I started reading the brochures because they were the thinnest. My plan was to start with the smallest pieces and work my way up to the thick ones.

I was looking at the fuzzy pictures of men and women smiling at sleeping babies when the unwelcome thump of a person sitting down intruded. It was a middle-aged man; specks of beer foam stuck to his bushy mustache. I looked at his beige polyester jacket, red-and-white striped tie, and green shirt and knew he was single. No woman would let her husband out of the house in that outfit—not even on Halloween.

I wrinkled my nose and said, "Look, buddy. I'm not interested. When I want company, I'll ask for it. Believe me, I won't call you."

He smiled; his teeth were the same color as his jacket. "I wanna talk to you. My name's Tomlinson." Shifting the beer mug he was carrying from his right hand to his left, he took a torn leather case from his inside breast pocket and flashed a gold shield at me.

"I'm not impressed. Any idiot can buy one of those things in any novelty shop in the city."

Tomlinson leaned back against the booth's cushions. "Cut the shit. I've been following you, waiting for a chance to talk to you."

"If you've been following me, then you know where I work. If you come to my office, I'll talk to you. But I'm off duty now, so leave me alone. I'll be in my office at nine tomorrow morning."

When he didn't answer, I snarled, "What do you want?"

"I want you to keep the fuck away from things that don't concern you. This is the one and only warning you're gonna get— and it's more than you deserve. But I'm a decent guy, I thought I'd give you a break."

"Be a real decent guy, give me a clue to what you're talking about."

Tomlinson leaned across the table until his face was inches from mine. When he opened his mouth, a blast of beer fumes jumped out and struck my face. I backed away and lit a cigarette to cover the odor.

"You need a clue? Here's your clue. Judith Marsden. Drop it."

"My client—"

"Your client is dead. I'm telling you to drop it. Drop it before you piss me off."

I ignored the gob of beer that flew out of his mouth and landed next to the ashtray. "I'm not dropping my case. Judith hired me to find her son—"

"What are you, a lunatic? Judith Marsden didn't have any kids. I'm warning you, leave it alone or someone might decide to stop you. Permanently."

"What about the fertility clinic? Have you talked to them? Their surrogate mother had a strong motive for killing Judith. Why don't you question her instead of hanging out in bars and making stupid threats? Aren't you concerned about letting a killer get off?"

"Your information is screwed. Judith Marsden wasn't killed. The autopsy said natural causes. So do yourself a favor. Quit running around town stirring up trouble where trouble don't exist."

Tomlinson's smug smile infuriated me more than his threats did. "I think your autopsy missed something. Maybe I'll have a chat with your boss."

Tomlinson slammed his beer mug against the table. "Listen to me, you nosy bitch. I know all about you. You killed a cop. Do you think my boss would talk to you? He'll throw your ass out his window—and his office is on the top floor."

It's impossible to reason with someone as angry as Tomlinson, but I tried. "Believe me, I spend every day wishing it never happened. When I turn off the lights and try to sleep, I replay it again and again, hoping the ending will be different. Trying to see if there was another way. There wasn't. He was going to kill me."

"Yeah, yeah, I heard that story."

"Well, hear it again. Try listening this time. That cop was corrupt. He sold out a federal drug investigation because he owed money to a bookie. An agent—my husband—got killed . . ." I thought of the miscarriage and the destructive years of drinking that followed. Would those painful wounds ever heal?

"When I got close to the truth, that cop tried to kill me. He shot me. I shot back. He died . . ."

Tomlinson swallowed a mouthful of beer and licked his lips. "Your smart-mouthed lawyer got you off by crying self-defense. No one believes that lie. Lots of guys would love to see you hang. Your attorney too."

We were running on the edge of an all-out war. I took a deep breath and ordered myself to relax. "You want to know what I think?"

Tomlinson rocked forward and banged his fist on the table. He spat at me and yelled, "You fucking bitch. I don't care what you think."

Bobby and Ryan don't allow troublemakers in their bar. As soon as Tomlinson raised his voice, Bobby dropped the rag he was using to wipe the bar and vaulted over the counter—an easy feat for a six-foot-eleven-inch guy. Bobby's extra-long legs carried him across the floor in three strides. He dropped a hand on Tomlinson's shoulder and squeezed.

"Is everything okay here, Blaine? Is this scumbag bothering you? 'Cause if he is, he's outta here. Want me to throw him out?"

"It's okay, Bobby. My friend's had a little too much to drink. He didn't mean to raise his voice. I'm sure he's sorry."

Bobby reluctantly took his hand from Tomlinson's shoulder. "Listen, partner, this lady is one of our friends. Watch your mouth and keep your voice down."

The detective mumbled under his breath, but had enough sense to not argue. I nodded my thanks to Bobby and waited for him to walk away.

"Detective Tomlinson, we've run out of things to say. Why don't you get out of here before Bobby changes his mind and throws you out?"

Tomlinson didn't move. "I'll leave when I'm ready. If that faggot thinks he can throw me out, he'd better think again."

I clenched my fists under the table. I wanted to smash his face—and he knew it. Tomlinson grinned and waited to see if I'd react. I didn't. I was mad, not stupid. If I even tapped Tomlinson with my pinkie, he'd happily arrest me. By the time Eileen bailed me out, I'd have collected a few bruises that would be explained away as the result of resisting arrest. I relaxed my fists and held up a hand.

"Listen to me." I popped my thumb in the air. "One: My client is dead. I'm not burying her until I'm convinced she wasn't murdered."

I held up my index finger. "Two: Judith Marsden's child is missing. I'm going to find him. Maybe I'll get lucky and solve Judith's murder at the same time.

"Three . . ." I held up my middle finger. "You have a foul mouth, but you haven't said anything that scares me. Keep away from me and I'll keep away from you."

Tomlinson was the type of guy who needs to have the last word. His were beauties. "You're a faggot-loving, cop-killing bitch. If you keep fucking around my case, you're gonna be sorry."

"What case?" I smiled innocently. "You said Judith died of natural causes, why is there a case?"

"Not one cop in this city will mourn if you disappear forever. This cop would be happy to do the job." He slid from the booth and was gone before I swallowed my anger.

Tomlinson shoved aside a woman who stood in his path and walked out the door. Once he was gone, I tried to concentrate on my reading; I spent more time thinking about the detective's message.

In the six months following the night when I became what Tomlinson called a cop-killer, I'd gone through guilt and depression and worked back to normalcy. I was still dealing with other related problems. All my sources in New York City's police department disappeared. They refused to talk to me. They turned away when they spotted me. When I entered a room, they left. I couldn't even get a clerk to check a license plate number for me.

Another shadow fell across the table. Expecting more trouble, I looked up. Bobby put a fresh mug of seltzer in front of me and sat. He awkwardly folded his legs under the table and grimaced as he banged his knee.

"This one's on the house. Is everything okay with you, hon?

That guy was throwing off mighty bad vibes, I was ready to call the cops."

"It's a good thing you didn't. That guy is a cop."

"He's a cop? He looked like a nut case, not a cop. Do they really let a guy like him carry a gun?" I laughed, Bobby wasn't amused. "Look, Blaine, I'm leaving early tonight. Why don't you hang around another hour and wait for me? I'll walk you home. You know, just in case that asshole is hanging around."

"Do I look like a helpless female? First you rescue me, now you want to escort me home in case the bad guy is hiding in the bushes. I'd better go spend some time in the gym and build up my muscles." I realized how nasty I sounded and stopped talking.

Bobby patted my hand. "That's okay. You're having a tough day."

"You're too sweet to put up with people like me. I don't mean to sound like an ungrateful shrew. I appreciate your concern. As always."

"Sure you won't hang around?"

I turned him down, politely this time, and went home. After carefully locking the doors and windows, I hid in my last refuge: the bathtub. It was the only place where I knew I wouldn't be disturbed.

I filled the tub and soaked in the hot water until the steam cleared my head. A plan slowly formed as the bubbles evaporated and the water cooled.

Tomlinson would have to be ignored. All I could do was stay out of his way as much as possible. If he was going to bust me, I wouldn't be able to stop him.

The disappearing credit line was another thing to ignore. If we didn't get our clients back, or quickly replace them, Eileen and I would have to use our savings to keep the company running, lay people off, or close down entirely. I added another burst of hot water to the tub and decided to stop worrying; it wouldn't change anything. The bankers would come back once the crisis passed and we didn't need them.

I slipped down in the tub until the bubbles touched my chin and thought about the missing surrogate and the fertility clinic.

Grace's papers were interesting, but not very informative. I needed to know more about the clinic.

The bathwater cooled before I convinced myself that my plan to raid the clinic was good. I flipped the drain and sat in the tub, watching the water swirl down. If I bothered to consult Eileen, she would have pointed out that I could be throwing our business out with the bathwater.

Chapter 28

• • • • • • • • • • •

I dressed in black corduroy jeans and a sweatshirt and filled a pack with a flashlight and other tools. Then I sat down on the living room sofa, planning to read until it was late enough to resume my career as a burglar. My peace and quiet was short-lived. Moments after I started reading the clinic's annual report, the telephone rang.

"Hey, Babe. Brad here. Hope I'm not interrupting anything romantic. I haven't seen you around, so I'm figuring you got something good going."

"If I had something good going, I wouldn't have answered the phone—especially if I knew you were calling. I've been busy working. How about you? Where are you?"

He sighed. "I'm in my car. I'm working, Babe. I took a shift tailing your cleaning lady. Decided it would be a good idea to practice. You know, in case I have to get a real job again."

"Are you calling to tell me you're working? Remind me to give you a gold star in the morning. What's Nikki up to?"

"She's up to the house next door to yours. Seems to me like she's decided to get to work too. I'm calling to give you a little advance warning. I'm glad you're home. My brilliant plan ended with this call."

It had been days since I'd seen Nikki. Days in which I'd learned many of her secrets. How many were left? "Brad, thanks for the forewarning. Stick around, she might not be here long."

"Okay, Babe. Scream if you need help. I'll be parked outside. Maybe you'd like me to visit?"

Boredom, not concern, prompted Brad's offer. His attitude would be less relaxed if he'd heard Father Timothy's story about the baseball bat. "No, thanks. I can handle her. Take a nap. I'll give you a wake-up call when she leaves."

"You're the boss. Will I see you tomorrow? I think you need to make an appearance at the office, Babe. Rumors are flying."

The front door opened. "Sorry, big guy, I can't play games with you. My company just arrived. Talk to you later." I hung up and went to confront Nikki.

She greeted me with her usual lively smile. "Hey, Blaine. I came to work on the basement. Hope you don't mind that I didn't call."

Her smile was warm; her blue eyes were icy cold. I decided to slap her with a dose of honesty. The jolt might force something useful from her. "Nikki, I received a letter from your sister yesterday. She asked me to leave her alone. She didn't put a return address on the envelope, so I can't write back."

Nikki took off her down parka and turned away to hang it in the closet. "I don't know what you're talking about. My sister doesn't know you. Why would she write a letter to you? Why should you leave her alone?"

"Yesterday was an eventful day. Several unsettling things happened. For instance, I had trouble with my computer last night."

Her back stiffened. "Really? That's interesting. I hope it wasn't serious."

"Somebody was looking at my files. He, or she, did it on a day when I was out of town. No one broke in. Someone with a key did the snooping." I paused and leaned against the railing, watching her reaction.

Nikki answered with a taut, ready-to-snap, voice. "Doesn't your boyfriend have a key? Why don't you go accuse him of using your computer?"

"I don't think so."

She whirled around. Her face was crimson, her eyes volcanic. "Are you accusing me of stealing? If you don't trust me, why don't you just fire me?"

Now that I had her on the verge of exploding, I pushed. "You and your sister are on the threshold of a great deal of trouble. I want to help you before you go over the edge and can't climb back. Nikki, I was working for Judith Marsden before she died. I still am; her estate hired me. I know your sister's pregnant with Judith's child."

Nikki panted from the effort of controlling her temper. Her eyes darted around the hallway looking for an escape—or a weapon. I could imagine Nikki striking her father's skull until it burst. Baseball season was still a few months away; I was safe.

"You're getting deeper and deeper into a situation you won't be able to get out of. I know you're hiding your sister so she can keep the baby. I know you printed a list of my clients and gave it to Dr. Nelson."

"You don't know anything. I'll look out for my sister. I've done it all my life. I'm not going to stop now. I can take care of any trouble."

"Just like you took care of your father?" Nikki gasped. A punch to her solar plexus couldn't have stopped her breath faster. "I took a ride to Beaver Ridge yesterday—the town where you supposedly grew up. I also visited a priest in Brooklyn."

Nikki grunted and struggled to get air into her lungs. I took a step closer to her and changed my voice from harsh to gentle. "Why don't you tell me your real name? You can't hide for the rest of your life."

Moving with an athlete's speed and strength, Nikki shoved me against the wall. My feet slipped on a throw rug; I struggled to keep my balance. Nikki kicked. Her heavy boots connected with my shin. I toppled over and cracked my head on the floor. My eyes watered. Through the teary haze, I watched Nikki grab her coat and rush out of the house. Scrambling to my feet, I ran after her.

Brad was parked out front as promised; the engine was already running. I dove into the car and slammed the door. Nikki ran along Barrow Street, heading for Seventh Avenue South. Brad pulled away from the curb and slowly followed. We crept along the narrow street, looking like a car searching for a parking spot.

"Don't lose her. If she goes into the subway, you take the subway. I'll take the car. I don't want her to see me. Do you have to-kens?"

"Yes, ma'am. I also have that cellular phone you've been teas-ing me about. I bet you'll change your tune before this night ends. What happened? When that little girl came flying out of your house, I was afraid I'd go in and find your body."

"I pushed her; she fought back. I'm hoping she'll run to her sister."

"Are you okay?"

I massaged the tender spot on the back of my head and winced. A lump was already rising. "The head is hard—I'll sur-vive."

Brad squinted through the windshield and concentrated on keeping Nikki in sight. As Nikki approached Seventh Avenue, she slowed to a fast walk. She was either confident, or uncon-cerned about being followed; Nikki never glanced around to see if anyone was chasing her.

"You took a gamble, Babe. What about the back-up you're al-ways preaching about?"

I found a crumpled pack of cigarettes and lighter in my sweatshirt pocket. I lit a cigarette, took a drag, and said, "I was ad-libbing. If I had more than thirty seconds to plan, I would have done a better job."

Nikki stopped at the corner and looked around. Brad pulled into an empty spot in front of a fire hydrant. After a slight hes-itation, Nikki strolled into a bar near the end of the block. Brad and I spoke at the same time. "Damn."

Brad found a Yankees cap in the backseat. He pulled it on and opened the door. "Guess I'll go have a drink. Take good care of my car. Don't go too far."

"Good luck." I ran around to sit behind the wheel and amused myself by playing with the radio. I found "Stairway to Heaven," a twenty-year-old Allman Brothers song, a talk show with the usual assortment of lunatics and outraged citizens, and an opera. I gave up and smoked my last cigarette.

An hour later, Brad came out of the bar and knocked on the window on the passenger's side. I opened, it, he stuck his head inside and threw a pack of cigarettes at me.

"I brought you a treat. I figured you were down to filters by now."

"Thanks." I tossed the cigarettes on the dashboard. "What's going on inside?"

"Not much. That is one weird chick. She's been sitting at the end of the bar drinking coffee and making evil faces at anyone who gets near her. Our girl made a phone call a few minutes ago. Now she can't keep her eyes off her watch. My finely turned deductive skills tell me she's waiting for someone."

I wiped the smoke film off the windshield with the back of my hand and peered at the man walking down the street. His brisk gait was vaguely familiar. I squinted and tried to get a clear view of his face, but the light was too dim. I pointed at the shadowy figure. "Break's over, Brad. That's Nikki's mystery date."

Brad looked over his shoulder. "Do you know him?"

The man walked past us without even a glance in our direction and went inside the bar. The light from the open door illuminated his face. I sat back and said, "Yeah, I know him." I had been expecting to see the priest. I was surprised to see the doctor.

Chapter 29

● ● ● ● ● ● ● ● ● ● ●

Brad waited until Nelson was inside before moving. He jammed his baseball cap in his coat pocket, then walked into the bar. I watched the door close behind him and started worrying. I wanted to be in there with Brad, but knew it was impossible. None of the hats in Brad's backseat collection could hide my red hair and the not quite six feet of body beneath it.

Within minutes, Nikki and the doctor walked out. I slumped down in the seat and watched them walk down the street. I started the engine in case they decided to flag down a cab. A few seconds later, a group of semidrunken people came out of the bar. Brad was with them, blending into the crowd.

The mob turned left. Brad paused, swiveled his head to look in both directions, then went to the right to follow his quarry.

Near the end of the block, the couple abruptly darted across the street and walked north on Seventh Avenue. Brad spun around and followed; he waved as he passed the car. I twisted around in the seat to watch them.

It was an odd trio. The doctor and Nikki on one side of the street, Brad on the opposite side. Both sides appeared to be unaware of the other. Nelson and Nikki disappeared into a black hole that led to the subway. Brad trotted across the street and followed them below ground.

I watched for a few minutes to see if anyone emerged. When no one did, I drove home and parked the car. Breaking into the clinic would have to wait for another night, I would spend the rest of the evening waiting for Brad's call.

Brad called an hour later. He sounded cheerful. "Babe, I hope you're warmer than I am."

"Where are you? Are they still together?"

"Yeah, so far. I'm standing outside the clinic. I would have called sooner, but I've been on a tour of the subway system. We went uptown, we went downtown, we went crosstown. It's beautiful this time of night. Filled with stinking drunks. The odd couple just went inside the clinic. I'm going to hang out here and see what happens next. If they leave separately, I'm going after the girl. Okay?"

"Okay. Do you need help? I can be there in about half an hour."

"No need, Babe, I've got things under control. Sit tight. Don't come up here and jinx my operation. Whoops, the door's opening. I gotta go." The dial tone sounded in my ear before I could respond.

I sat in the kitchen with Grace's material, a pot of coffee, and a silent telephone for company. The phone rang at twelve-thirty.

"Babe, is that you? I hope I didn't wake you. You're going to be mad enough when you hear my news."

"What happened? Did you—"

"Yeah, I lost her. She left the clinic alone. I followed her to Coney Island and back. I had a lot of trouble keeping out of sight. The train was almost empty—it's too cold for the sunbathers."

"Where did you lose her?"

"She lost me. We rode the F train back to Manhattan. At Rockefeller Center, she slipped out through the closing doors. I couldn't get out. She gave me the finger as the train pulled out of the station."

"How long ago?"

"Five minutes. I got out at the next stop. Babe, I'm really sorry. I blew it—"

"Forget it, Brad. I've done it too many times to get mad at you." I sighed. "Let's hope she goes home. I'll cover her apartment. Go home and get some sleep; you sound beat."

"Depressed, not tired. Let me watch her building. I'm closer. Besides, I need to be doing something. If I go home, I'll spend the rest of the night calling myself an ass and getting drunk. Might as well do something useful. I'll pick my car up in the morning."

If Brad wanted to do penance, I wouldn't interfere. After making him promise to call if Nikki showed, I hung up and went back to my reading. Three hours later, I gave up and went to bed. The phone never rang.

When I walked into the office, the inactivity startled me. The lobby was empty, the telephones weren't ringing, the typewriters were silent. Marcella was watering the plants near her desk, trying to keep busy. Even the plants looked depressed.

Marcella didn't smile when I greeted her. I asked if Brad had called. She shook her head. "No one calls. It is too quiet."

I cut her short—I didn't want to hear more bad news. I smiled at Marcella, told her everything would be better soon, and went to my office. I dragged a beeper out of my desk so Marcella could find me if Brad called, ripped a list of Brooklyn hospitals from the telephone book, and left.

According to the quick count I made in the elevator, Brooklyn had a dozen hospitals. If my theory about Hannah's hiding out near Father Timothy was correct, I could eliminate half the list.

I decided to start with the most likely places. I'd get to the rest if I had time.

Driving in New York City is something I avoid whenever possible. But when I thought of the distance I had to cover, and my unfamiliarity with the Brooklyn subways, I decided to drive. I didn't fume at the traffic tie-ups on the Brooklyn Bridge; I used the time to create a story. It had to be simple and close to the truth. As a back-up, I planned to offer a thousand-dollar reward. If the story didn't work, the money might. By the time I got to the first hospital on Atlantic Avenue, I was ready.

Seven hours later, hungry, tired, and not sure I had accomplished a thing, I dragged myself back to my office. Marcella was still grumpy. I waved at her dour face and grabbed my messages from the top of her desk as I stumbled past. I looked in Brad's office. It was empty.

I walked by Eileen's office and peeked in the open doorway. Her chair was turned away from the desk; she was sitting and staring out the window. The telephone, which is usually attached to Eileen's ear, sat in its cradle.

I tapped on the door. Eileen didn't move. Her voice floated over the back of the chair. "Could you come back later? I'm busy at the moment."

Eileen's slumping shoulders matched her dispirited voice. I stepped inside and gently closed the door. "Busy doing what? Did we get a city contract to count pedestrians?"

"It's almost four. Where have you been—out looking for a job like the others?"

When I'm angry or upset, I blow up and let it out. My sister is different. Eileen withdraws and twists her problem until her brain gets knotted up worse than a pretzel. Getting Eileen untwisted without causing an explosion is a delicate operation.

After dumping my coat on a chair, I sat on the edge of Eileen's desk and joined her vigil at the window. "I've been working. Hanging out in hospitals. Pounding my feet on Brooklyn's frozen sidewalks, trying to find a place to park where the car wouldn't get stolen, searching for our missing surrogate. Who's out looking for a new job?"

"Take a walk around and count the empty desks."

"Is that what you've been doing all day—counting empty desks? No wonder you're depressed. Who's missing, your kids or mine?"

Eileen slowly mentioned a few names. I listened for a few seconds, then started laughing. "You idiot. You spent the entire day thinking my staff had gone out on job interviews. Then you decided I was out setting up my own agency."

She mumbled, "You're wrong . . ."

"You're lying." A blush spread across Eileen's face and neck. I was uncomfortably close to the truth. "Everyone who's out is out working on the Marsden case. Since we have only one good client left, I decided to put everyone to work on it. It's better than having people sitting around letting their overactive imaginations make up wild stories."

"Like I've been doing."

"Yep, just like you've been doing. What else did you do today? Something positive, I hope."

Eileen rubbed her forehead. "I've been on the phone all day, talking to anyone who would take my call. I had a long conversation with Stan Adams from CIG."

I took a cigarette from the pack on Eileen's desk and lit it. "Stan loves to gossip. I bet he was drooling, waiting for your call. I'm surprised he didn't call you. What did Stan tell you?"

"The pressure to get rid of us came from an investment banking firm. Lazarus, Reed and Milkman. The president of the firm is the brother of Stan's boss."

"They're also the lead firm in the consortium that's getting new investors for the fertility clinic. I read about them last night while I was waiting for . . ."

Eileen wasn't in the mood to hear about my newest missing person. I took a deep drag on my cigarette and blew out a cloud of smoke. "Grace told me about it. They're raising money to open clinics all over the country."

Eileen didn't notice my abrupt switch. "Why are they afraid of us? It must be more than a fear of bad publicity about a missing surrogate. What else is the clinic involved in?"

"Quite a few things. Expansion is their main priority. They're anxious to develop new properties. They hope to have the limited partners' money together by July so they can start. Let me try making a few calls. I want to see if Lazarus has ties to anyone else."

"Could the directors of the clinic be afraid the bad publicity will make it difficult for them to raise the money? Are they desperate for cash? Could they need investors to keep the clinic operating?"

I hated to yank the flicker of hope away from Eileen, but I did. "I don't think so. The clinic has a lot of money available. Their parent company has another subsidiary that produces a fertility drug. It's used to stimulate their patients' ovaries. The drug is a moneymaker."

Eileen twirled a pencil on the top of her desk. "So we're back to a fear of publicity. If people hear about the clinic's renegade surrogate, they might be afraid to entrust Dr. Nelson with the task of finding a suitable woman for them. Speaking of finding surrogates, how is your search going?"

I told Eileen about my record-breaking feat of visiting ten out of twelve of the hospitals in Brooklyn in seven hours. "The last two were on the opposite end of the borough. I'm guessing they're too far away from Hannah's hideout. I was hungry and tired of getting lost. I'll have someone check them out tomorrow."

Eileen was impressed, but cautious. "I hope your efforts pay off. What tale did you tell? Do you think you managed to get the sympathy of overworked delivery room staff?"

"I found a picture of Hannah in Judith's photo album. I had copies made with my name and telephone number on the bottom. I said Hannah had run away and her family hired me to find her. Hannah's an heiress to an oil fortune. The disconsolate, but wealthy, family will generously reward any compassionate person who helps get their daughter home again."

"Did anybody believe you?"

"People were interested. I passed out dozens of flyers, talked to the heads of departments and emergency room nurses, and stressed the need to be sure Hannah doesn't find out that someone's looking for her. I'll make the rounds again next week and remind people that I'm still looking."

"All we have to do is hope our luck changes." Eileen grinned. "We're due for a break; maybe this will do it."

"Hope so, I'm tired of the long faces around here." I ground the cigarette out and slid to my feet. "I'm going to see if I can get some work done." I went back to my office and worried.

Chapter 30

• • • • • • • • • • • •

I stared at the telephone, hating it because it was silent. If no one would call me, I'd burn up the outgoing lines. I found Johnnie Bramble's card in my briefcase and made my first call. With luck I'd catch him at his desk rewriting his copy before the six o'clock news.

The reporter's deep voice greeted me. "Bramble here." When I identified myself, the friendly tone became cautious. "I'm sorry. This isn't a good time to talk. I'm getting ready to go on the air."

"You have an hour and a half before the news comes on. This won't take that long. The package you promised me hasn't arrived. Where is it?'

"Ahh . . . I've been meaning to call you. There's a slight problem. My producer wants me to back off. The autopsy said the death was a suicide. There isn't any sense in pushing it. Not unless you have a new angle."

So that's why there weren't any reporters lurking in my waiting room. "You people are fickle. One day you won't leave me alone. The next day you're out chasing another bloody story."

"Look, what can I do? The report says suicide. My boss says let it drop."

"Hasn't your boss heard about detectives who convince medical examiners to say a death was due to natural causes, suicide, or an accident? Hasn't your boss heard how affable medical examiners agree? Case closed. No messy, potentially unsolvable murder to bring down your closure rate."

"Tell it to the movie-of-the-week people. I report news, not suspicions. If you uncover something solid, call me. Otherwise, I can't help you."

"Let me get this straight, Bramble. You're the big, bad investigative reporter who's backing away from a hot story because his boss said to give it up. What if Woodward and Bernstein had listened to their boss? No one would have heard of Watergate."

Bramble hurried to let me know he wasn't blowing me off. "Hey, Blaine, don't get me wrong. I'm behind you. I want to work with you, but my hands are tied. You know how these network guys are. If I start chasing down stories that never make it on the air, they'll get nervous and wonder if I can cut it. I'll take a risk and push for you—when you give me something concrete."

I silently wished him plunging ratings, then politely said goodbye. Johnnie sounded relieved. I knew he was regretting his impulsive decision to give me his telephone number. Next time I used it, I'd be greeted by a secretary screening pesky callers.

The gloomy atmosphere of the office closed around me. The walls pressed in on me, making it difficult to breathe. I decided to go home. The fresh air and exercise would clear my head and maybe drive away the claustrophobic feelings that were suffocating me.

After filling my briefcase with work, I said good night to Eileen and started to leave the office. Marcella stopped me before I could walk out the front door.

"I have been searching for you. You have a call. She will not give her name. She tells me it's important. I tell her that everyone says that. She tells me it's about a missing baby."

I dropped my briefcase and grabbed the telephone on Marcella's desk. "This is Blaine Stewart. How can I help you?"

"Miss Stewart, I'd like to see you. Talk to you." The whispery voice was familiar. I took a guess. "Nikki, is that you? What's wrong?"

"No, this is Hannah. My sister gave me your telephone

number. I hope I'm not bothering you. It's really important. I have to make you understand . . ."

She hesitated. Afraid she'd hang up, I said, "Why don't we meet face-to-face. It's easier that way. Where are you? I'll come to you."

"Oh no. I can't do that. I can't tell you where I'm living." I held my breath and prayed she wouldn't hang up. "But I want to see you. If we meet, maybe you'll have different feelings." Hannah's voice grew stronger, more assertive. "Do you know the museum on Fifth Avenue? You know, the one by the clinic."

I felt like a person hearing Lotto's winning numbers and realizing they matched those on the ticket in her wallet. "The Metropolitan? Sure, I know it. The museum's open late tonight. Not many people go there on a Friday night, we won't be disturbed. What time? I'll meet you inside the main entrance."

"I like the room with the temple. I go there sometimes just to sit. It's real peaceful. I can be there in an hour. Is that okay with you?"

"No problem. I'll meet you at the Metropolitan Museum at the Temple of Dendur in an hour—okay?"

"Okay. Well, maybe an hour and an half. You know, in case the trains get mixed up. Will you wait?"

"Hannah, don't worry. I'll wait in the museum until the guards throw me out. If you get stuck, call again. My office will be able to find me."

Beepers are horrible inventions designed to torture those of us who just want to be left alone. I recently—and reluctantly— became a slave to technology. When I wasn't involved in an important case, my beeper resided in the top drawer of my desk, buried under paper clips and rubber bands. I'd taken it out briefly for my hospital visits and thrown it back inside the drawer when I finished. I dug the ugly thing out again, dropped it in my jacket pocket, and walked out the door.

In 15 B.C., the Emperor Augustus built a shrine on the banks of the Nile River at a place called Dendur, about six hundred miles south of Cairo. The temple, built to honor the goddess Isis, lasted through wars, floods, and the erosion of time—until the twentieth century and modern man's version of progress.

In the early 1900s, a dam was built at Aswan. When the Nile rose during the rainy season, its waves lapped at, and sometimes poured into, the temple. The water slowly receded when the river shrank back to its normal boundaries.

In 1960, the engineers started building a second dam, the High Dam. When the dam was finished, the Temple of Dendur would disappear forever, covered by the lake that rose behind the concrete barrier. Isis's holy place would cease to exist. What the gods couldn't take away, the engineers would.

Instead of letting the temple be engulfed, Egypt gifted it to the American people. The plaque says the gift was in recognition of the U.S. contributions to UNESCO. The temple was taken apart, shipped overseas, and reassembled at the Metropolitan. In 1978, its new home opened to the public.

Isis was one of ancient Egypt's most important goddesses. She cured the sick, brought the dead to life, and had powers superior to all the other gods. What did Isis think of New York City? I had a lot of time to learn the temple's history and think about Isis's reaction to the Big Apple. I was early; Hannah was late.

The gray granite temple, and the tall columns of its gateway, sits on a platform in the center of a large, airy hall. A pool of water symbolizing the Nile forms a U around the front half of the platform.

You climb a few stairs to the patio where the temple sits and admire the shrine from a respectful distance—the sanctuary is off-limits to visitors. Visitors have the nasty habit of scribbling their names on the ancient stones. Granite benches are built into the low wall lining the dais; a perfect place to sit and watch. You can gaze at the temple or look at the glass wall on the north side of the temple.

The wall slopes from the roof to the ground, giving a view of the lawn and the traffic on the Eighty-sixth Street transverse that cuts through Central Park to the West Side. Quite a difference from the banks of the Nile River.

I walked around the hall and read every word on every plaque and every poster describing the evacuation of the temple. Four times. Then I gave up.

Sackler Hall, where the temple is located, has three entrances. It's impossible to find a place where all three are visible, but I found a seat on the granite benches that gave me a view of two entrances.

After another half hour of waiting, I thought about going back to the main entrance, but didn't. I was afraid I'd miss Hannah in the twisting corridors of the exhibits. By eight-fifteen, I admitted that I had been stood up. Half an hour later, a guard chased me out. The museum was closing.

I paused at the top of the stairs and looked across the street at the clinic. It was dark and quiet. Perfect for a break-in. Sighing, I walked down the stairs. I wasn't prepared to be a burglar. Going home and taking a bath was all I was prepared to do.

Taxis always line up at the foot of the museum's stairs to wait for a fare. I got into the first one in line and settled back against the cushions. It had been a long day; I'd earned an evening off.

Living alone never bothers me—except on cold winter nights when the sun goes down before five o'clock. I hate walking into a dark house. In addition to the standard fears about robbers and bogeymen, I don't like to be reminded that the house is empty, that no one is waiting for me.

Because my hours are irregular, I keep a small lamp on a table in the hallway attached to an automatic sensor. As soon as it gets dark, the light goes on. It helps a little, but doesn't take the ache away.

From the moment I climbed the steps to unlock the door, I knew something was wrong. My light wasn't on.

Most people would have shrugged it off as nothing more than a burned-out bulb. I didn't. My afternoon of dodging bullets in a cemetery had made me a suspicious woman.

I put my briefcase on the floor and quietly closed the door. Hailstones rattled against the windows, covering an intruder's noise. I slid my pistol from its holster and waited.

You can stand in a dark corner holding your breath and waiting for the monsters to grab you for only a few seconds. Then you start to feel like a baby waiting to be rescued by its mother. Then you start to feel silly. I grinned and flipped the switch for the overhead light.

The harsh light made me blink. My eyes adjusted and took in the scene before me. I gasped. My reliable lantern had been shattered; pieces of the porcelain littered the floor. The table rested on its side. The drawer where I toss my bills until it's time to pay them hung open. Envelopes, a few of them torn in half, littered the floor.

Cursing the inadequate locks on my door, and wondering if my thieves had managed to breach my gun safe, I ran up the stairs to my bedroom. I stopped in the doorway and grabbed the wooden frame for support. The destruction made my head spin.

Furniture had been upended, pictures pulled from the wall, the glass and frames broken, clothes and shoes thrown across the floor. The sheets and blankets had been ripped from the bed. Holes were torn in the pillows. Feathers floated on the air currents stirred by my entrance.

Shaking with anger, I stepped over the piles of clothes and broken glass to check the tiny vault that was built into the wall. My backup pistol was still inside. I slammed the door and twisted the knob, locking it back in. I was mad enough to kill anyone I discovered in the house. I didn't need a gun; I could do it with my hands.

Before going back down to survey the damage and see what had been stolen, I checked my office. I didn't have to go inside the room; I could see the vandalism from the hall.

Files were strewn on the floor. Their edges were charred from an attempt to set them on fire. My computer had been tossed from the desk and landed on the floor beneath the window.

The unit had been kicked apart. A shaky wire connected the hard drive to the computer; the monitor sat in the center of the room. Its screen was shattered, the plastic casing split. The edge of the keyboard stuck out from beneath the desk. Coiled snakes of cable were in the corner of the room.

Wiping tears of frustration and rage from my eyes, I slowly walked down the stairs. The upstairs mess didn't prepare me for the havoc I found in the dining room. Every piece of crystal and china I owned had been smashed against the wall, not a single dish or glass escaped. I looked at the pile of shards. Hatred blistered my stomach.

Two more rooms. Ready to see a smashed television and stereo, I stumbled to the living room. The compact discs that had been broken in two and flung across the room, the plants that had been ripped from their pots, and the books thrown on the floor with their covers torn off didn't surprise me.

But I wasn't ready for what I found in the fireplace. Nothing could have prepared me. The bastards had pulled my wedding picture from its place of honor in the center of the mantel, ripped it from the frame, and shredded it. The twisted frame crookedly propped against the wall proclaimed this was not an accident. The pieces of the picture had been thrown on the ashes from the previous night's fire.

I knelt on the brick hearth and gently stirred the debris. My hands shook as I plucked the fragments out from the ashes.

I wanted to cry. I wanted to find the bastards and rip them apart, just like they had done to my picture. All I could do was gather the scraps of my picture and make a little pile on the floor.

Once I rescued as many pieces as possible, I awkwardly got to my feet and looked around. Shock numbed my brain. I couldn't think of anything except the pile of confetti in front of the fireplace.

The telephone was the only undamaged thing in the room. It had been carefully placed in the corner near the hallway, out of the path of the destructive force. I picked up the receiver, listened to the dial tone, then dropped it in its cradle. Who was I going to call? The police? What would they do after they shook their heads, took fingerprints, and filled out their reports?

One more room. I went to the kitchen, glad I'd put off grocery shopping. At least I wouldn't have to scrape fresh food off the walls and floor. Condiments, coffee beans, orange juice, and a few hard bagels were the only things that had been in the refrigerator. The cupboards were equally bare.

The pattern held. Cabinet doors were flung open, their contents swept to the floor. The refrigerator door was ajar and everything spilled out on the floor. Puddles of ketchup and juice were drying to a tacky cover on the tiles. I leaned against the wall and stared at a broken coffee mug, too shocked to move.

The telephone rang. I roused myself from my stupor and forced my legs to move. The phone rang four times before I got myself across the room.

A raspy voice greeted me. "How do you like our work?"

I didn't recognize the voice. It was impossible to decide if my caller was male or female. I closed my eyes and asked, "Who is this?"

He/she chuckled. "Your new interior decorator."

Bile rose in my stomach. I gripped the receiver and bit my lip to hold back the obscenity I wanted to shout. I didn't; I listened to the voice say, "You're working too hard. Take a vacation. If you don't, our next visit will be at night—when you're home."

"Fuck you . . ."

The voice hardened. "You don't like living, do you? Check your basement. The same thing could happen to you."

The phone went dead.

Chapter 31

• • • • • • • • • • • •

I sat cross-legged on the floor with the telephone in my lap. Countless horror movies where the helpless victim gets chopped up by a lunatic with an ax, ran through my mind. I felt trapped in an underground version of *Psycho*. In my version, the madman would be in the basement, not the shower. Suddenly, I wanted someone in the house with me.

Without thinking, I dialed Dennis's office. He answered on the first ring. I said hello and heard a smile spread across his face. "Blaine, what a nice way to end a lousy day. I was just getting ready to leave. Do you want—"

I interrupted. "Dennis, I'm at home. Can you come over? Right away."

"What's wrong? Are you in trouble?"

How could I explain? "Dennis, please . . ."

"I'm putting my coat on. As soon as we hang up, I'm out the door. It'll take me at least half an hour to get up there. Is that okay?"

"Yeah, sure. I'll be fine. Just hurry."

I put the telephone back on the floor and leaned against the wall. The wreckage surrounded me, mocking the illusion of my home being a haven from the insanity of the city. Anger simmered inside me, boiling away the remnants of shock and pushing me to my feet. I wasn't going to hide in a corner, trembling and waiting to be rescued.

I was almost certain the house was empty, but I wasn't going to take a chance. I took my gun from its holster again and made sure it was fully loaded.

My basement is like millions of basements in America. It's dusty, cluttered with things I'm planning to give away, throw away, or get fixed, and hiding treasures too precious to throw away.

With a flashlight in my left hand, in case I had to search dark places, and my pistol in the right, in case I had to shoot whatever I found in those dark places, I crept down the stairs. A light was on, spotlighting the body laid out in front of the washing machine. I stopped and inhaled sharply.

The body was face down on the concrete. The back of its head was matted with blood. I recognized the jacket on the torso. I dropped the flashlight and ran down the stairs.

It was Nikki. She was dead.

Chapter 32

• • • • • • • • • • • •

I knelt beside Nikki, but didn't roll her over—it would have been a meaningless gesture. There was no sign of life. Splinters of bone from her crushed skull pierced her skin. I slowly realized that my knees were wet. Splatters of blood covered the washing machine, the dryer, and the floor. I had knelt in the puddle around the body.

Nausea threatened to overwhelm me. I fought it down and jumped to my feet. Forcing myself to act professional, I retrieved my flashlight from beneath the stairs and searched the cellar, carefully avoiding the quickest glimpse of Nikki's body.

I found a baseball bat wedged behind the hot water heater. Dried blood obscured the name on the label that was burned into the wood. I didn't want to see anything else. I left the bat and went upstairs to wait for Dennis.

I sat on the stairs leading to the second floor and smoked until the doorbell rang. I stamped the cigarette out in the broken mug I was using for an ashtray and opened the door.

Dennis looked over my shoulder. "Jesus, what happened? It looks like a plane crashed in here." His eyes focused on the bloodstains on my skirt and my legs. "What happened? Did you walk in on a robbery? Are you hurt? Did you call the police?"

"No. No. No. Listen to me. I'm not hurt. It's Nikki. She's downstairs. She's dead."

Dennis wrapped his arms around me in a tight embrace. He repeated, "What happened?"

I rested my head on his chest for a minute, then pushed myself away. Dennis didn't want to let me go; he held on to my arm and listened to my rushed explanation. "I came in and found this. Whoever wrecked the place didn't miss a thing. Everything's been trashed. Everything but the telephone; that still works. I got a call. It was a threat and a suggestion that I look downstairs. I called you. Then I found Nikki. She's dead."

Dennis tightened his grip on my arm. "Are you sure you're not hurt?"

I ran my fingers through my hair and looked down at my skirt. For a second I couldn't figure out how the blood had gotten on my clothes. Then I remembered and shuddered. "I'm okay. Shaky, but okay. I wanted someone with me when I call the police. You know, in case there's any trouble."

Dennis usually calls me paranoid. He didn't this time. He dropped my arm and put his hands in his pockets. "I'll make the call. Give me a few minutes to look around first. Wait here. I'll be right back."

Of course, I couldn't wait. I followed Dennis to the basement, sat on the stairs, and watched. Dennis checked the body, then quickly looked at me. "Where's your gun?"

"Here." I patted my jacket pocket. "They've done enough for one night. I didn't think they'd be back, but . . ." Dennis walked around the basement, casually looking behind boxes. "If you're looking for a murder weapon, look over there." I pointed at the boiler. "They didn't use a gun."

Dennis followed my directions. "A baseball bat? No wonder her head . . . " He glanced at the wan expression on my face. "Forget it. Is this your bat?"

"No, I don't play baseball. But Nikki did, softball too. Maybe it belonged to her. Have you seen enough?"

"More than enough. Come on, let's go call the cops. Do you want to call Eileen too?"

Dennis's innocent question made me lose my temper. "Why? Do you think I need an attorney? I found the body. I didn't put it there. Do you think I killed her and want you to help me cover it up?"

Taking my arm, Dennis led me up the stairs. "You're entitled to think whatever you want. Just don't ask stupid questions about what I think. I do think you'd better calm down and get hold of yourself before the cops get here. Shouting at them won't make anything easier."

I sat on the stairs again and smoked another cigarette while Dennis made his call. He hung up and peered at me between the railing. "There's no reason to bother nine-one-one. I called the local precinct. A detective and the crime scene unit should be here soon."

I didn't answer. Dennis walked around inspecting the damage. I listened to his feet crunching broken glass and tried to keep myself from imagining the violent scene that had taken place. Dennis came back and sat next to me. He put an arm around my shoulders. "Is the upstairs as bad as this?"

"It's worse. My clothes are in a pile in the center of the floor. They dumped my bath powder on the floor and mixed the shampoo into it. Then they spread it around. My bathroom floor is covered with a thick white paste . . ." I closed my eyes.

Dennis squeezed my hand. "Thieves who kill someone during a robbery don't call back to make threats. What do you think? Is this connected to the clinic?"

"I've been trying to decide if the voice on the phone belonged to Dr. Nelson. I don't know."

The doorbell rang. Dennis pressed my shoulder. "Blaine, let me handle as much of this as possible. Keep quiet unless someone asks you a question." He gently kissed my cheek and said, "Let the FBI take care of this one."

I don't usually sit back and let someone else take care of my problems, but this time I agreed. I was willing to do anything to speed the process of getting the body out of the house. I went to the living room, cleared a space on the sofa by pushing the garbage to the floor, and sat.

The uniformed police came first. Dennis identified himself. He accounted for my blank face with one word, "Shock." Happy to ignore the potentially hysterical female, the cops left me alone. Dennis took them to the kitchen and explained the situation.

One cop went with Dennis to the basement; the other went upstairs. I listened to crackling sounds of radios and glass underfoot and kept my mind blank. I could think later—when I couldn't sleep.

The three men reappeared at the same time. They formed a semicircle in front of me. I opened my eyes and waited. Before any questions were asked, the doorbell rang again.

Someone opened the door. I heard a familiar voice and thanked God for the small bit of good fortune sent my way. The willowy detective who walked in was a friend. Irma listened to the two cops give their preliminary report, then came over to me.

"Blaine—I thought this was your neighborhood. I didn't think I'd be coming to your house. What happened?"

"Irma, I—"

"Wait, don't tell me. Let me take a look before the guys with the cameras and fingerprint stuff get here. We'll have plenty of time to talk later. I know you have all kinds of theories."

Waves of people arrived and started working. I ignored them;

154 • Sharon Zukowski

they ignored me. Dennis, his work as unofficial host done, sat next to me and held my hand. I rested my head on the back of the sofa and stared at the ceiling. It was the only thing in the house left intact.

Staring at the ceiling lulled my anxious nerves; fatigue took over. I was about to pass out when Irma returned. The grave smile on her face woke me up. She pointedly said "Excuse us" to Dennis and waited for him to leave before saying anything else.

"FBI boyfriend. How convenient."

"He tries. Where's your partner? Or are you working alone these days?"

"I told my partner to go home. He was spending the evening puking his guts out. We're fresh out of substitutes. Everybody's got the flu. So I'm on my own tonight. Let's get this over with so I can go home."

Irma sat down beside me and went into the good cop routine. She smiled at me. "It's been a while since I've seen you in the pool. Did you decide you don't need to exercise anymore?"

We met at the local Y. Our friendship developed from heated competition in the swimming pool. Irma, who could have been an Olympic champion if she'd been able to find swimming lessons in the South Bronx, usually won. As a result, I usually paid for breakfast.

I shrugged. "You know how it is. I've been busy."

"Girl, you should get unbusy. The exercise would do you good. It's been months since I had a good race. Come to think of it, it's been months since I had a good breakfast." Irma glanced at the notebook in her hand. "So, it looks like your cleaning lady threw a fit, tore your house apart, then beat herself to death as punishment. How do you manage to get yourself in the middle of shit like this?"

I shrugged again. "Ask me something I can answer."

"Whose fingerprints are we going to find around here? Beside yours and your cleaning lady's. Anyone you know? Anyone we know?"

"I have no idea. Don't ask me if anything's been stolen. It's kind of hard to tell."

"What are you working on?"

"A missing person."

"Who?"

"The dead girl's sister."

"Who's looking for her, and why?"

"I can't answer that. You'll have to wait until I talk to my client."

Irma's eyes narrowed. "Are we going to waste time going around the old confidentiality dodge?"

"If we have to. If you don't want to waste time, don't ask questions I can't answer."

"Can I be straight with you? I'm one of the few friends you have left in the department. Don't add to your troubles by playing games. It's just luck that I got this call. It could have been someone else."

"Someone less friendly? Someone like Tomlinson?"

"Are you going after another cop? Wasn't one enough? Lady, you'd better pray we don't find a remote connection between you and that body downstairs. If we do, my boss is going to be all over me, demanding your ass in a jail cell. It's going to be impossible for me to talk him out of it."

"Irma, I'm tired of that threat. You should hold a contest to see if someone can think of a better one."

"Some people think a night or two in jail would improve your attitude. Sometimes you make it hard for me to disagree." Irma stood up. She pulled a large plastic evidence bag from her jacket pocket and tossed it in my lap. "Change your clothes. I want the lab to take a look at those stains you're wearing."

Chapter 33

Dennis lurked in the hallway, listening to our conversation. As Irma walked past, Dennis stopped her and asked a question. She frowned and answered. Dennis frowned; he didn't like the answer. They started a heated, but muted, discussion. I watched their bowed heads and angry gestures and tried to eavesdrop. No luck, they were too experienced at whispering in front of anxious listeners to raise their voices loud enough to be overheard.

Neither face looked victorious when they broke away. I couldn't tell who won the fight. Irma went to the kitchen. Dennis came back to me.

"Go change your clothes. And pack a bag, you'll have to stay with me for a few days."

"So I'm being released in your custody. When did I become a suspect? Is that my choice: go with you or get arrested?"

Dennis leaned down until his face was inches from mine. I didn't see any love, any compassion. Anger was the only thing I saw in his brown eyes. "Will you shut up? Look around; you can't stay here."

His brusque voice stung harder than a slap across the face. My head cleared. Embarrassed by my outburst, I went to my bedroom, picked up enough clothes from the floor to last a few days, and stuffed them in a suitcase.

Irma waited for me at the foot of the stairs. I gave her the evidence bag filled with my bloody clothes, and a set of house keys. Dennis took my suitcase with one hand, grabbed my arm with the other, and led me outside.

We didn't talk until we were in his apartment, the world securely locked outside. Dennis went to the kitchen. I followed and watched him take eggs, cheese, and butter from the refrigerator.

After digging a frying pan out of a cabinet and putting it on the stove, I sat and lit a cigarette. "I'm not hungry."

Dennis didn't stop slicing cheese. "I am. It's been a long time since lunch." He cracked eggs into a bowl and vigorously beat them with a fork. "Blaine, I'm sorry I yelled at you. I wanted to get you out of there before anything happened."

I watched the cigarette smoke spiral to the ceiling. "Don't apologize. I'm glad you stopped me before I said, or did, something stupid."

He pulled an envelope from his pocket and gave it to me.

"What . . ."

"Open it."

I followed his instructions. Pieces of the torn picture spilled out on the table. Tears filled my eyes.

Dennis turned away and poured eggs into the pan. "I found them in front of the fireplace while you were upstairs changing. When I realized what they were, I stuck them in an envelope. I decided the cops didn't need to see it."

"Thanks. I'm not sure anyone knows where the negative is . . ." I scooped the fragments up and stuffed them back in the envelope.

Dennis finished cooking his omelet and took it to the living room so he could watch the news while he ate. The smell turned my stomach. While he ate, I wandered through the apartment looking for something to distract me. Nothing worked; my mind kept flashing back to Nikki's body. All I succeeded in doing was annoying Dennis, so I gave up. I said good night and went to bed.

I didn't sleep. I stared at the sliver of light coming in from behind the curtains and tried to make sense of the maelstrom I was trapped in. The bedroom door opened. Taking great pains to not disturb me, Dennis quietly walked in and eased into the bed.

Without rolling over, I said, "Thank you for tiptoeing around in the dark, but I'm awake. Wide awake. Did I make the news?"

"Not tonight. The snow was the big story. A plane slid off a runway at JFK. There were a few injuries, nothing serious. The reporters had a grand time interviewing the passengers and their families. When that got boring, they dragged out old footage of the last big plane crash. A body in a basement can't compete with a flaming jet. Irma promised to keep it quiet if she could. I guess the crash helped."

"What else did you two talk about?"

"You. Irma's afraid you're going to hold information back. She thinks you'll go out on your own, find out who did it and go after him."

Dennis touched my rigid back and kneaded the tense muscles. "Stay out of it."

"I can't. Two people are dead. Hannah's still missing. They trashed my house. They're trying to take my business. Dennis, what am I supposed to do—let them take everything?"

Dennis's hands stopped moving. "Don't . . . I don't know what to tell you. I don't want you to get hurt."

I didn't answer. Dennis's hand tightened on my shoulder. I waited to hear what was on his mind. Instead of talking, Dennis kissed my neck and rolled back to his side of the bed. My tense muscles gradually relaxed and I fell asleep.

I woke early, before Dennis was awake, with a clear head and a rumbling stomach. I took a shower and dressed as quietly as possible. Dennis slept through it all. I didn't bother him—it was the least I could do—and went to the kitchen.

The sight of the fully stocked refrigerator made me smile; it was nice to be in a house with food. I stood in front of the toaster and drank a glass of orange juice while I watched a bagel brown.

The sound of the toaster popping brought Dennis out of the bedroom. I was spreading a thick layer of cream cheese on the bagel when he shuffled into the kitchen.

He yawned and ran his hands through his hair. "You're up early. I thought you'd sleep until noon."

"I want to get an early start. I have a lot of things to do today."

Dennis tightened the belt on his robe. "It's Saturday. Where are you going so early in the morning?"

Giving him half the bagel, I said, "I'm going to the library. I have to do some research."

"Can't your scholarly urges wait? I thought we could stand in line at TKTS and get tickets to a matinee. You know, take a day off and have some fun. After we see what Broadway has to offer, we can have an early dinner, then come back here to spend a quiet evening. Alone. I think we can find a way to amuse ourselves."

I ruffled his hair on my way past him to the coffeepot. "That's what I like about you, you're always thinking. Don't stop. I should be back in a few hours."

He grabbed my hand. "Blaine, are you really going to the library? Why do I have a bad feeling?"

"Because you're hungry. Hunger always makes you suspicious. Didn't your mother tell you to have a good breakfast before you start being distrustful? Eat your bagel or I will."

Dennis dropped my hand and grabbed the bagel before I could get it. "Please tell me what you're up to so I know how much worrying I should do. I'd like to plan my day around when I'm going to have to post bail for you."

"I had a weird dream last night. It featured two-headed babies and witches. There was a lot of singing and dancing."

"That explains the twitching. You kept rolling into me. I almost kicked you out of bed."

"Stop laughing. You asked a question. I'm trying to answer it. The witches came from *Macbeth*. The deformed babies were . . . real. Cute little things, if you ignored the two heads growing out of one neck."

"Is that why you're going to the library? To find a book to interpret your dreams and solve your case? What's next, a psychic? Drink your coffee. I think you're still dreaming."

"I think you should put extra sugar in your coffee; you're too acerbic this morning. While you're up, I could use a refill."

Dennis brought the coffeepot to the table and put it in front of me. "Help yourself. Why is your dream sending you to the library?"

"Birth defects. When I was in the shower, I started wondering about why babies are born with deformities. I don't know what I'm looking for, but I want to do some research. Then I'm going to the office."

Dennis's face fell. I laughed. "I won't be gone long, I promise. I want to catch up on a few things I left behind on my desk. If

Eileen's there, I want to tell her about last night. If she isn't, I won't bother her until Monday. She might as well have a peaceful weekend."

"Is that all? Your eyes say you have something else on your agenda. You're not going to your house to poke around the rubble, are you?"

I thought of the wreckage I'd left behind and shuddered. "No way. I have no intention of setting foot in that house unless I have a battalion of cleaning people behind me. Besides, didn't Irma say she wanted me to stay away for a few days so they can be sure they haven't overlooked anything?"

Dennis laughed so hard that he choked on his bagel. After he caught his breath, he tried to apologize. "I'm sorry. This is the first time I ever heard you worry about what the cops want. You must be getting old."

I stood up and dumped my coffee down the drain. "I'm getting old sitting around here providing you with comedic material." Before Dennis repeated his question about my other plans, I left.

The library was closed, a victim of New York City's latest round of fiscal belt-tightening. An elderly man huddled in the doorway, seeking shelter from the wind. He coughed and told me to come back in April when the library was scheduled to re-open on Saturdays.

I thanked him and went to a bookstore on Fifth Avenue near the Flatiron Building that carries medical textbooks. I purchased books on birth defects, drug testing, and fertility, and went to the office. The place was empty; I was the only workaholic in sight. I spent an uninterrupted afternoon flipping through the books. When I got tired of reading about oocytes and embryos, I perfected my plan to break into the clinic.

Chapter 34

When I walked into the apartment, Dennis was laid out on the sofa watching television. He waved at me. "Look at the depths to which you have pushed me. I spent the entire day right here on the couch, waiting for you. I missed you so much, I couldn't do anything else."

"It's nice to be missed." I hung up my coat and dropped my bag of books on the floor. After kissing Dennis's cheek, I pushed his feet aside to make room to sit. I glanced at the television. "Bowling—I didn't know you're a fan."

Dennis put his feet in my lap. "I can't find anything else to watch except old movies. I hate old movies. They were bad when they were made. Fifty years later, they put color in them, but they're still awful. There isn't any more football until next year. It's too early for baseball. What's left? Bowling."

I laughed. Dennis shook his head. "It's not funny. You are looking at a man who's in the terminal stages of sports with-drawal. Take me away from this sad place. Museum, movie, the-ater, nightclub, restaurant. You decide. Just get me out of here before I lose my mind."

I looked at my watch. My break-in at the clinic couldn't take place until late in the evening—after everyone had gone. We had plenty of time to go out.

"Can you refrain from having a nervous breakdown long enough for me to shower and change clothes? I promise I won't take long."

Dennis lifted his feet to release me. "Hurry. Ice dancing comes on in twenty minutes. I may change my mind and decide to watch it."

I promised to be quick. I was rinsing conditioner from my hair when the bathroom door opened. Shaking water from my face, I yelled, "I'm hurrying. Go back to your ice dancing. Better yet, take your clothes off and join me. We can forget about going out."

Dennis pushed the shower curtain aside. He held a thick bath towel. His face was somber. "You didn't hear the bell. We have company."

"Can't our company wait until I'm clean?"

"No. Come on, you have to hurry. This guy isn't here on a social call."

"Trouble?"

"It's the police. You're about to be arrested for murdering Nikki Wyrick."

"You're kidding. Is this Irma's idea of a joke?"

Dennis didn't smile. "It's not a joke and it's not Irma. It's some guy dressed in bad clothes. He has a badge. He has a warrant. They're real. He's not very patient. If you're not out in five minutes, he's going to drag you out, dripping wet and buck-naked. That's a quote."

"Tomlinson. Is he alone?" I turned the water off and took the towel.

Dennis nodded. "His partner's waiting in the car. He said he didn't want to make too much of a fuss."

I cursed. Afraid of Dennis's reaction, I cut myself off before I blurted out Tomlinson's threats. "Keep him happy while I get dressed."

"I don't like this guy. There's something slimy about him—I'm going with you."

"There's no law that says slimy people can't be cops. You know you can't tag along, so don't try. Don't interfere. You'll only make more trouble for me."

Dennis wasn't convinced. "Then I'll follow you . . ."

I dried myself as I talked. "What would that accomplish? You always tell me to go by the book—take your own advice. Let this guy do his job. If you want to help, stay here. Call Eileen as soon as we leave. Tell her to meet me at Central Booking and get me released. This won't hold up."

Sharp pains hammered my stomach. I managed to sound calm. "Dennis, find Irma too. Tell her what's happening. I'm

sure she doesn't know. If she did, she'd be making the arrest herself."

Dennis hugged me. I kissed him, then pushed him away.
"Don't worry, I can take care of myself. Just make those calls. I'll
be back as soon as Eileen works her magic."

The clothes I'd been wearing were on the floor. They were
wrinkled and soiled—perfect for jail. I dressed and tried to blot
my hair dry with a towel. I was using Dennis's comb to untangle
my curls when a fist pounded on the door.

"Hurry up. You got another thirty seconds." I dropped the
towel on the floor and opened the door.

Tomlinson was standing in the hallway. Dennis stood a few
feet away glaring at him. When I stepped out of the steamy
room, Tomlinson grinned. He pulled a set of handcuffs from his
jacket pocket.

"Let's go. You know the routine."

"Is that necessary? She's not going to attack you."

Dennis's hands were at his sides, clenched in tight fists. Sensing
trouble, Tomlinson's grin deepened.

"Dennis, don't make trouble."

"Yeah, buddy. Do as the lady says. Just because she's your
girlfriend doesn't mean she gets special attention. I'm following
standard procedure. Just like the manual says." Tomlinson rattled
the handcuffs. "Come on. Let's get going."

Dennis ignored my earlier warning. He stepped closer to the
detective. In a harsh voice, he said, "It's freezing outside. Aren't
you going to let her put a coat on before you drag her out in
handcuffs?"

The men glowered at each other. I picked my coat off the rack
near the door, slipped it on, and held out my hands.

"Turn around." Flashing a warning look at Dennis, I turned to
face the wall. Tomlinson tightened the handcuffs around my
wrists and frisked me. When his hands touched me, my stomach
turned. I bit my lip and forced myself to remain still.

Dennis's face burned with anger. He took another step toward
Tomlinson. I decided to get out of the apartment before Dennis
took a swing at him. I spun around. "Let's go. The sooner you
book me, the sooner I get out."

"Don't count on it, honey. Say good-bye to your boyfriend. It's going to be a long time before you see him again." He nodded at Dennis and led me from the apartment.

Dennis stood in the open doorway, watching as we waited for the elevator. I looked back and tried to smile. Tomlinson chewed on a dirty toothpick and hummed the theme song to *Jeopardy*. The elevator arrived before the song ended.

Two couples stood inside, blocking our way. Neither pair wanted to relinquish their space to newcomers looking as unsavory as we did. Tomlinson's trench coat was rumpled and stained; my hair hung in wet strands.

Tomlinson waved his badge at them and snarled, "Step aside. Police business. Step aside."

The shield worked. The couples cleared a space in the center of the car for us. They stood in opposite corners of the elevator and carefully avoided brushing against me.

The yuppies in jogging outfits openly stared, enjoying the spectacle. The senior citizens discussed restaurants and watched from the corners of their eyes. I bowed my head and tried to ignore the gapers. Tomlinson enjoyed the attention. He kept a tight grip on my arm and a satisfied grin on his face.

The doorman scrambled to hold the door open. His eyes opened wide. Delight at witnessing gossip in the making shone in his eyes. Any person passing his station would hear his story. The tale would get more outlandish with each telling. Dennis's reputation would be ruined in hours.

Tomlinson had parked in front of the building, blocking a fire hydrant. I didn't see any sign of a waiting partner. Not wanting to be alone with him, I tried to hang back. Tomlinson opened the door on the passenger's side and pushed me in. He slammed the door and hurried around to the driver's side.

He started the engine and pulled away from the curb. I asked, "Where's your partner? What about the standard procedure from your manual?"

"The manual says a lot of things. It also says murder one is serious. You're going to have trouble wiggling out of this one. Wasn't it kind of stupid to kill the girl in your own house? Why didn't you do it someplace else?"

"I have the right to remain silent. Anything I say may be used against me in a court of law. I have the right to consult with an attorney before speaking to the police and to have that attorney present during questioning. I can afford an attorney, so we can skip that one. I think that's it. Detective Tomlinson, I'm officially requesting that you allow me to consult with my attorney."

He grunted. "Like I said, there's a lot of stuff in the manual. Some people read it. Other people do things their own way. Before we consult anybody, we're gonna take a little ride."

I tried to find a way to sit that would ease the ache on my shoulders and waited. As long as the car was moving, I wasn't too worried. The trouble would begin when we stopped.

We drove a few blocks. Tomlinson was remarkably quiet for a man who claimed he wanted to talk. We drove down Second Avenue. I convinced myself that the detective had decided to bypass the precinct house and take me directly to the Central Booking Unit on Centre Street.

I was wrong. He drove into Chinatown and wound through the narrow streets, turning away from police headquarters and heading north again.

The streets were crowded with hungry people searching for dinner. I watched them walk past the telephone booth pagodas, the sidewalk fish markets, the vegetable stands, and the sidewalk vendors selling cheap watches and handbags.

How could I attract their attention? I twisted and strained to reach the door handle. Tomlinson noticed. He grinned and moved his left hand from the steering wheel to the arm rest. The locks clicked.

We wove through poorly lit streets, zigzagging across Manhattan until we were in the shadows of the World Trade Center. Without warning, Tomlinson turned and drove uptown.

I broke the silence. "Thanks for the tour, but I'm tired of sightseeing. Can we get on with this big bust? This expedition has worn me out."

He made a noise. It could have been a word, or a belch. I didn't ask for a translation.

"Come on, man. We can't drive around all night—"

"Shut up. I'm thinking."

"Think about how you abducted me from the apartment of an FBI agent. He wasn't thrilled. I bet your bosses won't be thrilled when they find out you used a fake warrant. It is a fake, isn't it?"

Tomlinson grunted again. He swerved to avoid a pothole and cursed the broken pavement. He turned onto Fourteenth Street and headed west to the Hudson River.

"You better pray they don't take your driver's license when they pull your badge. You're going to need it—driving a cab is the only job you'll be able to get."

"Your boyfriend, he's a Feebie?"

Hearing a slight tinge of uncertainty in his voice, I pressed. "Worse than that. He's a Feebie who holds a grudge. While we take this grand sightseeing tour, he's burning up the phone calling every agency in this city. When he's done with them, he'll call Albany. Then he'll call Washington. Dennis might even call the White House. I wonder if Bill and Hillary are home tonight."

The car bounced over the century-old cobblestones that had broken through the asphalt. The signs on the buildings advertised Ed's Boxed Beef, Prime Meats, Excelsior Provisions, and Frozen Meats. We were in the center of the meat-packing district. During the daytime the streets would be clogged by tractor trailers delivering beef carcasses. The sidewalks would be crowded with butchers, their white smocks stained with blood from the steaks and ribs they were carving.

On a Saturday evening, the streets were deserted. Thick iron curtains were rolled down over the doors and windows until Monday morning. We stopped for a traffic light. I looked at the Sunoco station on the corner. It was closed. Nothing was open in this forsaken part of town.

Tomlinson drummed his fingers against the steering wheel, waiting for the light to change. I stared across the intersection at the rows of buses parked in front of the Marine and Aviation Pier.

"Take a deep breath, detective. It smells like the inside of a garbage can that's been sitting out in the sun too long, doesn't it? It's not. Take another deep breath. That's the smell of your ass frying."

Tomlinson shot across Eleventh Avenue into a narrow lot on

the side of the road. He slammed the car into park and turned the engine off. "This should do."

My stomach pains started again.

He got out and hurried around to my side of the car. When he opened the door, I twisted away and tried to scramble to the other side of the car. Tomlinson, his pudgy body belying his strength, jerked me from the car.

I dragged my feet on the ground, trying to find an anchor in the tufts of weeds growing through the cracked blacktop. My feet slipped on the frozen gravel. Strong fingers wrapped around my arm and kept me from falling.

Tomlinson hauled me through a gap in the chain-link fence to a jetty that stretched out into the river. I hooked my legs around a fence post and tried to hang on. He pried me loose and pulled me through the hole. Regretting the sneakers I'd put on, I kicked at his legs.

I hit the back of his knee. Tomlinson's leg buckled, but he didn't fall. He spun around and raised his hand. I braced myself for the blow. Instead of slapping me, Tomlinson pushed me in front of him.

We struggled through another gap in another fence to the long wooden pier. The boards sagged under the weight of the construction equipment crowded on the jetty. Tomlinson shoved me through a narrow pathway between cement mixers, spools of cable, and sections of pipes and crane derricks. A rotten board gave way under my feet and fell into the river. My foot slid through the hole. Tomlinson tightened his grip on my arm and pulled me along.

As we wove through the maze of equipment, I threw a steady flow of warnings about the futility of his actions over my shoulder. Sharp jabs in my back were Tomlinson's only response.

By the time we reached the end of the quay, we were panting from the struggle. Tomlinson thrust me against the railing. "Kneel down."

"Don't be stupid. Let me go before this gets out of control. No hard feelings."

The detective stepped closer. I lowered my head and butted

his chest with my shoulder. He rocked back on his heels and flailed his arms, fighting to regain his balance.

I ducked under his outstretched arms and ran. Tomlinson recovered, grabbed my legs, and tackled me. I fell, landing flat on my face. Cold river air seeped through the cracks in the boards.

Tomlinson didn't waste time celebrating the sack. He jumped on my back and pinned me to the rough planks. I tried to roll away. Tomlinson ground his knee into my back to keep me down and opened the left cuff. My hand swung free.

He kept a tight grip on my right arm and tried to loop the handcuff over the lower rung of the railing. I groped behind me, searching for his holster. Tomlinson fought to get my wrist locked up again.

My fingers brushed the cold barrel of his revolver. I pulled at the grip and felt it move from the holster. Tomlinson realized he was about to lose his gun. He quickly snapped the open handcuff around the railing and batted my hand away from the revolver. He drew the pistol. Without warning, Tomlinson lunged forward and shot.

Chapter 35

I didn't have time to watch my life pass before my eyes. The bullet landed inches from my head. The board splintered. Pieces of wood hit my face. I closed my eyes and waited for a second shot.

My ears rang. Through a thick layer of cotton, I heard Tomlinson laugh. My breath came back in an angry rush. My legs twitched. I wanted to jump up and strangle him. I forced myself to remain still.

Tomlinson fired again. The shell flew by my head and splashed in the Hudson. The noise roused a family of sea gulls. They circled over us, squawking their displeasure at having their rest disturbed. I struggled to sit up.

"You're messing around in family business. You won't get another warning." Tomlinson stepped back a few paces. "The company that owns this place went out of business a few years ago. Gangs hang out here now, smoking crack and shooting up. But don't worry, nobody comes around when it's cold. It'll be days, maybe longer, before anybody bothers you."

He walked away. I listened to his footsteps until they became too faint to hear. I wondered if he was waiting at the end of the pier. If he'd change his mind and come back to kill me. My wondering ended when I heard the faint sound of a car starting and driving away.

My pockets were empty. No hat. No gloves. No picks. Twisting around, I clawed at the handcuffs with stiff fingers. The locks held.

The cold wind pushed aside my open coat and sliced through my sweater. I fumbled with the zipper. Uncontrollable shivers ran through my body by the time I managed to pull it up. My hands and ears went numb.

The dock could have been a nice place to sit and sniff the salty air, dream of ocean voyages, and admire the lights of Manhattan. But I couldn't find anything to enjoy. It was twenty degrees. The freezing wind blowing off the river froze the wet ends of my hair. Tiny icicles hit my cheeks every time I moved my head.

A few hundred yards of coal-black water separated me from the tugboats moored at a neighboring pier. I yelled for help. The waves lapping at the pilings muted the sounds of the city, just as they muted the sound of my voice. The wind whipped my words back into my face, mocking my efforts. My voice got hoarse; my yelling faded to a croak.

Frustrated, cold, and furious, I shook the railing. It moved slightly—enough to make me think I had a chance. Maybe I wouldn't freeze to death.

I peered behind the center post. Two rusty nails fixed the weathered two-by-four to the pillar. I smashed my fist against the railing. I hit it again and again until my hand swelled. The nails didn't move.

Closing my eyes, I rested my head on the board. My throat ached. My toes were frozen lumps in my sneakers. Every part of my body was cold. Newspaper stories about hypothermia scrolled through my mind. I was too discouraged to care. Why did I talk Dennis out of following me?

Claws scratching across the wooden planks stirred me from my lethargy. Visions of rats nibbling on my frozen body scared me more than any story about hypothermia. Dragging the hand-cuff behind me, I crawled to the opposite end of the railing and pounded on the crossbar.

One-handed hammering was stupid, but it gave the illusion of action. My hand throbbed each time I struck the wood. I kept on until a long splinter broke off and dug into my palm. Tiny drop-lets of blood froze on my skin. Promising that my break would last only a few minutes, I paused. I huddled with my knees drawn up to my chest and wished for a hammer.

My eyes focused on a pyramid in the corner. I squinted in the darkness. Sections of pipes, each about six inches thick, were stacked in neat rows. A single pipe capped the two-foot high pile.

I stretched out as far as possible and groped with my free hand. My wrist and arm screamed from the tension. My shoul-der popped. The tips of my fingers didn't come close. There was a gap—six inches wide according to a ruler, as wide as the Grand Canyon to my eyes—between my fingers and the pipes.

I rolled over on my stomach and kicked out with my legs. My toes hooked a pipe at the base of the stack. I pulled. The pyra-mid collapsed. Pipes tumbled down and bounced across the wooden deck. They rolled in every direction. A few spun over the side.

One hit my ankle. I hooked my foot over it and carefully rolled it back until I was able to grab hold with my outstretched hand and pick it up.

Cradling the pipe in my arms like a newborn infant, I got to my knees and hammered at the board. Each blow sent burning vibrations through my hand, throwing off my aim. Every few minutes I'd stop and shake the board to measure my progress. There wasn't any. The board stubbornly refused to move.

Snow started falling. At first, only tiny particles came down, but the flakes quickly grew larger. Within minutes, a thin layer of cold, slippery snow covered everything on the pier, including my head. A winter wonderland.

The pipe slipped from my hand. In slow motion, it bounced on the dock and rolled into the Hudson. I awkwardly dove for it—and missed. The splash was louder than any gunshot I'd ever heard. My stomach sank along with the pipe.

At that moment, I was the loneliest person on earth. I remembered Eileen quoting Coleridge to me after our father died, "So lonely 'twas that God himself/Scarce seemed there to be," and felt my eyes fill with tears.

The tears made me mad. I turned and slammed my hand against the board. Time didn't matter. The snow didn't matter. The cold didn't matter. The wood was the only thing that mattered.

The grunting noise made by the nails pulling away from the column was the happiest sound I've ever heard. I kicked the board loose and slipped the handcuff off the railing.

I was free.

Chapter 36

• • • • • • • • • • • •

I ran across the street and tried the phone at the gas station. It didn't work. I slammed the receiver down and went on a telephone search. I found one on Ninth Avenue. It worked. I dialed the operator and told him I wanted to make a collect call.

Dennis answered before the phone finished its first ring. He shouted, "Yes, yes. I'll accept the call. Blaine, where are you? You've been gone for hours. We've been going crazy trying to find you. Are you—"

I couldn't stop shivering. I bounced up and down, trying to get the blood moving in my frozen feet.

"Will you stop and listen to me. I'm fine. I'm on Ninth and . . ." I looked up, saw the giant cow sitting on top of the marquee of the building on the other side of the street, and

172 • Sharon Zukowski

smiled. "Ninth Avenue and Fourteenth Street. Across the street from the Old Homestead."

"What are you doing there? Never mind. Stay where you are. I'll come get you."

"Dennis, don't. By the time you get here, I'll be an ice statue. I'll find a taxi. Leave some money with your doorman so I can pay the driver." I wanted to get out of the cold, but was reluctant to break the connection. "Have you talked to Eileen?"

"Every ten minutes. She's at Police Plaza, raising hell with everyone. I'm not sure the building's still standing. She even tried to get hold of the mayor. The supervisor found Tomlinson. The asshole claims he's been sitting in a bar all evening and has a room full of witnesses to back him up. He suggested that you're pulling a wild publicity stunt. I think Eileen had to be restrained. She was going to rip his head off."

"And people think Eileen's the mild-mannered sister. Tell her to back off." I thought of Eileen tearing up police headquarters, and sighed. "You'd better invite her over for a cup of coffee. You know Eileen, she won't leave us alone until she's convinced I'm okay."

Other than giving the address and asking the cabbie to turn the heat up as high as it would go, I didn't talk. As soon as the taxi stopped at the curb, Dennis ran out of the building. He pulled the door open before the car stopped moving.

I slid across the seat. In a heavily accented voice, the cabbie growled, "Hey lady, where you going? Eleven seventy-five. Who's going to pay?"

Dennis dug a handful of money from the hip pocket of his jeans. He threw a twenty dollar bill at the man. "Keep it. Come on, Blaine, let's get inside."

I clumsily got out of the cab. My frozen feet clumped on the sidewalk. Dennis wrapped his arm around me and escorted me into the building. We walked past the doorman, into the elevator. Disappointment flashed on the doorman's face, my return ruined his evening of speculation and gossip.

Dennis didn't talk; the concern in his eyes was fierce. When the elevator door closed, I touched his arm with my left hand. "Dennis, it's okay. You can stop worrying."

"What's wrong with your other hand? Is it hurt? Do you need to see a doctor?"

I lifted my hand from my coat pocket. Tomlinson's cuffs dangled from my wrist. "No doctor. I couldn't get these things off. It's hard enough to find a taxi in this city. No one would have picked me up if I looked like an escaped prisoner. Did you get hold of Eileen?"

"I beeped her as soon as we hung up. She should be here any minute. She's still steaming."

The elevator stopped at the fourth floor to pick up more passengers. I quickly stuffed my hand back in my pocket. Dennis unobtrusively moved his arm to hide the silver around my wrist. He smiled and said, "You look cold . . ."

Dennis locked the door and took my coat. I went to the bedroom. Dennis followed. He stood in the doorway and watched me pull my suitcase from the floor of the closet.

"Are you leaving?"

"Don't be silly. I'm looking for my pick. When Irma left me alone to pack, I decided to throw it in the suitcase. It would have been awkward to explain how a SuperPick came to be hidden in the back of the linen closet. My guns are in here too." Dennis shook his head and walked out of the room.

I found my picks and sat at the kitchen table working at the lock while Dennis hovered behind me, offering to help and getting in my way. The doorbell rang. Dennis didn't move. I tugged on his flannel shirt to wake him from his overprotective trance.

"That's probably Eileen. Why don't you let her in? That will give me a few minutes to get out of these things."

By the time he returned with Eileen, I had freed myself. Dennis had an afghan tucked under his arm. He draped it over my shoulders and stepped aside so Eileen could get a look at me. She wasn't happy with what she saw.

"You look awful. I think we should get you checked out by a doctor before we do anything else."

I snapped. "I'm fine. Back off and let me breathe. I'm cold—not dead."

Eileen smiled. She looked over my head and talked to Dennis. "When Blaine's cranky, it means she's okay. You have to worry when she's being sweet."

"Thank you, Eileen. I appreciate your compliment. Tomlinson was better company than you two."

Dennis ignored our bickering—he'd heard it before. He took three mugs from the cabinet and started pouring coffee. Eileen's eyes went from the pick and handcuffs on the table to the mugs to the coffeepot. "Dennis, do you have anything stronger? I'd like a real drink."

They looked at me as if asking permission. "Don't swing your guilty faces in my direction. You're both crazy to drink coffee when you want whiskey. Go ahead, Dennis, break out the bottle. I can handle it."

They drank brandy. I drank coffee. They listened while I told them about my excursion to the waterfront and my brief conversation with Tomlinson.

Dennis swirled the brandy snifter and frowned. "Family business. Could the clinic have ties to organized crime? First thing on Monday, I'll check with our task force to see if they've heard anything. Maybe we should take a look at the clinic."

"Maybe we're getting too complicated." I looked across the table to Eileen. "When you talked with Judith's attorney, did you ask who inherits the estate if the baby isn't found?"

Eileen wrinkled her forehead. "That's such a simple question—you would think I'd have asked it. It won't be too difficult to find out. All I have to do is make a call."

Dennis pointed to a telephone on the wall next to the refrigerator. "Help yourself."

I protested. "It's Saturday night. You don't expect to find that poor guy in his office, do you?"

"Nope." Eileen pulled an address book from her handbag and walked over to the telephone. "I have his home number. I know he's there. They had a baby about six months ago. Charlie was complaining that since the baby arrived they never go out."

As Eileen predicted, Charlie answered the telephone. I pulled the afghan around my shoulders and tried to keep from shivering. Eileen repeated my question, listened to his lengthy answer, then said. "Thanks, Charlie. Sorry I interrupted your evening." Eileen laughed at his response and hung up.

Eileen was still smiling when she returned to the table. "Charlie's having a hard time with fatherhood. He's amazed by the noise one little baby can make."

"How sweet. Who gets the money?"

The smile disappeared from Eileen's face. "Jerry Marsden was an only child. His parents died about ten years ago. Judith's parents died around the same time. If you don't locate Jerry Junior, the money goes to Judith's sister and adopted brother. The sister lives in New Mexico. The brother lives in Queens. He uses the name of his natural parents: Tomlinson."

Dennis whistled. "John Tomlinson. A detective with the NYPD. Twenty million reasons to want Blaine off the case. Is the sister still alive? Tomlinson may have arranged a convenient accident."

"I don't know. I'll call Charlie tomorrow to see if he's had any contact with her since Judith died."

I cradled the warm coffee mug in my hands and felt the icicles begin to melt. "You might diplomatically suggest that Charlie warn her to be extra careful. After the evening I spent with her brother, I wouldn't be surprised to hear he's planning to be the sole heir."

Eileen drained her glass. Dennis quickly refilled it. "Blaine, I'm sorry. I would have saved you a lot of trouble if I'd thought to ask about the other heirs. Do you want me to file a false arrest complaint against Tomlinson? I can get him thrown off the force. We could file criminal charges too."

"Let me find the baby before you do anything. Taking the money away from Tomlinson will be better revenge than an official reprimand. That's good enough for me."

I caught a glimpse of the anger that had been fueling Eileen's rampage at Central Booking. Eileen shook her head and said, "It's not enough for me. Are you going to let this man get away with killing his sister? What about Nikki? Dennis told me about her. Are you going to let Tomlinson get away with killing her too?"

I pulled the afghan tighter around my shoulders. "I'm not convinced Tomlinson murdered anyone. If he poisoned Judith and beat Nikki to death, why didn't he kill me? A guy that violent would have done something more deadly than cuffing me to a fence."

Dennis gently rubbed the raw bruises on my wrist. "I think he intended to kill you, but he was afraid to leave his bullet in your body. Everything, except a slug from his gun in your brain, could be explained away. If you froze to death, he wouldn't have mourned."

Eileen agreed with Dennis. They spoke at the same time, trying to convince me to let Eileen take legal action. I refused to listen.

"I'm not ready to make a complaint against anyone. I have more pressing problems to deal with at the moment."

I stood up and said, "I'm freezing. You people can sit here and plot ways to change my mind. I'm going to sit in a tub of hot, soapy water until I thaw. Shoot anyone who comes to arrest me."

Chapter 37

• • • • • • • • • • • •

I was sitting on the floor, leaning against the sofa with an afghan spread over my bare legs and trying to understand the medical language in the textbook on my lap. An empty coffee cup and full ashtray sat on the carpet next to me. I heard a noise and looked up. It was four a.m.; the apartment should have been quiet.

Dennis, his hair tousled and his eyes sleepy, walked out of the bedroom. He belted his robe and sat down next to me. "When I went to bed, you were sound asleep. I thought you'd be out until noon. What's wrong? More nightmares?"

"The nightmares never had a chance." I rested my head

against the cushions. "I slept for about fifteen minutes. After that, I couldn't sleep. My nerves were jumping. I didn't want to bother you, so I decided to get up and read."

Dennis pushed the book back to look at the title. *"Modern Fertility.* If that hasn't put you to sleep, nothing will. I won't even offer you a cup of hot milk."

"You never get up in the middle of the night. What's wrong with you?"

"Things caught up to me too. I couldn't stop myself from thinking. I rolled over and you weren't there. I was afraid you were gone again."

Dennis put his arm around me. I covered his legs with the afghan—it's always nice to share.

"Blaine, I don't ever want to go through another night like tonight. Waiting helplessly. Not knowing what to do. I was so mad at myself for not following you."

"I asked you not to, remember? If you want to be mad at someone, be mad at me."

Dennis took my hand. He traced the scratches and bruises with his index finger. "Your life frightens me . . ."

I tried to pull my hand away. Dennis wouldn't let it go. "Don't run away like you always do. I know why you're afraid to marry me. It's the same reason why I was afraid to ask you."

I didn't want to have this conversation, but I didn't have a choice. Dennis was a man on a mission. He gripped my hand tighter.

I stopped trying to get away and said, "Oh? What reason did you come up with?"

"It's because of nights like this. You dread the telephone call as much as I do—maybe more because you've been through it. I know what can happen. My vivid imagination supplies all the bloody details."

I listened in amazed silence. Dennis must have eavesdropped on the conversation I'd had with my pillow.

He rubbed my hand. "So what are we supposed to do? I've been lying awake, asking myself that question . . ."

He stopped talking. I couldn't interpret the expression in his veiled eyes. My stomach twisted. "Don't leave me in suspense.

What answer did you come up with? Did you decide you'd be better off without the anxiety?"

"I don't want to wake up every morning afraid something is going to happen to you. I do want to wake up every morning and find you next to me. I love you. If I have to worry, I'll worry. It's worth the risk."

Dennis slipped his hand inside my robe. My breath caught in my throat. I turned to him. The book slid to the floor. We kissed; all our fears disappeared. Our robes and the afghan got in the way of our hands. We tore them off, not caring if the material ripped. Nothing else mattered—only the urgent need for skin to touch skin.

I rested my head on Dennis's chest and listened to his heart gradually slow. He stroked my hair and stared at the ceiling. I watched his face. He suddenly grimaced and clutched his back. Concerned, I lifted my head. "What's wrong?"

"This." He pulled my textbook out from beneath his back and held it in the air. "I thought I felt something poking me."

The cover was bent; a few pages were torn. Dennis laughed and tossed the book on the sofa. "Modern fertility. I hope we didn't challenge the gods to teach us we shouldn't make love on their bible. Come on, let's go to bed."

"No, I don't want to move . . ."

We woke at dawn and found ourselves sprawled across the floor, muscles complaining about the hard wood beneath the carpet.

Dennis groaned. I kissed his chest. "If we're going to do this again, you'll have to get a bearskin rug and a fireplace. I'm too old for this. I don't think I can move."

"Don't try. Let's just stay here for a while. Our muscles should loosen up in a day or two."

"I can't. I have to get up." I kissed him again. "Would you mind if I left you for a few hours? I want to go sit in a whirlpool at the Y until my aches go away."

"I'll go with you."

"They won't let you in—the other ladies might get jealous. I can go by myself; I don't need a guard."

"I'm hurt. My offer was made because I'm hungry, not because I want to be your bodyguard. I'll walk you to the Y, buy the *Times,* and have breakfast while you get your muscles working again. After that—"

"After that, I'm going to church to have another talk with Father Timmy. I'm hoping that if I catch him after Mass, he'll be in a more talkative mood. Your presence won't do a thing to encourage his cooperation. Why don't you wait here? I'll be back as soon as I can."

"So it's business as usual again. Are you going to pretend nothing happened last night?"

I sat up. "No, Dennis, I'm not going to pretend anything. I need to think—maybe I should stay with Eileen for a few days."

Dennis laughed. "That should be fun. You can sleep on Eileen's sofa and try to ignore her daughter when she wants to play at six in the morning."

"Sandy's cute—"

"That's not what you told me the last time she woke you up for a predawn Barbie wedding. Don't go hide out at your sister's house. I'll wait. I'll wait until your case is finished and you can think with a clear head."

"Is that an ultimatum?"

"No." Dennis found a robe under the sofa and draped it over my shoulders. "I'll wait patiently until this case is over. Then I'm going to ask you to marry me."

"This is a ridiculous discussion for two naked people to be having. You don't look patient."

Dennis pulled me down. "I'm not. You're not going to be as early as you thought."

The locker room still smelled like pine-scented disinfectant. Sweaty body odor wouldn't overpower it until later in the day, when Sunday brunch was over and people straggled in to work off the cholesterol from their eggs Benedict and the alcohol from their Bloody Marys.

The only woman in the locker room was standing in front of the mirrors at the back of the room, drying her hair. I tossed my knapsack on the bench and called out over the noise, "Hey,

Irma. I didn't expect to see you here. I thought Sunday was your day of rest."

Irma turned the dryer off and walked over to greet me. "Talk about surprises—you're the last person I expected to see. Glad you're here. I was going to try to find you later today. Saves me the trouble of tracking you down."

I snapped, "Your fellow detective didn't have any trouble finding me last night. Why didn't you call him? He could have given you directions."

Irma tossed her towel on the floor and sat down next to me. "Look, Blaine, this isn't much of an apology, but I am sorry about what happened last night. My son was sick yesterday and I couldn't find a sitter. So I took a personal day. Tomlinson went through my desk. He read my files. That's how he found out where you were staying. As for the rest . . ."

"He forged an arrest warrant and kidnapped me. What was going through the man's mind? Did he think he was going to get away with it?"

"Tomlinson's been doing a lot of drinking since his sister died. It's not an excuse, but he got it in his head that you're an anticop monster who's gotten away with murder. Tomlinson liquored himself up and decided to play Dirty Harry—"

"There's more to it than drinking—"

"I expected you to be more understanding."

"Because I used to drink? When I was drunk, the only person I ever tried to kill was myself. This guy's trying to kill other people and he's blaming it on drinking. I don't accept boozers' excuses."

Irma's eyes narrowed. "So, what are you going to do about it?"

"At the moment, nothing. How about you? What are you doing?"

"That man knows I'll kill him if he so much as breathes the air over my desk. If he touches anything, I'll pull his fingers off with a staple remover and stuff them down his throat."

"What about your boss? What's he doing?"

"They put him out on sick leave. The man's got a bad heart. They said the alcohol didn't mix with the pills. I heard they're waiting to see how much of a fuss you make."

"Eileen wants to slap him and the department with all kinds of suits. I'm still thinking about it."

Irma hesitated, then said, "We have to talk."

"We are talking. What's on your mind?"

"The scene at your house is on my mind. What's the girl's real name? It isn't Nikki Wyrick. How much do you know about her?"

"Probably less than you do. I just found out a few days ago that she was using fake ID. I don't know her real name." Irma's suspicious expression made me laugh. "Trust me, I'm not holding back. What else did you find?"

"A puzzle. I was joking about her trashing your house, then killing herself. The technicians tell me I was close to the truth. We found a lot of her fingerprints. Tons of yours. A few unidentified prints—probably your boyfriend's. No sign of anything being wiped clean. It looks as if Nikki, or whatever her name is, did the damage."

It didn't make sense, but few things made sense these days. "Then who killed her? What about the bat? Are there any prints on it?"

"No, the handle was wiped clean. It was the only clean thing in the house. Is it your bat?"

"Nope. I watch baseball, I don't play it. Nikki did. It might be hers. Maybe she used it to smash up my house."

"Maybe." Irma's candid approach disappeared. She kicked at a piece of lint on the floor and avoided my eyes. "There's another problem . . ."

"Let me guess. I've been promoted to the top of the list of suspects."

Irma nodded unhappily. "It's a short list. Your name is the only one on it. I've been advised to take a closer look at you. Nothing's gone to the D.A. But I have to warn you—"

"If I make a fuss about Tomlinson, somebody's going to decide there's enough to charge me." I shook my head. "Serve and protect. You guys should change your motto to 'We serve ourselves and we protect ourselves.' Everyone else better take care of themselves."

"It's uncomfortable being stuck in the middle. Help me. Answer my questions so I can write a nice long report for my boss. If he reads it, he might just leave me—and you—alone. Where were you Friday between the time you left your office and the time you arrived at your house?"

"I was at a museum. The Met. I have a receipt." Allowing myself to be set up. "I hung out at the Temple of Dendur. The guard might remember me. We talked about graffiti."

"Graffiti?"

"You can't go into the temple, or get too close to it, because people write their names on the walls. The guard showed me century-old graffiti left by tourists when the temple was still in Egypt."

"Fascinating. I'll check this out. I don't want to, but . . . What else did you do?"

"The museum closed. I took a cab home. That's it, my big evening out. The life of a single nineties woman."

"I need more than that. Did you remember the cab number or the hack's license number?"

I laughed. "Sure, I always memorize the license number of the cabs I ride in. Don't you?"

"I'm doing my own single thing. I'm a single mom trying to raise a kid and put away enough money to get him through college." Irma frowned. "I can't remember the last time I rode in a cab. Some kind of number would help me track this down."

"How about a receipt? Would that help? Force of habit—I get a receipt for everything."

She didn't laugh. "What were you doing at the museum?"

I didn't want to tell Irma anything that would lead her to Judith's missing baby and Tomlinson's involvement. It would put both of us on a path to trouble. I wasn't sure Irma could overcome her loyalties to a fellow cop.

Without any of the hesitation that signals a lie, I said, "It was a rough week. The museum is a great place to recharge. You should try it sometime."

"In my next life. I don't have the time or the money for culture. Is this all you can tell me?"

I told her it was, and added, "I'm tired of living out of a suitcase. When can I have my house back?"

"Three, four days. Maybe a week. We may need to take a second and third look to be sure we didn't miss anything."

Irma looked at her watch and excused herself. "I'm late. Come earlier next time; we can do some laps together."

"Yeah sure." While Irma finished dressing, I sat on the bench. My energy disappeared. The walls of the locker room closed in around me. I lost interest in sitting in the whirlpool.

I needed to be out in the cold air. After saying good-bye to Irma, I grabbed my knapsack and hurried out. A subway ride to Brooklyn was just the thing to clear my head.

By the time I got to the church, the last Mass was over. Father Timmy wasn't at the church. He wasn't at the rectory. I couldn't find anyone to tell me where the priest had gone.

I added another missing person to the list and took the subway back to Manhattan. During the long ride, I amused myself by staring at the advertisements.

Hemorrhoid removal, acne treatments, abortions, living room furniture, credit counseling. Every problem solved. I looked, but didn't spot any cards advertising help for a befuddled private investigator who was losing people, not finding them.

I didn't want to go back to Dennis and reopen our discussion about love and marriage. I needed to be alone, so I went to the office. It was the loneliest place I knew.

Chapter 38

••••••••••••

I unlocked the door to our office suite. Mick Jagger's voice blasted from somewhere in the back. I followed the noise to a private office and peered around the partially opened door. I saw Brad sitting at his desk and frowning at the legal pad on top of his desk.

"Can't get no satisfaction—sounds like bad news to me."

Brad started. He reached behind him and snapped off the tape player. "Sorry, Babe. I thought I was alone. It's Sunday. What are you doing here?"

Brad's curly hair was more disheveled than usual. Deep purple circles ringed his eyes.

"I thought this would be a quiet place to do some reading." I couldn't hold back a giggle. "You look like a punk raccoon. Why are you here? A sexy guy like you should have your entire weekend taken up by an equally sexy blond."

"She's working. Flight attendant. I had to get serious with a lady who works on Sundays." Brad sighed.

"Listen, Blaine, one of my friends at the *Post* called me this morning. He told me what happened at your house. They're not running the story—not enough blood—but he was hoping I knew something juicy. What gives?"

I draped my coat over the back of a chair and sat. "I'm sorry. I should have called you. You wouldn't believe how insane my life has become. I haven't had time to do anything."

Brad opened his mouth. I raised my hand to stop him and told him about Tomlinson. When I finished, Brad smiled. "So we have a brand-new suspect. Good, I was afraid we were going to run out of things to keep us busy. What do you want me to do?"

"Check Tomlinson out. I want to know everything about him. His shoe size, the brand of beer he drinks, what he eats for breakfast. Why he needs twenty million dollars. Everything."

Brad saluted. "Whatever you say, Babe. I'll get right on it. It'll be fun to have some real work to do."

I stood up and tucked my coat under my arm. I didn't want to listen to jokes about our disappearing business. "Great. Now I'm going to do a little reading."

"Wait a second, Babe. I took a message for you." Brad rooted around in the stacks of paper on his desk.

"The lady was surprised to have a real person answer the phone. She seems to think Manhattan closes for the weekend."

"Did you tell her that only happens during the summer? We tend to stick around in the winter and hibernate. Who was it?"

Brad found the errant message on the floor and passed it across the desk to me. "Don't know why she called if she didn't think anyone would answer. It's a five-oh-five area code. Where's that?"

I had no idea until I read the message. "Olivia L'Ameillaud. Please call. As soon as possible." Eileen must have given a sinister message to Charlie Spragge. "Five-oh-five is in New Mexico. I really need to talk to this lady. Did she say she'd be home today?"

"Yep, all day . . ."

I hurried out before Brad finished. The sound of the Rolling Stones followed me. I smiled as I walked down the hallway to my office. Brad wasn't the only one who couldn't get satisfaction.

A softer, more formal version of Judith Marsden's voice answered my call. When I introduced myself, I heard a sigh. It could have been relief. It could have been dread.

"Thank you for returning my telephone call so quickly. The gentleman who answered your phone was so polite. You should be commended for hiring such mannerly employees. In today's rush, rush society, it's a delightful surprise to be treated with courtesy."

I had the strange feeling of talking to someone born in another earlier generation. Her politeness was contagious. I made a gracious reply, told the woman I was surprised by her call, then asked if I was interrupting her Sunday afternoon.

"Not at all, I'm done for the day. I do most of my work early in the morning. That's when the light is at its best."

"The light?"

"I'm a painter. Judith and Johnnie always teased me about moving to New Mexico to do the Georgia O'Keeffe thing. Especially Johnnie. He tells me I'll never find a good husband if I hide in the desert for the rest of my life."

I heard the tiny sigh again. "What has Johnnie done? Mr. Spragge hinted there was some trouble. When I questioned him, he suggested that I call you directly."

God bless Mr. Spragge for being a chicken. I lit a cigarette and reminded myself to be diplomatic. "Has your brother been in trouble before?"

My ears caught the momentary hesitation while Olivia picked the right words. I tapped the cigarette against the side of the ashtray and patiently waited.

"As a child, Johnnie never got into real trouble, but he was involved in many fights. You have to understand, Johnnie has an appalling temper. But he would never knowingly hurt anyone. After he loses his temper, he's so remorseful."

I hadn't seen any remorse on Tomlinson's face—maybe the light on the pier hadn't been strong enough. "Olivia, have you spoken to your brother recently?"

"We were never close. I'm much younger than Judith and Johnnie. We've always labored under the strain of being rooted in different generations. I haven't talked to Johnnie since the service . . ." Her voice broke.

While Olivia fought her tears, I decided to follow a less upsetting path. "Did Mr. Spragge explain that I was working for your sister? I still am. I'm looking for her son."

"Judith wanted that child more than anything in the world. She was heartbroken when she died. What can I do to help?"

Olivia sniffled. It didn't take great detecting skills to guess that she was crying. I listened to her quiet sobs; my hopes of learning anything useful faded. I tried to end the conversation. "I'm sorry, Olivia. It wasn't my intention to upset you. Why don't I call you back later, or tomorrow?"

Olivia answered in a ragged voice. "No, ask your questions. Mr. Spragge said it was important that I do my best to help you. I'm going to raise the boy, did Mr. Spragge tell you that? I'll do whatever I can to help you find him."

"Did Judith mention that she was writing an article about the fertility clinic? I looked through Judith's papers, but didn't find anything."

"Judith kept a journal. Actually, it was a manuscript. She thought it might be published some day." Olivia's voice shook from the effort of holding back tears. "Judith sent me a copy. She said it was a backup in case something happened to the original . . ."

Where was the original? Not in Judith's house—I wouldn't have missed it.

". . . I haven't been able to force myself to look at any of it. Do you think the manuscript might be useful?"

"It might."

Olivia quickly said, "I'll take it to the Federal Express office tomorrow. You'll have it Tuesday morning." The prospect of action brought vigor back to Olivia's voice. "You don't think my sister took her life."

"I didn't say that."

"People think painters are only interested in filling a canvas. They're wrong. A painter's also fascinated by the empty spaces on that canvas. Ms. Stewart, the things you don't say are more intriguing than the things you say. I spoke with my sister early in the morning of the day she died. What do you want to know?"

"Did you talk about her problems? How did she sound?"

"Judith was worried, but she had hope. She told me there was a good lead and she was waiting for a report. I will not accept the finding that she committed suicide. Will you?"

I didn't answer. I didn't want to share my theories with Olivia; her motive for murder was as strong as her brother's. What if they had formed a deadly partnership.

"I think she was killed."

My cigarette smoldered on the edge of the ashtray. I stubbed it out before it tumbled over and set my desk on fire. "What makes you think Judith was murdered?"

"Because I can't believe what the doctors are telling me. Because I'm afraid I missed a warning from Judith. My new paintings are filled with guilty and confused faces. One of them is mine. I don't want to spend the rest of my life painting a guilty self-portrait. I have to know the truth of my sister's death."

Chapter 39

The words were sincere, but Olivia's voice didn't have a tone of conviction. That's the problem with interviewing people over the telephone, you can't see their eyes. You don't have any way to judge the truth of their words. Trying to keep suspicion out of my own voice, I asked, "Why does your brother use a different surname?"

Olivia's courtliness disappeared. She snapped, "Why do your questions resolve around my brother? Isn't it enough that my sister is dead? Are you blaming her death on what's left of my family?"

"I'm not trying to make your brother the guilty party. We had an argument. He never mentioned he was Judith's brother. I'm curious why he omitted that fact, that's all."

"What do you mean by an argument?"

"Nothing serious, just a disagreement about my involvement in the case." I quickly asked, "Why would anyone want to kill Judith? Who would benefit from her death?"

"Are you saying that Johnnie killed my—his—sister? I find that suggestion revolting. How could you think such a thing?"

"I'm not suggesting anything." I stopped to pull my temper back under control. "You just finished telling me you think Judith was killed. Why are you getting so upset when I asked who might have done it?"

"I find this difficult to discuss over the telephone. Especially with a complete stranger."

"It's too bad I don't have the time to fly to New Mexico to make your acquaintance. We're on the same side. Isn't that enough?"

Olivia didn't answer. How would I act if a complete stranger asked me if my brother murdered my sister? I'd be angry and upset—just like Olivia. "I'm sorry. Working on Sunday doesn't seem to agree with me." I rubbed my forehead and looked in my desk drawer for the aspirin bottle.

"Johnnie is the oldest. He was adopted after my parents gave up hope of ever having children of their own." Olivia laughed. "Those stories you hear about a couple adopting and suddenly having a baby came true. Judith was born a year after the adoption. I was born ten years after Judith—I was truly a surprise."

I found the aspirin, popped three in my mouth, and washed them down with a mouthful of coffee. Olivia continued talking.

"When Johnnie was a teenager, I was a toddler. He was a wonderful older brother. I have many vague, but happy memories of him. I don't believe my sister committed suicide. At the same time, I don't believe my brother killed her. Someone else must be responsible for her death. If you suspect Johnnie, you are wasting your time."

That was it. Olivia refused to extend the discussion. After promising to send Judith's diary, she hung up. I put my feet up on my desk and listened to the faint sounds of the Rolling Stones filter down the hallway. Brad was still listening to Mick complain that he couldn't get any satisfaction. Brad's love life must be as confused as mine.

I looked at the telephone and smiled. If the Stones had recorded "Can't Get No Answers," I'd be wearing it out.

I found Dennis sprawled on the couch, watching basketball. Despite his protestations, I was convinced he had spent the entire day on the sofa, channel-surfing the afternoon away. We ended the weekend with dinner and a dull movie that had gotten rave reviews from the critics. The prospect of early meetings on the next morning sent us to bed before eleven.

Monday disappeared in a flurry of meetings with prospective clients, all of them small accounts—the type we found when first beginning our business—and another fruitless round of visits to clinics. At six-thirty, after my last visit to a Brooklyn hospital where no one could remember seeing Hannah, I went to Dennis's apartment, exhausted and wanting nothing more than sleep.

Dennis was working late and couldn't interfere with my plans. After eating a container of yogurt, I went to bed.

The package arrived Tuesday morning, just as Olivia had promised. I picked up the bulky envelope from Jona's desk and locked myself in my office.

I opened the envelope and shook out a thick stack of unbound papers typed in faded ink. Two hundred pages with no happy ending.

A note was clipped to the top sheet. Olivia's bold handwriting told me to keep the manuscript as long as necessary. There was no reference to our conversation, no offer of additional help. After pouring a cup of coffee, I started reading.

Chapter 40

"Months before he died, I promised Jerry I'd give him a son. Today is the day I carry out that promise. It's been a year since Jerry died, but I felt him at my side as I climbed the stairs.

"The surrogate passed all the tests. The screening is over. The real work begins today. Even though I understand the technical aspects—the need to stimulate the growth of mature eggs—the thought of dozens of injections a day frightens me. I remind myself why I'm doing this and enter my brave new world with resolve.

"The doctors started preparing Hannah for the pregnancy. I feel a deep emotional attachment to her. The pull of our bodies getting in synch is too strong to ignore. Whenever I see Hannah, a deep pang of jealousy strikes. It's the same every time. I envy her. I'll never feel my baby grow inside me. I'll never feel my baby's kick as he turns in my womb."

Judith's envies made me uncomfortably aware of the turns my life had taken. I didn't want any reminders. I flipped the page over.

"I join the hopeful faces in the waiting room. We don't talk. We don't acknowledge the presence of another barren body. I read the magazines, but can't remember what I've read. When my name is finally called, I jump up and run across the floor. I'm too excited to walk calmly to the lab."

The next few pages repeated a nurse's instructions for giving injections. I skipped them and looked for more interesting entries.

"I'm lying in bed, depressed and sick again, writing this. The month of drugs didn't work. My stubborn ovaries refuse to produce. The doctors shook their heads. I closed my eyes and silently repeated: I am more than just an egg factory. I am more than just an egg factory.

"They sent me home with another box of syringes and vials of drugs. I am more than just an egg factory."

The next three days were marked by nothing but the date and a recurring notation: Sick. The fourth day had a longer text:

"The shots are making me ill again. Just as they have been doing all week. My head is aching. My stomach is spinning.

"Jerry's robe is casually slung over the back of a chair—I've taken to wearing it around the house. I can almost fool myself into thinking Jerry will walk in and tease me for wearing his clothes. I know that won't happen, but I need to have something that once held his arms wrapped around my shoulders. If I close my eyes, I can smell his after-shave. Maybe I'm imagining the smell, but I'm not imagining the way I feel.

"The only way I can stop the nausea is to curl up in a fetal position and think about the baby I'm trying to make. My eyes fix on his robe. Would I have the strength to go through another cycle of needles and tests if it wasn't for my promise to Jerry? No."

"Dr. Nelson lost his temper today. I told him I wanted to stop. I can't give myself another needle. The worry keeps me awake at night. Am I injecting myself with a drug that will cause a cancer to form somewhere inside my body?

"He told me I'm paranoid because cancer killed Jerry. Dr. Nelson is right. After watching Jerry die, I'm afraid the same thing will happen to me.

" 'I wouldn't do anything to endanger you. There are no long-term health effects.' Dr. Nelson's paternal reassurances didn't alleviate my concerns.

"A simple reporter's question came to mind. *What studies have been done?* Before it came out of my mouth, Dr. Nelson reminded me that I was fulfilling Jerry's last wish. My question died on my lips, not in my mind.

"I took the kit, but I didn't go home. I went to the library. I searched the medical journals until closing time. No studies. Nothing to put my mind to rest. Still, I fill the needle with the syrupy liquid, twist around, and stick it in my buttocks. The needle pierces my skin. I ask myself why and collapse on the bed as the dizziness carries me away."

The next ten or twelve pages repeated Judith's complaints about what she called her morning sickness, likening it to the discomfort suffered by a pregnant woman and wishing it was morning sickness. After a week of curt reports about headaches and vomiting, the tone of Judith's entries changed from peevish to slightly hopeful.

"Dr. Nelson is changing my medication. 'We're going to make a switch. Your ovaries haven't responded as we had hoped. I'm putting you on Digomethate to give your ovaries extra stimulation so they produce enough ripe eggs for us to harvest. I think this will do the trick.' "

Days went by before there was another entry. The tone, even the handwriting, was stronger: "My hopes are soaring—again. This injection didn't make me sick. My depression is gone. I found the energy to go outside today. I went shopping and bought a stroller for the baby. Tomorrow, I'm going to hire painters for the nursery."

The euphoria lasted a week. In those seven days, Judith hired painters, filled the nursery with toys, and wrote page after page about her hopefulness. The journal then skipped a few days. I recognized the pattern. Whenever Judith faced a crisis, she didn't write about it for a few days, until she was ready to face the uncertainty.

"The letters are blurry again tonight. I'm having trouble seeing these words appear on the page. I'm sick and tired all the time and trying to ignore it. But it doesn't matter. Anything to get those eggs growing.

"We increased the dosage again today. Despite my fears, I do whatever the doctors tell me. I leave the clinic, unasked questions burning my lips. Why am I so timid? I am more than just an egg factory."

I don't know how Judith dealt with the recurrence of the side effects because she didn't write about it. She didn't write about anything for weeks. What emotions had she been fighting?

"I spent the afternoon at the clinic, getting ready. One last shot, one last ultrasound, and an antibiotic to prevent any infections. I can't sleep. Tomorrow morning is the first harvest. My ovaries are finally filled.

"I stay awake and wonder if Hannah is tossing and turning, worrying about tomorrow as much as I am. She brushed my questions aside with a curt shake of her head. Dr. Nelson says it's a sign that Hannah won't become attached to the child. I pray he's right."

"I thought I'd endured every indignity the doctors had been able to invent—I was wrong. The briefings didn't prepare me.

"The anesthetic dripping in my arm dulled the pain, but left me keenly aware. I have nothing left. All my privacy is gone.

"The doctors said, 'Let's go fishing.' Everyone laughed at his joke. They were still laughing when he inserted the tools. First an ultrasound probe, then a suction tube with a needle at the end to pierce the ovaries and suck the eggs out.

"I closed my eyes. The low hum of the vacuum covered the voices of the doctor and his assistants. Test tubes—one two three four; I stopped counting—were filled and rushed across the hall to the lab. Sharp eyes examined them to see if the fluid contained eggs that could be fertilized with Jerry's sperm.

"Dr. Nelson snapped his fingers, impatient with the delay. No one spoke. I kept my eyes tightly closed and tried to picture myself holding my baby.

"Someone crept back into the room and delivered the bad news. 'They want more.'

"Another failure. My eyes flew open. A nurse patted my arm.

'Don't worry, dear. It's routine. The lab always wants more. Just in case.'

"The vacuum started again. I closed my eyes and tried to relax.

"The harvest left me sick and drowsy. Cramps kept me doubled up. I clutched my abdomen and slept through the historic moment when the eggs were fertilized.

"After a few hours I was sent home, still feeling the cramps and the nausea. Before collapsing on my bed, I went to the bathroom and threw away all the needles, all the drugs. I'm done. I am no longer just an egg factory.

"All of Jerry's sperm has been used to fertilize the eggs. Now we wait for embryos to form. Some will be implanted immediately. Then we wait for Hannah to become pregnant. The rest of the embryos will be frozen—just in case. All I can do is pray. And worry."

"It's been a week since I could force a sheet of paper into the typewriter. A week of elation when the embryos were transferred. Disappointment when the doctor called with the bad news.

"I hung up and cried. After going through a box of tissues, my disappointment turned to rage. Rage at myself for being defective. Rage at Jerry for leaving me to face this alone. I cried myself to sleep."

I stopped reading to fill my coffee cup and wash the image of Judith mourning her lost baby from my mind. When I returned to my desk, I skimmed the manuscript without paying much attention to the words until a name jumped out at me. *Johnnie*. I turned back to the previous page to find the beginning of the sentence.

"Johnnie called last night. He asked why I was crying. I tried to explain, but Johnnie doesn't understand. He called it Frankenstein science fiction and hung up. . . ."

I skipped the complaints about her brother's lack of compassion and dropped to the next paragraph to find the reason for Johnnie's call. My hopes of discovering an outright threat faded.

I read of a continuing squabble about selling the family home, but not a single worry about Johnnie.

The manuscript resumed with a tedious litany of embryo transplants and failures. The repetition grew dull until I realized Judith's lack of emotion was deliberate. How else could she report the anticipation that followed each embryo transplant and the crushing grief that followed each miscarriage?

"I'll be relieved when tomorrow's attempt fails. It will be over. No more holding my breath and crossing my fingers. No more reciting prayers and dreading the news that the implantation failed. No more embryos. No more sperm. No more heartache.

"Dr. Nelson can't tell me why the other attempts didn't work. At least he didn't look at his watch and hurry me out of his office like he did last time.

"I'm a nuisance who won't cooperate by having another success for the bulletin board. Without saying a word, he makes me feel like the failures have been caused by a hidden deficiency in my eggs. In me."

The notation ended on the bottom of the page. I was afraid to turn to the next one. I didn't want to read about another lost baby.

"I've given up hope, but I'm afraid to leave the telephone. I've spent the past weeks wandering from room to room, looking at the reminders of my life with Jerry. It will all die with me. There won't be anyone to receive the pieces of our lives. No son. No daughter. Nothing."

"We're pregnant!"

Chapter 41

• • • • • • • • • • •

"Elation. Now I understand the meaning of the word. It's the feeling I have when I think about my baby. I can't stop thinking about him. All the discomfort from the shots fades when I look at the blob on the Polaroid snapshot. The blob is my son. My son."

I scanned the pages that described the surrogate's pregnancy for another reference to the fertility drugs. After fifty pages about decorating the nursery and buying baby clothes, I found it.

"My worries about the drugs I shot into my body rushed back today. It happened at the dentist's office. I was looking at a magazine while I waited. A sentence in the middle of an article jumped out at me.

"Certain fertility drugs have been linked to birth defects.

"A pain worse than I ever experienced ran through me. I dropped the magazine on the floor. Thinking I was ill, the receptionist rushed over to me. I managed to choke out the words to cancel my appointment and fled.

"Birth defects."

"What if I've harmed my baby? What are the chances of his being born with a birth defect? No one will answer my questions. Dr. Nelson told me to let him do the worrying. He reached out to pat my hand, or my head, but drew back. If he touched me, I would have bitten him. Nelson must have seen the danger in my eyes. He repeated that I should stop worrying. 'Let me do my job. I wouldn't do anything that was dangerous for you or your baby.'

"My worries are expanding faster than Hannah's waistline. I've been talking to the other women who shared the reception area with me on those mornings when we waited to be called for our ultrasounds and desperately tried to divert our minds from our full bladders.

"Most of them don't have any worries—because they don't have any babies. But I listen to the gossip in the waiting room. I've heard names whispered by women with panic shining in their eyes. After they're out of the room, I write the names in my notebook and vow to find them.

"Horrible names have entered my vocabulary. Spinal bifida. Missing limbs. Anencephaly—I imagine the baby being born with a head so small that the brain doesn't have room to grow. And then I cry."

"I asked the doctor one last question. His answer gave no comfort: Any birth defects that may have occurred have been attributed to genetic failures in the women, not to any treatment they received at the clinic.

"According to Dr. Nelson, my questions have no merit. I wanted to shout, *Are you experimenting on my baby?*

"I accepted Nelson's appeasement without saying a word. Inside, I seethed. How dare he blame the women for having faulty genes?"

"A mother, one whose child was born without a brain, talked to the doctors at the clinic. She told them I called to ask about her baby. Dr. Nelson and I had a discussion about my snooping. I've been warned . . ."

The manuscript ended in mid-sentence. Disgusted, I threw the last page on my desk.

Chapter 42

• • • • • • • • • • • •

I ignored the gentle tap on my door. The knock was louder the second time. When I didn't respond, the door opened. Eileen stuck her head inside. "Jona warned me that you were refusing to see anyone or take any calls. What's going on? Are you hiding?"

"I thought I was solving a case. But I'm not; I'm wasting time. This case keeps taking me away from the baby—not closer to it. The worst thing is that I'm not sure I want to find the baby. He might be better off with the surrogate."

Eileen knows when she's supposed to give a pep talk. She didn't let me down. She walked in and closed the door behind her. "You're supposed to be looking for a missing person, not deciding the question of motherhood. The courts have ruled that the genetic parents are *the* parents. Leave the philosophical problems to someone else. Find the kid. Then we can concentrate on getting this business going again."

Eileen sat down and pointed at the papers scattered across the top of my desk. "What's that, the reason for your depression?"

"Judith's memoirs." I made a neat stack of the manuscript and pushed it to the center of the desk. "There are a lot of innuendoes about problems with the drugs the clinic prescribed. Judith was investigating. Nelson was pressuring her to drop it. Unfortunately, there's no proof of anything."

"What next? How close are you to wrapping this thing up?" Eileen crossed her legs and tried to look casual. She only succeeded in making me tense. "I hate to bring this up and put more pressure on you, but . . ." I braced myself for whatever bad news she was going to deliver. "We lost another client today."

"Don't tell me who it is, I don't want to know. What else? I know there's more, I can see it in your face."

"The bank won't even discuss reopening our credit line. They sent a form letter blaming the economy in response to my call. I'm going to try to establish credit at another bank. Any suggestions? We can't be blacklisted with everyone in this town."

"Yes, we can." Eileen looked startled. "When I got tired of reading Judith's life story, I called friends who know people who know people in the companies we lost."

"What do they know?"

"Nothing that can be proved. A common rumor is swirling around town. The scuttlebutt says the order to dump us came down from upper management in every company. A lot of our customers are involved in the underwriting of the clinic's new stock offering."

When Eileen didn't comment, I said, "Think about it. Our clients are law firms, investment bankers, insurance companies—people who will profit from the clinic's business. The rumor says we pissed someone off. Someone who let it be known their business would go to another firm unless we were thrown overboard."

"You're going for the paranoid conspiracy theory. That's

unusual. You generally ridicule people who see conspirators beneath every desk."

"They haven't been sitting under my desk before. If Nelson is pulling strings, there isn't a damn thing we can do about it. Except stay in business and put him out of business."

"Okay, Ms. Sherlock, where are your bright ideas? You're running full blast into solid brick walls and you don't have any plan on how to get around them."

I had a plan, but I wouldn't discuss it with Eileen. I was too discouraged to argue about the legalities of breaking into the clinic. "I'm going to take a closer look at Nelson's operation. It's been on my agenda, but murders, break-ins, and bogus arrests have been getting in the way."

Eileen guessed my plan. She started her customary lecture about not breaking the law and being careful, but the telephone interrupted her. I grabbed the phone and mouthed "Yeah, yeah," at Eileen while I listened to my caller. I jotted the name and address she gave me on a legal pad, thanked her, and hung up.

"A break?"

"I doubt it. Breaks don't get called in; you have to find them yourself. That was Judith's sister, Olivia. She found a package of Judith's notes. It had the name of a couple Judith questioned about the clinic. Olivia thought it was important."

"Is it?"

I shrugged. "Who knows. I'll visit them on my way home tonight. Maybe I'll be surprised."

I was surprised. Unfortunately, it wasn't a pleasant surprise.

The door opened as wide as the chain would allow. A brown eye peered through the small opening. "Yes?"

"My name is Blaine Stewart. I'd like to speak with Mrs. Wonder. Is she available?"

New Yorkers are a suspicious bunch. The woman curtly asked, "What do you want? Look, this isn't a good time. I don't want to be rude, but I'm not interested in buying anything. My husband wants his dinner and my kid is crying. So go away and leave us alone."

The woman moved to close the door. I leaned against it so she couldn't.

"I've come to talk to you about your son. I'm a private investigator. You spoke with Judith Marsden about the fertility clinic."

I held an identification card up to the door and hoped it would prove my credibility. People seem to believe the laminated card with the horrible picture—it looks official.

"Is this about our lawsuit?"

This was the first time I'd ever heard about a lawsuit—so I lied. "Yes, it is. I'm sorry to bother you, but it's important. I have to talk to you."

"Wait a second." She pulled the license from my fingers and walked away from the door. At least she didn't try to slam it against my face. I leaned against the door and tried to understand the murmuring voices coming from the apartment.

After a muted discussion, the woman returned. "Okay. My husband says I should let you in. But you can't stay long. It's almost time for the baby's bath."

The door opened. The woman who stood behind it was in her mid-forties and wearing a standard dark business suit; dark roots streaked across her close-cropped blond hair. Her head was level with mine; if she took off her heels she'd shrink from five-eleven to less than five-nine. She led me into a large foyer decorated with sleek chrome and glass tables, huge vases filled with silk flowers, and large abstract paintings.

Everything looked expensive. I wasn't surprised; the clinic didn't have many low-income clients.

"How did you get past the doorman? We're supposed to have twenty-four-hour security."

"Your security guard was busy shoveling snow. I slipped inside when he had his back turned."

The woman smiled. The faint worry lines around her eyes didn't go away. "I'm Wanda. Let me take your coat."

I slipped out of my coat and apologized for showing up on her doorstep without warning. "Your name just surfaced in Judith's notes. I wanted to interview you and your husband as soon as possible."

Wanda led me to a living room. She introduced me to her husband, Frank. I was too busy looking at the baby in his arms to notice him.

"That's Rob. I assume he's the reason why our name is in Judith's notes. We talked with her several times about the clinic. He's also the reason for the lawsuit."

Frank quickly reminded her, "We're not suing anymore, remember? We settled. We shouldn't even be talking about the case."

"I'm not here to talk about your lawsuit. I'm following up on the research Judith Marsden was doing. You were patients at the Metropolitan Fertility Clinic?"

We stood in a tight circle in front of the sofa. Every eye focused on the baby. The infant was dressed in a blue sleeper, ready for bed. His eyes were dark, like his dad's. He watched his father's face and smiled.

No matter how hard I tried to keep them away, my eyes wouldn't stay away from the baby's empty sleeves. They hung in the air and swung with each tiny movement. There was no way to camouflage the missing arms.

Wanda broke the silence. She took the infant from her husband and said, "Please, sit down. My maternity leave just ended. This is my first week back at work. We're having trouble adjusting to our new schedule."

Frank and I sat on the couch. Wanda and the baby settled into a chair across from us. She smoothed her son's hair. "He has little flippers . . ."

Her voice faded. The air in the apartment was crackling with emotion, making the hair on the back of my neck bristle—just as it does before lightning hits. "Did the clinic prescribe Digomethate to stimulate your ovaries?"

Wanda answered in a defensive, challenging tone. "I did what the doctors told me. We wanted a baby. I was ready to give up. Frank convinced me to stick with it for a few more months. Dr. Nelson convinced me to try the new drug. Frank doesn't sleep at night. He feels guilty—"

"How should I feel?" Frank rushed out of the room. Wanda shrugged and tried to smile to hide her embarrassment.

Frank returned a few moments later, clutching a tumbler filled with an amber liquid. I recognized the death grip he had on the glass. Scotch, bourbon, or whiskey—I couldn't tell, but it wasn't Frank's first drink of the evening and it wouldn't be his last. He stood behind the couch and gazed at his family.

"You said it yourself. I talked you into it."

"We *both* decided."

Finding myself an unwilling spectator at their encounter session, I interrupted. "How long did you take the drug? Was your dosage increased?"

"I . . . I took it for about six months. We increased the dosage once. The ultrasound showed there was a problem. The doctors told us to have an abortion. They offered to do it. No charge. We chose to have the baby."

Frank stared at me through the bottom of the glass as he drained the drink. I looked away. I knew too well how life looked through the bottom of an empty glass to make any comment.

"We shouldn't be talking to you. The settlement included a clause that said we wouldn't discuss the case."

I made believe I didn't hear the belligerence in his statement. "When did you settle?"

Wanda answered. "Last week. The clinic made an offer. We decided to accept it. We wanted to get on with our lives. The settlement will be enough to be sure Rob has whatever he needs—"

"The bastards should be put out of business."

"Frank, we've been through this. I don't care about the others. I only care about Rob . . ."

"What do the doctors say about Rob's future?"

"They're not sure there haven't been other . . ." Wanda chewed on her bottom lip. ". . . other types of damage."

Frank snorted. "Why don't you tell her what the doctors really said? Tell her about brain damage and arrested development."

"What do you want me to say, Frank? Do you want me to say that I don't know what's going to happen? Will that make you happy? Okay, I'll say it. I don't know what's going to happen . . ."

Wanda furiously blinked her tears back into her eyes. She stared at Frank. He turned away as if to go refill his glass.

I squirmed. All I wanted to do was get out of that apartment. I said something about leaving; Frank stopped me.

"Would talking to other parents convince you to go after the clinic? Our attorneys talked to a few couples whose children . . ." His voice cracked ". . . whose children have worse deformities. I'll give you their names. I want those bastards out of business."

He pulled an address book from a briefcase that was on the floor next to the sofa and quickly ran through a list of names. I half-heartedly recorded them in my notebook, even though I knew I wouldn't make any attempt to contact them. I'd seen enough.

Chapter 43

• • • • • • • • • • •

Dennis was waiting—not very patiently. He was at the door before I was able to get the key out of the lock. "Where have you been? I expected you—"

"Hours ago." I kicked my boots off and let Dennis take my coat. I didn't explain that I'd walked home, slowly, from the Wonders' apartment near Central Park, and wondered if I wanted to lead a crusade to close down the clinic.

Dennis stood with my coat slung over his arm, waiting for an explanation. I ran my fingers through my hair and tried to remember if I had promised to be home earlier. "I'm sorry. You look angry. Did I forget something important?"

"No, I'm trying to keep you from thinking that I was sitting here for the past two hours worrying about you. Bad day, I assume. You look wiped out."

"I am." I went to the bedroom and sat on the bed to take my sneakers off. "I want to change my clothes and forget everything."

Forgetting he was still holding my coat, Dennis stood in the doorway and watched me. "It's after eight. Did you eat dinner? If you don't feel like going out, I can cook something."

I squinted at Dennis. "You can't be real. I come home grumpy and tired. Here you are, sweet and understanding."

Blushing, Dennis draped my coat over the back of a chair and sat next to me. "Why are you grumpy and tired?"

"Judith's sister called me again. A package of Judith's notes turned up. I went to interview one of the families mentioned. The baby . . . " I shook my head. "I don't want to talk about it."

Dennis put his arms around me. I leaned against him and closed my eyes. He rubbed his hand up and down my back. The vision of the baby's flapping sleeves wouldn't go away.

"I don't want to talk about it. I don't want to even think about it. But I can't stop; it keeps coming back."

"Let's think about something else." He kissed me and helped me undress.

After you've made love, it's difficult to climb out of bed and excuse yourself to go play burglar. It's difficult, but not impossible. Thinking Dennis was asleep, I tried to ease myself from the bed. I was wrong. Dennis was awake. He grabbed my arm and held me back.

"Where are you going? To the kitchen for a snack, I hope."

What could I tell him? I sat on the edge of the bed and rubbed the hair on Dennis's forearm. "Sorry, no snack. I have to go out. Work."

"You must be crazy. It's the middle of the night. What—"

"Don't ask."

I slid away from him and turned on a lamp. We both squinted against the light. Dennis watched me dress in jeans and a sweatshirt. I didn't like the silence. "I'm sorry. I have to go out. I'll be back in a few hours."

"Should I worry?"

"No more than usual." I found my sneakers and sat down on the edge of the bed to put them on. "We agreed we wouldn't argue about work, remember?"

"I'm not prying into your business, Blaine. But I want to be sure you have proper back-up. Does anyone know where you're going—in case you disappear again?"

That uncomfortable silence filled the bedroom again. A wrong answer would destroy the shaky foundation Dennis and I were building. It was time to start trusting Dennis. "I'm going to the clinic."

Dennis rolled over onto his back and laughed. "What a pair we make. You're crazy. I'm crazy. Don't forget your picks. Take a quarter, too. Call me when you get busted."

"Is that all you're going to say? No lecture?"

"Nope. I'm not your attorney. Your sister would give you an earful, but . . . I'll be waiting—as usual."

I tied my sneakers and leaned over to kiss Dennis. "Thank you." After another kiss, I pushed myself away. I found my picks and left before I changed my mind.

A cab was lurking outside Dennis's apartment. I rode up to Seventy-fifth Street and Madison Avenue and walked the last six or seven blocks to the clinic. When you break into a building, it isn't a good idea to arrive at the front door in a taxi.

The streets were almost empty. I passed a couple strolling home from a late evening in the clubs and several people walking their dogs before turning in for the evening. I walked faster, hopeful that this was going to be my lucky evening.

It wasn't. The sight of the brightly lit building hit me in the pit of my stomach. It was after midnight, didn't those people ever go home?

I stood in the doorway of a building on the other side of the street, shivered, and watched the clinic. I couldn't see any movement in the offices, but I wasn't going to take the chance. Don't break into a building when all the lights are on is the second rule of successful burglars.

I stayed long enough to smoke two cigarettes. The cold began to ooze through my clothes, bringing back unpleasant memories of the pier. During that time, no one entered, or left, the clinic. After flicking my cigarette butt into a snowbank lining the curb, I crossed the street to take a closer look.

A low wrought-iron fence blocked a narrow alley between the clinic and its next-door neighbor. It would be so easy to jump it and pick the padlock hanging on the door. So easy. I decided to try.

I was near the top of the fence, about to scramble over the top, when headlights swept around the corner. I jumped down and tried to look innocent.

A cab turned the corner and stopped at the curb. The two men who got out didn't pay attention to me. My hair was stuffed under a dark wool cap; I was wearing a ratty coat and dark jeans. I looked like just another homeless person searching for a warm grate to call home for the evening. A sneeze tickled my nose. I clamped my jaws shut and buried my face in my hands.

They hurried past without giving me a second glance. To their eyes, I was invisible—or they were afraid I'd ask for a handout.

I recognized one of the men and drew into the shadows of the building before he looked at me. Why was Dr. Nelson going to work in the middle of the night? Was he an incurable workaholic bringing a companion for a late-night conference?

I hung out on the cold street corner for about an hour, waiting to see if Nelson and his friend would leave. They didn't.

Cold, frustrated, and disappointed, I finally gave up and went back to Dennis's apartment. Dennis, despite his vow to be awake and waiting, was sound asleep. I quietly stripped my clothes off, dumped them in an untidy pile on the floor, and slipped into the bed. Dennis never stirred.

Chapter 44

• • • • • • • • • • • •

Fragile from the beginning, my case shattered into a series of unconnected leads. For three days, I spent the daylight hours in the office, or library, becoming an expert on the FDA drug-approval process, birth defects, and fertility drugs.

When my studying gave me a headache, I made it worse by visiting the people whose names Frank had given me. I found infants with physical disabilities, angry or guilty parents. I found a lot of what Eileen called "circumstantial evidence," but no solid connections to the clinic's drugs. Images of deformed infants haunted my sleep.

I woke up every morning feeling groggy and depressed. I'd lie in bed and list the reasons. Hannah was still missing. Father Timmy wouldn't talk to me. Business was getting worse. Dennis was grouchy about my late-night stakeouts, but he never complained. Eileen complained because I arrived at the office later than usual.

On one of those mornings, I wandered in at ten-thirty, still yawning. Brad was sitting at Jona's desk reading a newspaper. He put aside the sports section and said, "Hey, Babe. What's happening?"

"Hey yourself. What did you do with my secretary? And what have you been up to? It's been a few days since I've seen you."

"I told Jona to go take a coffee break. That I would sit and answer the telephone. That's been an easy job 'cause no one's been calling. Anyway, I wanted to be sure to catch you today. I knew I wouldn't miss you if I sat in front of your door."

I slung my coat over my shoulder. "If you can tear yourself away from Charlie Brown and his pals, I'll give you my complete attention."

With great dignity, Brad said, "I read the comics hours ago. I'm up to the predictions for the baseball season."

"Great, maybe you can find a job with the Mets. We may all be looking for jobs by the time spring training starts."

Brad dropped the paper on the desk. He tucked a manila folder under his arm and followed me into my office. I tossed my coat on the sofa and leafed through the messages on my desk. That didn't take long.

Brad closed the door before squeezing into a chair. Brad has trouble sitting on normal-sized furniture. "So, Babe, I've got enough material on your detective friend to write an episode of *This Is Your Life*."

"And—what did you find?"

"No smoking gun. Tomlinson, as our beloved President Richard Nixon used to say, is not a crook."

"Please, Brad, don't give me any more bad news. I've had more than my share this week. What do you have?"

After a deep, theatrical sigh, Brad opened his file. He made a point of studying his notes. I waited—complaining would only prolong Brad's theatrics.

"John Tomlinson was born in Queens and adopted at birth. His natural mother was in the eighth grade. No one ever knew who the father was. Anyone who knew the truth has long since died. Family connections got the adoption deal done.

"Johnnie had a complex about being adopted. When he was a teenager he called himself Mr. Cinderella. He said his parents favored the real children—the girls—and treated him like Cinderella."

"Did they?"

Brad shook his head. "I don't think so. I talked to a teacher who's living in a local nursing home, someone who worked in the house, and an elderly couple who remembered them. They all said the family was close. So close you'd never know the boy was adopted."

"Who knows what happened when the family got behind closed doors. What else did you find out about Tomlinson?"

"He was a below-average student. A wanna-be jock who was never good enough to make a team. Not smart enough for college. He became a cop because it made him feel successful. Like he accomplished something his sisters couldn't."

I took a cigarette from a half-empty pack and tapped it on my desk. Brad frowned. "You're not going to light that, are you? I don't want to lecture, but I will. You're smoking too much, Babe."

Brad was right; my occasional cigarette was rapidly climbing to almost a pack a day. I dropped the cigarette on my desk. "What kind of cop has Tomlinson been?"

"Dull and unspectacular. A few excessive-force complaints in his file, every one dismissed as unfounded. Tomlinson's adopted parents told him the truth about his mother. He spent a lot of time trying to track her down but never found her. When he entered the academy, he changed his surname to his natural mother's. Said it was because her family and the people who adopted him pressured her into giving him up. He was showing solidarity with her. Although I'm not sure he knows what solidarity means."

"Did you get his credit report? Does Tomlinson need his sister's money?" I made a note to check Olivia's finances. Maybe the artist was starving and needed help with the rent.

"Got it. Pays his bills on time. He has a few credit cards, a car loan. He applied for a huge mortgage—"

I lifted my head. "Define huge."

"Half a mil. He wanted to buy a co-op on the Upper East Side. The banks turned him down. Not enough money for the down payment. Not enough income to pay the mortgage. Tomlinson did a lot of complaining as he sat on the stools in his favorite bars. He's still complaining. He asked Judith for a loan. She wouldn't give it to him."

"Do you think he snapped? When Judith wouldn't give him money, his resentment finally pushed him over the edge . . . He went berserk and killed Judith." I leaned back in my chair and played the scene out in my mind.

"Sorry, Babe. I hate to rain on your parade, but . . ."

I sat up and glared at Brad. "One more cliché and I'm lighting a cigarette. What's wrong with my theory?"

"It's nice, but you won't be able to prove it. Tomlinson was celebrating in the bars a few weeks ago. Not that he needs a reason to celebrate. This guy celebrates when the sun comes up and when the sun goes down."

I tried to push Brad back on course. "Why was he celebrating? Did he win the lottery?"

"Almost. His sister decided to give—not lend—him the money for his new house. He's gonna buy his dream cottage."

"Check it out. I want to know if he's really buying something."

"You're thinking I'll find that Judith reneged on her promise and the deal fell through. That drove Johnnie over the edge and he whacked her."

I muttered, "If we're lucky. But the way my luck's going, you'll probably find a huge deposit in his checking account and a closing set for next week. Take another look at his bank account."

"You got it, Babe. But I think you're sniffing around the wrong tree. Tomlinson just ain't smart enough to make his sister's death look like suicide and hide the baby so he can inherit the cash. What about the kid?"

I was getting sick of that question, I'd been asking it constantly. Brad watched my face flush. "That bad? I'm sorry I asked. Is there anything I could be doing?"

The thought of telling Brad about my plan to break into the clinic was appealing. Having him alongside me would be comforting. "Maybe there is . . ." I stopped and rolled the cigarette across the top of my desk while I thought.

Getting arrested is a risk I'm willing to take. Getting an employee arrested is a risk I won't take.

"Forget it. Keep after Tomlinson. Find out if he has a believable alibi for the night Judith died. Irma mentioned that he has a bad heart. Judith supposedly overdosed on medication used for high blood pressure. Check with Tomlinson's doctor. See if you can find out what he's taking. I tried, but didn't have any success; maybe you'll have better luck."

"You want me to look for the smoking pill bottle?"

"Exactly. Use your well-documented charm on a nurse. Get Tomlinson's medical records. I want to know what he's taking, how much he takes, when he takes it, and the last time he got a refill."

Brad saluted. After promising quick results, he pushed himself out of the chair and left. I dropped the cigarette into the garbage can and went back to work.

The only highlight of my week came a few minutes after Brad left my office. Irma called.

"You can have your house back. We're done." She said good-bye.

"Wait a second; you're not getting away without giving me a status report. What did you find? Any leads to the killer?"

Irma sighed. "I call to give you some good news. You reply by badgering me. Next thing, you'll be asking for a carbon copy of my reports. Better yet, why don't I send you the original? My boss can make do with a smudged copy."

"By the way you're running your mouth, I'd have to guess that you're stuck."

"Uh huh, we're stuck. I hate to admit it—especially to you—but we haven't turned up one solid lead."

"What about the clinic? That's a good lead."

Irma forced a laugh. "Now you're directing my case. The clinic's a dead end. There's no motive. No opportunity. Your cleaning lady worked at the clinic. You're working a case that involves the clinic. You're the only connection."

"What about . . ." I stopped. Irma's worn temper would snap if I suggested that Tomlinson was involved.

"What about this: Unknown assailant. A robber surprised in the act. Case closed."

I strangled the curse that flew in to my lips. "Is that official?"

"It is."

I waited for Irma to continue. When she did, she repeated a familiar litany. "You don't have many friends around here. The girl worked for you. She got killed in your house . . ."

I recognize a threat when I hear one. Even though red-hot anger bubbled inside my chest, I kept my voice calm. "Is that another official line?"

"Unofficial at this point. But it's lurking in the dim hallways of this precinct. No one's been pushing me for results, so I'm letting the file get buried."

"And I should take your advice and leave it buried? Or I'll find myself buried under a murder charge?" Irma's silence answered my question. I told her I got the message, thanked her, and hung up.

I tried to smile at the thought of getting my house back, but could only manage a frown. I wanted to go home. I needed to go home. Dennis wouldn't understand. How could he, when I didn't understand?

Dennis didn't understand. We went to an Indian restaurant in midtown that night. Dennis ordered appetizers after I told him to order whatever he liked, and idly talked about his day.

When the plate of food arrived, he ravenously attacked it. I ignored the *samosas* and *pakoras* and tore off a chunk of bread. While Dennis ate, I tore the *nan* into small pieces and rolled it between my fingers. Dennis glanced at the bread pellets on my plate and put his fork down.

"The turnovers and fritters are great—try them." I shook my head. "What's wrong? I thought you liked this restaurant."

The restaurant was one of my favorites. I loved the pastel colors and the folk carvings on the walls. The dining room was always crowded, but never cramped. We had one of our favorite tables in the back where you could look at the glass wall of the kitchen and watch the chefs take brightly colored food from the tandoori oven.

"I love this restaurant. I'm not very hungry." I sipped my water and thought, *Should I ruin the evening now, or should I wait until after dinner?* I'm not good at waiting. I put the glass down and said, "Irma called me this afternoon. She told me it was okay to go home. I'm going to go."

Dennis carefully swallowed a mouthful of beer. Glass in hand, he sat back. His eyes locked on mine; they were clouded by hurt. "This is sudden. I was hoping you'd decided to stay."

Showing impeccable timing, the waiter appeared with a tray of food. He didn't have any trouble picking up the anger swirling around the table. After quickly serving, he smiled and disappeared.

Dennis cut into his chicken. Without looking up from the plate, he asked, "When?"

"A cleaning crew is going there in the morning to put the place back together. I should be able to move back in after work tomorrow."

Dennis flinched. "That soon? You're in a hurry—"

"Please." I pushed the plate of lamb curry aside and leaned forward to touch Dennis's hand. "When I moved in, you knew it would only be for a week or ten days."

The rigid set of Dennis's jaw was one I hadn't seen since the day I told him I was getting married—to Jeff. Was Dennis reconsidering his impulsive proposal and our whole crazy affair?

"I'm tired of fighting with you. If you want to go, go. I won't stop you. Make sure you get your locks changed so I don't have to worry." Dennis jerked his hand in the air, motioning to the waiter for a check. The waiter and maitre d' instantly appeared at our table, asking why we were leaving our food untouched. Was there a problem?

"Not with the food." Dennis glanced at the check the waiter slipped onto the table and gave him a credit card. "I've lost my appetite and the lady has to leave."

I sat and mutely watched. My throat ached. I tried, but I couldn't force any words out. Dennis signed the credit card receipt, said he didn't want to take the leftovers home, and stood up. "Are you coming? Or have you decided to leave tonight, but forgotten to tell me?"

I didn't move. Dennis took two steps away from the table, turned and came back. "I'm sorry. You're probably thinking about crashing at your sister's house again. Don't bother; I'll behave."

Dennis's idea of behaving was to ignore me. To be honest, I didn't try very hard to break the silence. I let him sit as far away from me as possible in the taxi and stare out the window as if the passing scenery was something he'd never seen before. I followed him through the lobby to the elevator and stood by his side as he watched the numbers on the control panel light up.

Behaving meant politely holding the door open for me, helping me take my coat off, and hanging it in the closet. It meant cheerfully saying good night and coolly kissing my cheek before he went to the bedroom.

Sounds of Dennis walking around, opening and closing drawers, floated from the bedroom. I didn't move from the sofa. Sleeping there seemed to be a good idea. Dennis came out of the bedroom, carrying an envelope in his hand.

"Here," he tossed the envelope in my lap. "Don't forget to take this—you'll need it to keep you company."

I opened it. Torn pieces of my wedding picture spilled out in my lap. So much for being polite.

I didn't sleep on the sofa. Dennis didn't either. He balanced himself on the far edge of the bed, once again keeping as much distance as possible between us. I stared at his unbending back, then snapped the light off. I said good night to the darkness. He didn't answer. When I woke up at six o'clock the next morning, Dennis was gone.

Chapter 45

• • • • • • • • • • • •

The yellow crime-scene ribbons were gone. A thin layer of snow, hamburger wrappers from McDonald's, and menus from a Chinese restaurant covered the front steps. I stuffed the trash into a garbage can and dug my keys from my pocket. After a moment's hesitation, I unlocked the door and went inside.

The cleaning crew had done a great job. The floors shone from a new coat of wax. Every room smelled like the pine forest that used to be advertised on television. Upturned furniture had been righted and tears in the cushions repaired, pictures rehung on the walls, shards of glass and china swept up.

After ten days away, my memories of the destruction had faded. I thought I had recovered from the shock—I was wrong. No amount of wax and furniture polish could take away the feeling of having been violated. As I walked from room to room, inspecting the job, it rushed back. My legs trembled. Anger raged through me.

I stopped in the kitchen. The door leading to the basement was closed. I opened the door and switched the light on, but my shaky legs wouldn't move. I couldn't go down those stairs.

Chiding myself for being a coward, I drank of glass of juice—fresh-squeezed. My cleaning crew had even restocked my refrigerator with milk, juice, and other basics. I drank a second glass of juice and went upstairs to bed.

I tried to sleep. The bed was larger, and emptier, than I remembered. Every noise from the street was loud and sinister. My overactive imagination convinced me that every creak came from an intruder's foot. I finally got out of bed, pulled on a robe, and checked every door and every window—twice. I was halfway up the stairs to go back to bed when I heard a noise in the basement. I froze. My hand tightened on the bannister.

The furnace kicked on. I laughed at my jumpy nerves, but

went back to the kitchen to check the basement door. It was still locked. After one last mouthful of juice, I went to bed. This time I fell asleep immediately.

Too many sleepless nights and too much time in the cold caught up to me. The fever and chills hit a few hours before dawn. Pulling the comforter up to my ears, I curled up into a fetal position and tried to sleep. When daybreak arrived, I managed to call Eileen to tell her I wouldn't be at work, then spent the day shivering, shaking, and sweating.

I didn't hear the front door open. I did hear the third stair creak; it always complains when any weight is put on it. The fourth stair was silent—it never complains—the next two howled.

Someone had gotten into the house and I was too sick to do anything about it. My guns were in their place in the linen closet. I didn't even try to get up; I knew I'd never make it.

Killed in bed—naked and vomiting. What a way to go. I pulled the blanket up over my ears and waited.

Dennis walked into the room. If I felt any relief, I was too sick to notice. "How did you get in?"

He held a chain in the air. Silver keys dangled from it. "You didn't change the locks." Dennis stood at the foot of the bed, unsure of his next move. "You didn't go to work today. You didn't go yesterday either."

Had it been two days? Dennis had no reason to lie, so I believed him. "I'm sick."

"Is that all it is, sick?"

I lifted my head and glared at him. "Did you think of that on your own, or did my sister send you over here to smell my breath?"

"Your sister was worried when you called in sick yesterday. More worried when you didn't show up, or even call, today. So was I. You always go to work—"

"Except when I'm drunk." I turned over and buried my face in the pillow. The movement sent my stomach pitching and rolling. "Orange juice is the only thing I've been drinking. Go away. Leave me alone. Tell Eileen to leave me alone too. I wish you and my sister would stop checking up on me."

"No one's checking up on you. Eileen and I both tried calling. You didn't answer."

"I was sleeping. Won't anyone listen to me? I'm sick."

Dennis sat on the edge of the bed. I groaned as the mattress sunk under his weight. "Eileen was on her way to court. I volunteered to come over to see if you were okay."

I groaned again. My head pounded too hard to argue with Dennis. "Go away. Let me die in peace."

"I'm sorry for doubting you. But I was worried." His lips brushed the back of my neck and abruptly pulled away. "You're burning up. You *are* sick. Where's your thermometer?"

Dennis didn't wait for an answer. Which was a good idea, because I was too busy clenching my teeth and trying to regain control of my stomach to answer. Dennis rummaged in the bathroom. He found a thermometer I didn't know I had and came back to me. Ignoring my weak plea to be left alone, Dennis popped the stick in my mouth. I kept my eyes welded shut and concentrated on not throwing up.

When you're a private investigator who busted up a fraudulent five-million-dollar malpractice suit against your doctor, she's happy to make a house call. A cold stethoscope pressed against my chest woke me.

"Works every time." Dr. Mabe smiled at me. "Now, don't get mad at Dennis. You hit one-oh-four on the mercury. Dennis got nervous; he called me. I decided to stop by and see what was going on. It was a good excuse to get out of my office and enjoy the fresh snow."

Dennis murmured a question. The doctor cheerfully replied, "Looks like the flu to me." She jabbed a needle into my arm. "I'm going to take a little blood. Just to be sure it's nothing more serious. But I'm sure the tests will agree. In the meantime, this lady needs to stay in bed. You know the routine: stay in bed, keep warm, drink plenty of fluids."

They started a discussion about whether or not it was safe for Dennis to leave me alone while he went back to his office to take care of some business. Having a name for my illness didn't make me feel any better; I fell asleep.

★ ★ ★

A wrong number saved my life.

The ringing was loud. Painful. I opened my eyes. The room was dark and cold. I turned on the bedside lamp and grimaced. The intense pain in my head made my ears ring.

I finally got the telephone out of its cradle and fumbled with the switch that turned it on. A heavily accented voice greeted me. "Is Raul there?"

It was rude, but I hung up without saying a word. Dennis had thoughtfully left a pitcher of orange juice, a glass, and a note. He used a thick, black magic marker to print the note. I could read the writing without picking it up.

"Sorry, I had to go back to work. Things are happening on my case. I can't hide out here any longer. *Stay in bed.* I'll be back as soon as I can. —Love, Dennis."

The sight of the orange liquid and the moisture beaded on the glass made me gag. Irrational, but I had to get the orange juice out of sight. I sat up—slowly because my head spun with every movement—and grabbed the pitcher. My legs wobbled, but I managed to get down the stairs without sliding down on my face. I left splatters of juice behind, but I got to the kitchen without a major disaster. The disaster happened in the kitchen.

I intended to put the pitcher on the counter next to the sink. If my eyes had been open, I wouldn't have misjudged the distance. The pitcher fell to the floor and shattered. A puddle of juice quickly spread across the floor.

Roaches appear without warning in the city; you have to be quick or a family moves in within seconds. I pulled a towel from a drawer and dropped it on the puddle. Getting down on my knees, I carefully picked up the broken glass. My head pounded. I really missed Nikki. I closed my eyes and lackadaisically swabbed the mess.

My fingers touched a rounded piece of glass. I opened my eyes. A small brown bottle, the type drugstores use for prescription drugs, had wedged itself between the refrigerator and the wall. The stopper was missing.

I sniffed the bottle. A faint medicinal smell drifted into my nose. I brushed orange juice from the label and squinted at the typing.

Digomethate.

The flu hadn't made me sick; Dr. Nelson had.

I leaned against the cabinets and stared at the bottle. My head pounded, from anger, not illness. My home had been violated— again.

A stupid idea pulled me from the floor up to my bedroom. I dug a dark sweatshirt and jeans from the closet and tossed them on the bed. A black jacket, cap, wool socks, picks, and flashlight joined them. I thought about tossing my gun on the bed, but decided against it. I dressed and left the house before my sluggish brain told me I was making a mistake.

Chapter 46
• • • • • • • • • • • •

By the time I retrieved my car from its garage and made my way through the pretheater traffic, it was after seven. I found a parking space that was close enough to see the clinic, but far enough away to be inconspicuous.

A steady stream of patients went in and out the heavy oak doors. Watching was boring work; my head continued to pound. I closed my eyes—for a few minutes.

When I opened them, I felt stiff and sweaty from the fever. Sleeping in the front seat of a cold car probably didn't meet my doctor's definition of bed rest. I stretched—as much as you can in the front seat of a Porsche—and looked across the street. The clinic was dark.

The street was empty, but you can't count on any street in Manhattan remaining empty for more than thirty seconds. No matter what the time of day, or weather, a dog-walker, stroller, or messenger would hurry past. I hurried from the car to the shadows of the alley next to the clinic. The gate wasn't locked. I pushed it open and darted inside.

The narrow drive was barely wide enough for a truck to back up to the loading dock. The light over the doorway next to the loading bay was on. I unscrewed the bulb. The courtyard went dark. I cupped my hands around the lens of my flashlight and turned the thin band of light on the lock.

Too many businesses talk about security, then stick a two-dollar lock on the back door. The clinic was one of them. The lock popped open in seconds. I let the door swing open and held my breath.

I've lost count of the number of buildings I've broken into, but I still have a heart-stopping moment of fear when the locks click. I open the door. And wait for the alarm that says I've been caught.

Nothing happened. I stepped inside and smiled: My perfect record of never getting caught was intact. I closed the door and swung the cone of light around the room. Boxes and barrels marked "Medical Waste" filled the room. Keeping as much room as possible between me and the containers, I made my way to the door leading to the interior of the clinic. My nerves tightened with each step.

When I reached the door that led to the interior of the clinic, I stopped and thought. I thought about going home and crawling back into my warm bed. Then I thought about the empty medicine vial, and Judith, and Nikki, and the babies born without arms or legs, and my disappearing clients. I pushed the door open.

As I hoped and expected, the corridor was empty. I jogged to Nelson's office and stopped in front of the closed door. Pick in hand, I tried the knob. The door opened.

I slipped inside and quietly pulled the door closed behind me. The heavy curtains were closed, blocking all light from the outside. I flicked my flashlight on with my thumb and slowly shone it around the room. The beam settled on the chair behind the desk.

It shone on a man. His face was pulled into the strained grimace found on bodies laid out in their coffins. *Another corpse?* Then I realized I was wrong. Corpses don't hold pistols in their hands.

The overhead light flashed on. I blinked at the sudden glare; Nelson did too. My stomach lurched. I was starring in my worst break-in nightmare.

The revolver in Nelson's hand looked like a miniature silver cannon. I swiveled my head to the right and saw another man standing next to the light switch. The pistol in his hand wasn't as large as Nelson's, but it was large enough to frighten me.

I let the flashlight drop to the carpet and raised my hands. "I surrender. Call the cops."

"I don't think so. I don't wish to involve the police in this matter. We prefer to keep things . . . private." He nodded at his companion.

"I can save you the trouble. There are picks and keys in my pockets—nothing else."

Neither man believed me. Clumsy hands patted my pockets. He took my picks, but didn't bother with the car keys. Small comfort; the Porsche would be either towed away or stolen by the time I got back to it.

Nelson leaned back in his chair, a satisfied smile on his face. "You have a strong constitution. It was quite a surprise to see you sneaking in our courtyard. You really should be more aware of security cameras. But I guess your head might be a little fuzzy." He laughed. "I'm forgetting my manners. I don't think you've been properly introduced to my co-worker. This is Dr. Ling So. It's his drug you're trying to discredit."

"That's a relief. I was afraid you were wasting your money on a bargain-basement gumshoe. Speaking of shoes, give the poor guy a raise. His shoes are awful. His clothes are awful. He looks like he shops at Goodwill. Not the image you want to project for your tony clients." I looked at his black leather suit, black shirt, and white tie and shook my head. "Bruce Lee meets the Godfather."

"Save it, Ms. Stewart. We have better things to talk about than men's fashion."

"I agree. Let's talk about something else. How did you get into my house?"

"Your cleaning lady had a key. I thought it best to have a copy made." He polished his Rolex with a tissue and smiled. "I decided it was time to use that key."

"My doctor took blood samples. When an overdose of Digomethate shows up in my blood, she'll get suspicious. Especially since I've discussed your drug's problems with her."

"Don't worry. Digomethate won't kill you. We just wanted to slow you down and keep you away from us—"

"Until you finished shredding those papers." I pointed to the machine sitting on top of the garbage can. "Tell me, Dr. Nelson, are you destroying the results of your drug's field tests? The true results. The ones that show the real miscarriage rate of women who took Digomethate. How high is it?"

"Before we resolve our problem, I'd like to know exactly what you've learned. And who else knows."

I wasn't scared—yet. But being in a room with two gun-bearing amateurs pushed my fear closer to the surface. I tried to talk myself out of it. "It's not that easy, doctor. Too many people know about my investigation. Are you going to kill them one by one with a baseball bat, like you did Nikki, or poison, like you did Judith?"

"At the moment, you are my only concern. The others can be dealt with later. Perhaps your boyfriend is one of those people. I'm sure your sister is too."

I bit my lip. Nelson laughed and said, "My esteemed colleague is a renowned researcher. Just as you have been studying us, we have been studying you. I know your business is suffering."

"Thanks to your influence."

"Perhaps. Perhaps we can arrive at an understanding. You cherish your business as much as I cherish mine. Perhaps we can talk as business owner to business owner."

Nelson was serious. I choked down a laugh. "Perhaps we can negotiate. We can't do it while your esteemed colleague is sticking a gun in my back."

The pressure lessened. I didn't acknowledge the movement. Nelson waved his gun in the air; his casual handling of the firearm was unnerving. I kept my eye on the barrel and prepared to dive to the floor.

"Sit, please."

So we were going to pretend we were having a civilized visit. I sat and casually crossed my legs. Dr. So stationed himself behind my chair.

"Well, Ms. Stewart. I thought you'd be nothing more than a minor nuisance. I was mistaken. You've been quite persistent."

"I could say the same for you. It was a bold touch, using your brother's position as director of a brokerage firm, and your upcoming stock offering, to pressure our clients to fire us. The threat of losing big fees if you pulled your underwriting business made my clients jump."

Nelson grinned. "But you survived. You've been talking to a few of our . . . our unfortunate families. Of course, we share the sorrow of their misfortune. However, we cannot be forced to assume the guilt for their situation."

I wanted to call him a bastard, but I didn't. Don't argue with a guy who's pointing a gun at you. "There seems to be some disagreement about the side effects women have after taking your fertility drug."

"That's a blatant lie."

"I don't think so. The Food and Drug Administration will be interested in learning how its testing procedures were circumvented. The SEC will want to know more about the fraud you're selling to investors. And what about—"

The door crashed open. A shot was fired from behind me. I threw myself to the floor and covered my head with my hands. I heard the thunk of a gun dropping to the carpet, then silence. I lifted my head—and groaned.

Tomlinson stood in the doorway, waving his service revolver in a slow arc from Nelson to Bruce Lee. His police shield dangled from a chain around his neck.

Bruce's hands were already in the air, Nelson's mouth wouldn't close. The detective waved his gun at Nelson. "Put that gun down on top of the desk. Slowly and carefully." To me, he said, "Get up."

Since I was the only unarmed person in a roomful of nuts who'd love to see me dead, I didn't move. I planned to stay on the floor until I knew a gun battle wouldn't erupt.

Nelson tried a blustery protest. "Officer, we caught this

woman breaking into our clinic. We were only holding her until—"

"I know exactly what you were doing. Shut up and put that gun down."

When Nelson didn't follow his order, Tomlinson pointed his gun at the doctor and shot. I buried my head in my arms and tried to disappear into the carpet. The bullet hit the wall, close enough to Nelson's head to convince him. He tossed the gun on the desk. I flinched as the revolver hit the wood, afraid it would go off.

"Come on, Stewart, get up off the floor. All the fun is over."

Reluctantly, I scrambled to my feet. Neither doctor moved. Bruce's face had lost all its color; he looked ready to vomit. Nelson couldn't figure out what was going on—neither could I.

"I get it. You two are working together—"

"No!" Tomlinson and I answered simultaneously.

"It won't work. You can't expect me to sit by and let you two charge in and steal from my clinic. Just wait until—"

Smiling, Tomlinson interrupted. "Dr. Nelson, I'm a cop doing his job. I saw a break-in and I investigated. I found two men holding a woman at gunpoint. I'm sure neither of those guns are registered. Whadda yuh say? Let's all go down to the station and sort this out."

"Now, officer, let's not be hasty. There's no need for anything like that." Nelson's eyes flickered; an idea was forming in his slippery brain. "I commend you for doing your job. In fact, the commissioner and his wife are my patients. I'll call him in the morning. He'll be pleased to hear how you took control of a difficult situation. Now, if you'll arrest this woman for burglary, my colleague and I will go to our homes and try to salvage the rest of the evening."

The fire crackled under the frying pan. My heart raced. I couldn't imagine any pleasant way out of the clinic and Tomlinson's grasp.

"That would be a nice solution to your little problem, wouldn't it, doc? I get rid of your problem; you call my boss and tell him what a good boy I've been. Sounds like bribery to me. I got a better idea. This lady's looking for something. So am I. In fact, we're looking for the same thing. I want to make sure it's never found."

Bruce edged closer to the door. Tomlinson noticed. Without moving his eyes away from Nelson's face, he said, "You back there, you're making me nervous. Come here where I can see you. Sit down on that ledge behind your friend." Dr. So moved to where Tomlinson directed him. He sat and folded his hands in his lap.

I stayed in front of the desk where I'd been since Tomlinson told me to get to my feet. Nelson's gun sat in the center of his desk, inviting me to grab it.

Tomlinson turned to me. I caught a whiff of alcohol. He waved the revolver under my chin. "You—sit down. Keep your hands on the armrests so I can see them. Don't be stupid."

Don't do anything to make the situation worse. I heard Jeff's voice inside my head, giving me the advice he always offered. I glanced longingly at the pistol on the desk, it was so close.

Tomlinson, a drunk with a gun, grabbed the corner of the desk to steady himself. "Why don't you folks continue your conversation? I'll listen and jump in when I'm ready."

Nelson snorted. A blush of anger spread across his face and neck. "There isn't anything to discuss. This woman, this maniac, breaks in and accuses us of I don't know what. You come flying in, shooting your gun and making threats. Now I'm being held hostage for no reason. I demand that you—"

Tomlinson yelled, "Your demands don't mean shit to me. It's my demands you gotta worry about."

Nelson's flush deepened. Before he triggered Tomlinson's temper, I said, "Doctor, tell me about the fertility drug. I know it causes birth defects. How did you get it approved?"

"Do you honestly think I would admit to falsifying our testing results? Not that the drug causes birth defects."

"I wouldn't expect you to admit to anything. But Judith Marsden didn't believe you; she knew the drug was causing families—too many families—to have babies with serious birth defects. She also knew you falsified the results of your testing. From toxicity tests all the way through field tests—lies. It's one big, deadly hoax."

"What do you know about toxicity testing?"

Nelson's cool facade showed a few cracks. I happily added to his discomfort.

"More than you think. Before a new drug gets approved by the FDA, it has to undergo a series of tests. Toxicity testing is the first phase. Once you finish testing your drug on healthy volunteers, you give it to a few hundred patients under controlled situations. Then you increase the range so as many as two thousand women are receiving your fertility drug under field conditions. After that stage is complete, you file a new drug application and wait until the FDA says it's okay to market the drug.

"A lot of people are looking forward to it. Especially you. Analysts project worldwide revenues of about a billion dollars a year. You'll be a wealthy man. If I'm not mistaken, you're expecting your approval to arrive within weeks. Unless they find out you lied about the side effects."

"You have no proof."

"I have enough to get the FDA interested. Do you know that the investigation into Thalidomide led to criminal charges against the manufacturers? By the way, they were found guilty. What do you think will happen here?"

Nelson didn't react, or show any remorse. "Judith heard rumors and investigated them. Knowing Judith, she confronted you. I'm sure she couldn't believe her trusted doctor was lying and jeopardizing the lives of unborn children. When Judith wouldn't back off, you tried to blackmail her by having the surrogate—and Judith's baby—disappear. When that didn't work, you had her killed. I can't figure out why you killed Nikki. Was she blackmailing you too?"

Tomlinson growled a curse. "I don't give a damn about your theories. I want to know one thing: Where's the baby?"

Forgetting my intention to keep Tomlinson's temper from exploding, I swung around to him. "Isn't there a limit to how far you'll go? Are you going to kill a pregnant woman so you can inherit your sister's estate?"

Tomlinson was too busy thinking to answer me. He turned to

Nelson. "Is what she's saying about these drugs true? Did you cook the books?"

"Of course not. We would never—"

"Let's try this again, doc. Is she telling the truth? Are you selling bad drugs?"

"Bad is such a misleading word."

"Misleading, but true. You're nothing but a crook. An educated, fancy crook." Before Nelson protested, Tomlinson laughed. "I like that. Now I know what I'm dealing with."

My stomach lurched. A subtle change had taken place in the atmosphere—and I was going to be the loser.

Tomlinson continued. "You tell me where the girl is." He jerked his revolver in my direction. "You can have her. You forget about me. I'll forget about your drug. We'll forget about this conversation."

My stomach lurched. The shimmer of interest in Nelson's eyes scared me. He leaned forward slightly. "What makes you think I know where the surrogate is hiding?"

"Come on, doc. There's no need to shine your halo for me. When Judith got hold of something, she never gave up. I know 'cause I grew up with her." Nelson blinked with surprise, but didn't say anything. "Stewart's right. The only way you could shut Judith up was to take her baby away. It didn't work, did it?"

Nelson twisted his watch around on his wrist. He wouldn't look at Tomlinson. "The surrogate exhibited signs of emotional instability. We were afraid the trauma of surrendering the infant would have been too traumatic for her and the baby. So we arranged for her to get away until the pressure was off."

"You mean until the pressure was off you." I quickly added, "Hannah wouldn't come back until Judith dropped her investigation of Digomethate."

Tomlinson interrupted. "What the hell is Digo—whatever you said?"

Tomlinson wrapped his hand around the edge of the desk to steady himself. Hoping he'd pass out and fall down, I slowly explained. "Digomethate. It's the fertility drug that Dr. Nelson is pushing on his patients. The drug has one problem: It makes babies come out with no brains. Or no arms. Or no legs."

Tomlinson shrugged. Birth defects didn't interest him. Money did. "So, doc, where's the girl taking her vacation?"

"We placed her in an apartment in Brooklyn."

Tomlinson and I leaned forward. Nelson folded his hands in his lap. His eyes focused on the gun. We both calculated the odds of reaching it before Tomlinson could shoot him.

Nelson cleared his throat and said, "There's a slight problem. One which I know will be cleared up momentarily."

Tomlinson's voice swelled with menace. "What kind of fucking idiot do you take me for? We had a deal, doc. Now you're telling me you don't know where the girl is hiding."

"We still have a deal. I just can't deliver the entire package at this moment. You'll have to be patient. I know we'll locate her in another day or two. After all, the girl has no family, no money."

"I'll be the one to decide if we still have a deal. What *do* you know? Tell me everything."

It was my turn to stare at the pistol and calculate odds. They weren't good. Nelson talked about giving Hannah two thousand dollars and an apartment in Brooklyn. She disappeared the day after Nikki's death. She'd be back when she needed more money.

Tomlinson listened intently, then he looked at me. "Well, Stewart, you're awfully quiet. What do you think? Should I believe him?"

I shook my head. "Like anything I say is going to change your mind. Are you going to trust this guy? He doesn't want to help you. He wants to get rid of you."

"She's wrong. I'm trying to level with you, detective." The doctor sounded sincere. "There is one other thing . . ."

Tomlinson snapped, "What?"

Nelson didn't try to bluff or stall. "There's a priest in Brooklyn. Father Timothy, that's all I know. He'd be the one the girl ran to." Nelson rattled off the address of the parish and settled back in his chair. "Do we have a deal?"

Tomlinson lowered his gun to his side. I held my breath and gripped the armrests.

"If you're bullshitting me, I'll be back. Here's my phone number." He tossed a business card on the desk and grinned.

"You call me if the girl turns up. This one's yours." He strode out of the room and slammed the door behind him.

Chapter 47

• • • • • • • • • • • •

Nelson and I jumped for the gun on the desk. He grabbed it with both hands. I managed to get my right hand on the barrel. We fought for control. Our wrestling match ended when Bruce Lee retrieved his gun from the floor and stuck it in my ear.

I know when to give up. For the second time that evening I surrendered.

Re-armed, confidence returned to the men's faces. Sweat dripped down my back.

Nelson smirked. "No pleading or begging?"

I didn't bother to answer. I've never pleaded or begged for anything. I wasn't going to start with Dr. Nelson.

Bruce stationed himself at my side. His gun was casually pointed at me, but his attention was on his boss—not me. I watched him out of the corner of my eye. Did I have the guts to grab his gun?

Nelson pursed his lips. "Let me think for a moment. Ms. Stewart, you've placed me, and yourself, in a very ticklish situation. I think you'll agree. I can't let you walk out of here."

After you've been shot once or twice, you're an instant slower to act. You wait a heartbeat, feel that heartbeat inside your chest, and wonder if you'll feel the next one.

Ernest Hemingway once said, "Cowardice, as distinguished from panic, is almost always simply a lack of ability to suspend the functioning of the imagination." I stopped imagining, I moved. I flung myself at Bruce. The chair flew over on its side. The revolver flew from Bruce's hand, bounced once, and stopped near the door. We dove for it.

I landed on the gun; my stomach squarely on top of it. Bruce jumped on top of me. He yanked my hair, clawed at my eyes, and pounded his fists on my back. Anything to pull me off the gun. I fought back with one hand and tried to grab the pistol with the other.

Nelson shouted. All he received in reply was our grunts as we scuffled for the gun.

Nelson yelled again. Then he shot.

Bruce shuddered once. Thick, warm blood poured down on my neck and the back of my head.

I rolled and threw the weight off me. Bruce landed on his back. His head lolled to the side, giving me a nose-to-nose view of his bloody scalp and lifeless eyes. I froze.

Before I shook the horror, Nelson crossed the room. He scooped the gun from the floor and dropped it into his pocket. Then he stepped back out of reach and aimed his revolver at my chest. "Look what you did. You killed him."

I didn't waste my breath pointing out that he had fired the deadly shot. I was glad to still be alive—even if only for a few more seconds.

Moving slowly and deliberately, I sat, crossed my legs, and rested my hands on my knees. "Calm down. Haven't enough people died?"

"I haven't killed anyone—until now." His voice rose hysterically. "Look what you made me do . . . This is all your fault."

"What about Judith? Who killed her?"

"Not me. Nikki did. I planted the seed—and enough medication to spike everything in Judith's refrigerator. After Judith died, Nikki cleaned everything out before anyone got suspicious. Being the cleaning lady, the girl had a key and a reason to be in that house. Nikki was a willing—no she was an eager—participant. She was protecting her sister. I was protecting my clinic."

"What about Nikki? Are you going to tell me someone else is responsible for her death too?"

"It was an opportune moment. You can't succeed if you don't take advantage of circumstances." Nelson laughed. "Breaking into your house and tearing it apart was Nikki's idea. That girl had a wonderful imagination. I'll miss it. She thought it might convince you to give up your search for her sister. It was an opportunity to get rid of another problem—"

"Why was Nikki a problem? I thought she was an eager participant."

"Blackmail can be so ugly. She didn't understand that I was in control and that her demands were unreasonable. She threatened to go to the police, but she couldn't. You see, Nikki murdered Judith Marsden."

I have a rule that you should never call someone who's pointing a gun at you a bastard, but I broke my rule. "You bastard. You're just as guilty. You're guilty of pouring the poison down Judith's throat and cracking Nikki's skull with a baseball bat. You're as guilty as the one who actually did the killing."

As an afterthought I added, "Who was your batsman? Was it this poor bastard here?" I pointed at Dr. So.

"Another inventive compatriot. Dr. So was furious that his years of research and development were threatened. After you swallowed the set-up, he and Nikki worked on your house." Nelson shook his head. "What a shame it was wasted. I thought you'd be slowed down by the awkward situation of having a dead woman in your basement. And now this . . ."

He shook his head again. The gesture infuriated me. "You're not a bastard. You're a lunatic." Having my theories confirmed didn't bring any joy. I caught my breath and tried to sound calm, even friendly. "It's not too late. You can still salvage your clinic. Let me help you."

"Help me? You've done enough . . ." Nelson's voice cracked. His hand wavered, but not enough for me to move. "What I need to do is take care of you."

I shivered. Another round of fever and chills was about to hit. I leaned back against the wall. "It's getting easier and easier for you to pull that trigger, isn't it? Don't you want to end this bloody madness?"

I thought furiously, looking for a way to throw him off balance. "My legs are cramping. I'm going to stand up. Is that okay with you? I don't want to do anything—"

"Go ahead, get up." Nelson took a step back out of my reach. "Put your hands on top of your head."

"Come on, doctor. Don't make things worse."

"I'm trying to make them better. Put your hands on your head." The gun in his hand shook.

I put my hands on my head. My fingers touched a clump of hair matted with drying blood. I gagged. A tense silence filled the room.

Nelson snatched a white lab jacket from a hook on the back of the door and tossed it at me. I didn't move my hands. The jacket landed on my toes.

"Pick it up. Wrap it around his head. I don't want to leave a trail of blood."

I tried Jeff's line. "Don't make things worse—"

"Do it." His voice cracked. "Just do what I say. You're the one who's making things worse, not me. I'm trying to clean this mess up."

Nelson's trembling hand matched his shaky voice. I watched his Adam's apple bob up and down. Moving slowly and deliberately, I lowered my hands and bent to pick up the lab jacket from the floor.

Telling myself it didn't matter, that the body on the floor was an empty shell not a person, I wound the jacket around Bruce's head until it looked like a museum mummy and knotted the sleeves in the back.

Finished, I stood. Blood quickly seeped through the thin cotton jacket. I glanced at Nelson. He was still having trouble swallowing. He didn't have any trouble talking. "Grab him under his arms. We have to get him out of sight until I decide what to do."

"He's too heavy. I won't be able to move him."

"You look strong and he's not very big." Nelson gestured with his pistol. "Let's go. We're not going very far."

Since I couldn't think of anything that wouldn't make the situation worse, I followed Nelson's order and dragged the body behind me through the outer office to the corridor. Nelson hovered, just out of reach, and gave directions.

Turn left, turn right, don't let blood drip on the floor. Stop. Nelson twisted the knob on a scuffed metal door and opened the door. "Inside."

I dragged Bruce into the room. When the door slammed

against his heels, I wasn't surprised. I was sweating and shaking and angry at myself for walking into a trap.

The lights went off.

When I was seven years old, Eileen and I fought over a doll. She lost. Eileen pushed me in a closet with the doll for company. I was terrified. I sat with my arms wrapped around the doll and cried. Eileen, who thought she'd played a good joke, pulled the door open a few moments later and dragged me out.

The memories of those terrifying minutes returned the instant the door closed. The sound of a lock clicking amplified the terror.

Chapter 48

● ● ● ● ● ● ● ● ● ● ● ●

My wristwatch has a luminous dial. I forced myself to concentrate on following the second hand as it swept around the watch instead of thinking about the darkness. After two minutes of nearly uncontrolled panic, I forced myself back to reality.

I caught my breath and leaned against the door to think. Reality was frightening enough; I didn't have to add claustrophobic fears from my childhood to it. Reaching behind my back, I found the knob and turned it. It wouldn't move. The door was locked.

My car keys were in my hip pocket. I pulled them out and prayed that the penlight I kept on the key ring still worked. It did—barely. The faint light was no brighter than a candle. It wavered and threatened to quit at any moment. I kept it on long enough to sweep the room once.

I was in a tiny supply closet. Six paces brought me to the far wall. Three rows of metal shelves extended from the floor to the ceiling. Metal shelves also lined the outer walls. There was a small sink in the corner near the door. A dusty automatic coffee machine sat on the counter. No windows. No lights.

Swallowing hard, I forced myself to kneel beside the body and gingerly search his pockets. I pulled his jacket back to look for an inside pocket. My hand accidentally brushed against his neck. The flesh was still warm. I flinched and hopped away from the body.

It took thirty heart-pounding seconds to talk myself into resuming the search. I found a wallet, car keys, a fistful of change, and a Swiss Army knife. I left everything except the knife in his pockets.

The knife had two blades, a corkscrew, scissors, and a nail file. The blades were dull and would have had trouble cutting a ripe banana, but it was a knife.

I turned back to the door and wasted my precious flashlight battery examining the door. There was no keyhole. The door was locked from the outside by a dead bolt. I knelt in front of the door, held my flashlight in my teeth, jammed the knife in the slot between the door and the frame, and wiggled it. The blade snapped. The lock didn't move.

The flashlight blinked. I shut it off to conserve whatever power was left in the battery and sat for a few moments with my head in my hands. I thought about the boxes on the shelves. There had to be something in one of them that could be used to get the lock open.

Working in the dark as much as possible to save my penlight, I opened boxes and cautiously stuck my hands inside. I found medical supplies, office supplies, cleaning supplies, and supplies for the coffeemaker. No keys. No batteries. No lock smashers.

Admitting defeat, I sank to the floor and rested my head in my hands. What would Houdini have done? I let my mind wander, not at all confident it would float to a solution.

A boy's face kept coming to mind. A teenager whose pockmarked face had the first traces of a dark beard sprouting in the craters. Wayne—I couldn't remember his last name. Wayne, my high school lab partner. Someone I hadn't seen since . . . since the day we blew up the chemistry lab.

We were bored seniors, putting in time until graduation. As the weather got warmer and the calendar moved closer and closer to June, we had trouble making it to class and even more trouble paying attention if we got there.

The trouble started in the library. Wayne and I were looking for the answers to a take-home exam when we stumbled across *The Anarchist Cookbook*. We copied the chapter on bombs, stuck it in the back of our chemistry books, and decided to test the recipes the next time things got dull.

Our opportunity came a few weeks later. One day, when a substitute teacher was failing in her attempt to keep control of the class, we mixed one of the formulas, carefully following the directions on the crumpled paper.

The solution looked like thick, gritty leftover coffee. Disappointed, we dumped it in a trash can and forgot about it. Until a few minutes before the class ended.

Wayne crumpled a soda can and tossed it in the garbage. Without warning, the trash can exploded. I'll never forget that sound: a whoosh followed by a loud thump.

Flaming shreds of plastic and paper flew straight up in the air. Our classmates poured out into the hallway, shouting, *"Fire!"* Smoke and the stench of burning paper and melting plastic filled the classroom. The quick-thinking teacher grabbed a fire extinguisher and doused the flames. Astonished, Wayne and I watched with open mouths.

The lectures delivered by the teacher, the guidance counselors, the principal, and our parents all contained the same elements: We were fortunate no one was hurt. We were irresponsible. We didn't know how deadly and volatile that compound was. We were lucky to be suspended and not expelled. We were lucky to be alive.

Wayne's parents transferred him to another school, far away from my evil influence. The principal suspended me for two weeks; my parents made me get an after-school job to pay for my share of the damages. The memory of the garbage can's blowing up cheered me through the evenings of straightening socks in the local five and dime.

Could I do it again?

Using my cigarette lighter as a guide so I could save my flashlight for the critical work, I went back to the rows of shelves to gather the ingredients. I found ammonia in the janitor's supplies. The ether and alcohol came from the medical supplies. The iodine crystals were in the boxes of supplies for developing X-ray films. The Mister Coffee box had filters and a pot for mixing. I grabbed a handful of tongue depressors to stir the mixture and went to the sink.

More than twenty years had passed since our lab experiment, but I didn't have any trouble remembering the formula. Holding my penlight in my teeth, I stood over the sink, dumped the iodine crystals into the coffeepot, and slowly poured ammonia over them. I held my head back, away from the fumes, and hoped the mixture wouldn't explode in my hands.

The crystals gradually dissolved. A soupy, rust-colored sediment formed on the bottom of the coffeepot. I gently poured the soup into the coffee filter and then washed it, first with a bottle of rubbing alcohol, then with the ether.

I didn't know when the molecules would be transformed to an explosive. I was afraid every tremor of my hands would cause it to go off.

All I could hear was my heavy breathing and my chemistry teacher's voice: "You mixed one of the most hazardous explosive compounds . . . An extremely unstable compound . . . When it dries, it becomes hazardous and sensitive. So sensitive that the slightest friction, even a fly landing on it, could have set it off."

Wayne and I made enough to fill a shot glass. That explosive ounce blew up a garbage can and started a small fire. I finished with two cups of the brew.

I drizzled the sludge on the doorknob, the hinges, and the floor beneath the door. While it dried, I snatched a few rolls of adhesive tape from a box and stuffed them into my jacket pocket. Then I built a bunker out of cartons of copying machine paper and crouched behind it.

Mimicking the soldiers in all those Sunday afternoon war movies I watched as a kid, I lobbed the adhesive hand grenades over my flimsy breastwork and held my breath. The third roll connected.

The flash was blinding, the explosion deafening. The boxes of paper absorbed most of the shrapnel from the door. Small flaming pieces of the wood and metal flew overhead. I pushed the cartons aside and jumped over the row of flames to the corridor.

I ran out the loading bay door to the small courtyard. A man grabbed my arm. The shadows and the Knicks cap hid his face. The gun in his hand was all I could see.

Chapter 49

I tried to run, but the man caught me from behind. He wrapped his arms around me. I struggled to break free, but couldn't. His arms tightened around my chest. He hissed, "Blaine, stop fighting."

"Dennis? What—"

"I couldn't stop worrying about you. As soon as I could get away, I went back to your house. You were gone. Somehow I knew you'd be here. I heard an explosion . . ." His hands touched my hair. "Jesus, that's blood. Are you hurt?"

"I'm fine." I pulled Dennis away from the door and quickly explained.

When I finished, Dennis nodded. "Okay, let's get Nelson." I didn't move. Dennis said, "Blaine, let's go." His voice held a tinge of annoyance.

"I can't." I paused. I was about to ask Dennis to do something I'd never asked before: Break the rules.

The rules said I should go back inside with Dennis and wait for the police to arrive. After who knows how many hours of answering questions, they'd let me go. By then it would be too late. I took Dennis's arm and moved close until I was inches away from his face.

"Tomlinson knows Father Timmy is the only person who knows where Hannah is hiding. Tomlinson went to Brooklyn. He's going to force Father Timmy to reveal Hannah's hiding place. Then he's going to kill her. And the baby. He'll probably kill the priest too. I can't let that happen. Too many people have died."

Dennis didn't protest. He pressed a revolver into my hand.

"Take this, it's my back-up. Go. Call me when you know what's going on. You'll have to come back to talk to the cops. I'll tell them you were gone by the time I got here. I'll also see if I can get a patrol car to check out the situation."

I don't remember driving to Brooklyn. I remember gripping the steering wheel hard enough to make my hands ache. I remember lighting a cigarette; the smell of burning tobacco made my stomach roll. I flicked the cigarette out the open window and let the cold air fill the car. I remember cutting off a taxi at the entrance to the Brooklyn Bridge. He flipped his bright lights on and tried to ride my bumper. I pushed the accelerator to the floor. His wheezing cab couldn't keep up.

An internal automatic pilot, or a guardian angel, took over and guided the Porsche. I roared over the bridge at seventy, ran red lights, and swerved around slow-moving cars and trucks. I hit a patch of ice in front of the rectory and skidded to a stop near the curb. I left the car, nose pointing toward a fire hydrant and tail angled out into the street, and ran to the priest's house.

The door was partially open. I kicked it aside and ran down the hallway to the study. Dennis's gun was in my hand, ready for use.

I was too late. Father Timmy was lying on the floor behind his desk. Blood streamed from his shoulder.

I knelt beside him and felt his neck for a pulse. The priest's eyelids fluttered, then stayed opened. He groaned, "My rosary. In the desk. Get them."

I found a set of wooden rosary beads in the top drawer of his desk. I took them out, slammed the drawer shut, and went back to the priest.

He wrapped the beads around his hand and said, "Leave me. Let me die in peace . . ."

"Sorry, Father. You're not going to die. I've seen enough gunshot wounds to know. Yours hurts and you're doing a lot of bleeding, but you won't die. Was the police detective, Tomlinson, here? Did he shoot you?"

"God forgive him. It was an accident. My temper . . . I tried to fight with him. Pray with me."

"Where's the girl, Father?" Father Timmy closed his eyes, his lips moved in silent prayer. I lost my temper. "I hope you're praying for Hannah. You won't die tonight, but she will if Tomlinson finds her before I do. Tomlinson's going to kill her and that unborn child. Can you live with that?"

The priest grimaced and coughed. "She's with my sister. I thought it would be a safe place . . ."

"How long ago . . ."

I let the question fade. Father Timmy had lost consciousness. I checked his pulse again; it was strong and steady. I opened his shirt. The bullet had gouged a track across his shoulder, but the flow of blood from the wound had stopped. Father Timmy would live. I got to my feet and went to the telephone.

The 911 operator demanded to know my name. I didn't think it was important. After repeating the address, I hung up. I never considered waiting for the police. After checking Father Timmy one last time, I ran out to my car.

During this trip to Beaver Ridge, I didn't worry about the State Police. I didn't glance at the speedometer either. I didn't want to know how fast I was going.

The trees on the side of the road blurred into an unbroken wall. The headlights of the cars I passed quickly shrank to pinpricks of light, then disappeared. The dotted lines on the highway melted into a long solid line.

Hoping the cold air would keep me awake and cool my fever, I drove with the windows rolled down. I groped in the glove box and under the seats, but I couldn't find any cassettes. I had nothing but the radio, and my black thoughts, to keep me company.

Chapter 50

A row of pine trees lined the Wyricks' driveway. I drove between them and pulled in as far as possible. The Porsche would be hidden from anyone glancing out of the house's front windows. The thin, ice-crusted snow crunched beneath my tires. Using the trees for cover, I walked up to the house. A flashlight wasn't necessary; the full moon lit the way.

A car with New York Police Department plates was parked in front of the house. I touched the hood; it was cool, but not ice-cold.

The ground-floor lights of the house were on; the second floor was dark. I darted around the house to the back. A dog barked furiously. I ducked behind a rusting pick-up truck and waited for the dog to lose interest. By the time he decided I wasn't a threat I was shaking from the cold. My feet were freezing from standing in the snow.

Before the dog changed his mind and started barking again, I ran to the porch and took the stairs two at a time. The door wasn't locked—folks in Beaver Ridge hadn't learned to lock their doors yet. They'd start when word of this night's adventure got around town.

The kitchen was dark. I hung in the shadows near the door leading to the living room and tried to catch my breath without panting out loud. Dennis's revolver, a stubby little .38 Special, was in my hand. I cracked it open and counted the bullets. Six.

I heard a painful gasp. Ethel protested in a voice edged with anger and panic. "You have to let us go. Can't you see she's about to have a baby?"

A man's voice rumbled. The words weren't clear, but the threat was.

I crouched low to the floor and peered around the door frame. Two women sat on the sofa. I could see the backs of their heads. One was Ethel. I guessed the other was Hannah.

Tomlinson stood in front of them. He was holding a gun. Two hostages. One pregnant and in labor. I rocked back on my heels and thought. How could we end this without leaving any more bodies on the floor?

Hannah moaned again. Ethel stood. I think she intended to slap Tomlinson. He lifted his right hand until his service revolver was level with her chest.

A point-blank shot would kill her. I started to my feet. A sharp jab in my back knocked me to the floor. Ronald Wyrick, hunting rifle in hand, rushed past.

The sick feeling of once again being too late slammed into me. I yelled "Don't!" and pushed myself to my feet.

Ronald didn't listen. He drew the rifle up to a firing position. I jumped and hit his forearm just as he pulled the trigger. The shot went low. Instead of hitting Tomlinson in the head, the bullet hit his leg, inches below his knee. His leg buckled. Tomlinson crumpled to the floor; the gun flew from his hand.

Everyone except Ronald started screaming. Tomlinson yelled obscenities. Hannah alternated between yelling that she was having her baby and that no one would take it from her. Ethel yelled at Ronald. Ronald raised his hunting rifle again, determined to end the threat to his family.

Ethel and I yelled for Ronald to stop. He didn't listen. I punched him in the stomach. He doubled over and clutched his abdomen. I felt bad about punching the old man, but that didn't stop me from tearing the hunting rifle from his hands. Ronald added to the bedlam; he shouted for me to give the rifle back so he could finish his business.

That's when I yelled. "Shut up! Everybody shut up!" My voice carried over the others. The noise stopped. Even Tomlinson stopped yelling. Expectant faces looked at me. Cradling the rifle in my arms, I issued instructions. I sent Ronald to gather blankets and bandages, anything to get him out of the room. I kicked Tomlinson's gun across the room, far away from his outstretched hand. Finally, I sent Ethel to the telephone.

An ambulance took Hannah and Ethel away. A second one took Tomlinson and a police officer. The other cops took Ronald, but assured us he wouldn't be arrested. Self-defense would be their finding. They'd save their arresting for Tomlinson.

The sheriff decided that all he needed from me was my name, address, and telephone number. I was free to leave. It was a local matter. They'd call if my testimony was needed.

I stood on the icy porch and watched the patrol car drive away. My hands trembled as my adrenaline rush ended and the fever came rushing back. I went back inside and collapsed on the sofa—in the family room, not the living room where blood stained the floor—and started making telephone calls. I couldn't find Dennis. Eileen was also unreachable. Her husband told me she was out cleaning up a mess—the mess I left behind at the clinic and the rectory.

Information gave me Charlie Spragge's number. As I dialed, I looked at my watch. It was well past midnight, but I continued dialing. Charlie's sleepy voice lost its irritation when I told him where he'd find Jerry Marsden III. Charlie thanked me and said he'd be in Beaver Ridge in the morning. I closed my eyes and rested my head on the back of the sofa. My case was over.

The smell of mothballs woke me. Bright sunlight streamed through the windows. Someone, undoubtedly Ethel, had come in during the night and draped a scratchy green Army surplus blanket over me.

I found Ethel and Ronald in the kitchen eating a huge breakfast. The smell of bacon grease set my stomach off on a series of slow rolls. When I walked into the room, Ronald pushed himself away from the table and disappeared out the back door. Ethel wouldn't look at me. She used her fork to trace a free-form design in the yellow puddle left on her plate by her eggs.

I felt like an unwelcome guest who lingered too long after dinner. At the same time, I didn't feel like making apologies for staying too long. "How is Hannah? And the baby?"

"Marianne's fine. That's her real name, Marianne. The baby's fine too. I suppose you're going to take the baby."

I stood in the doorway and folded my arms across my chest. "That's not for me to decide. I'm not smart enough to decide. Ethel, I don't know what's right anymore. I only know too many people died."

Ethel's fork scraped against the plate. "When my brother showed up with Marianne, I thought, *I let him use my girls. How much more can I give?* I let him talk me into taking care of her. We fooled ourselves into thinking we had one of our girls back."

What could I say? Until the day she died, Ethel would still

mourn her girls, still hope they'd come up the drive laughing and talking about boys. The mourning never ends.

Dr. Mabe assured me there wouldn't be any lasting effects from my Digomethate overdose, but I'm still afraid I'll find out she's wrong. I wait for a strange lump or ache to appear without warning. I stopped smoking, started taking my vitamins, and got back to regular workouts in an attempt to defeat any mutant cells. That worry still keeps me from sleeping at night. The absence of the victorious feeling that usually comes after solving a case added to my insomnia.

By midweek, Nelson was out on bail, deploring the terrible accident that killed his colleague. The bureaucratic wheels wouldn't move; the FDA was reluctant to examine the results of Nelson's test of Digomethate.

Our business wasn't getting worse—but it wasn't improving. Eileen was impatient. I was depressed. The day the papers from the Metropolitan Fertility Clinic's attorneys arrived in our office informing me that I was being sued for slander was the day I decided to take action. I picked up the telephone and made a call.

Johnnie Bramble's earnest face stared at the camera. His smile was welcoming, but grave. He was happy we invited him in. Unfortunately, he didn't have good news.

"Good evening. We begin tonight with an exclusive NewsBreakers report. As a result of an on-going NewsBreakers investigation into one of New York City's leading fertility clinics, we have startling information on a troubling rate of birth defects caused by the clinic's patented fertility drug. We have also learned of a cover-up that extended to the highest levels of the clinic. Tonight, officials are charging the clinic with experimenting with the yet-to-be-born."

Bramble swallowed and fought to keep his voice calm. He lost. "This incredible story also includes murder, blackmail, and a newly born infant who will inherit one of the city's largest real estate fortunes."

A videotape of Bramble standing in front of the clinic appeared on the screen. The remote control was resting on the arm of the chair. I punched the power button; Bramble's smug face disappeared. I made another telephone call, then went to bed. For the first time in weeks, I slept through the night.

EPILOGUE

· · · · · · · · ·

The equipment lining the walls made the narrow corridor almost impassable. I pushed an incubator away from a window for a clear view of the nursery.

Gerald Marsden III was the only baby in the room. The other babies were having lunch with their mothers. He slept, a tiny fist jammed against his mouth, unaware of the storms surrounding his birth.

I watched him and wondered what Judith's sister would tell him about his prenatal adventure and how he would deal with it. I wondered if I'd ever forget the look on Hannah's face when I walked into the Wyricks' living room and she realized the baby wouldn't be hers any longer.

I silently wished him a good life and slowly walked away. I couldn't help but wonder if I had done the right thing.

Dennis said he'd wait in the lobby. He'd be leaning against the wall with his arms folded across his chest, watching the people walking by. He'd stay there as long as necessary. He'd always be there—unless I pushed him away.

I started walking faster. Dennis had waited long enough. It was time to answer his question.